YUMMY
the Last Days of a Southside Shorty

by G. Neri

illustrated by
Randy DuBurke

LEE & LOW BOOKS INC
New York

To J.F., for pulling me from the slush pile with this one and seeing it all the way throug
And of course, for Maggie and Zola, who keep me sane.—G.N.

To my two wonderful sons, Sakai and Matthias, and my equally wonderful and lovely wif
Olivia. Special thanks to Christy Hale and Laura Reder—R.D.

Text copyright © 2010 by G. Neri
Illustrations copyright © 2010 by Randy DuBurke

LEE & LOW BOOKS Inc., 95 Madison Avenue, New York, NY 10016
leeandlow.com

Manufactured in the United States of America by Worzalla Publishing Company, February 2011

Book design by Christy Hale
Book production by The Kids at Our House
The text is set in Opti Kartoon and Evil Genius
The illustrations are rendered in ink

10 9 8 7 6 5 4 3
First Edition
Library of Congress Cataloging-in-Publication Data
Neri, Greg.
Yummy : the last days of a Southside Shorty / by G. Neri ; illustrated by Randy DuBurke. — 1st ed.
p. cm.
Summary: "A graphic novel based on the true story of Robert 'Yummy' Sandifer, an eleven-year-old
African American gang member from Chicago who shot a young girl and was then shot by his own
gang members"—Provided by publisher.
ISBN 978-1-58430-267-4 (pbk.)
1. Sandifer, Robert—Comic books, strips, etc. 2. African American youth—Illinois—Chicago—
Biography—Comic books, strips, etc. 3. African American youth—Illinois—Chicago—Social conditions—
Comic books, strips, etc. 4. Gang members—Illinois—Chicago—Biography—Comic books, strips, etc.
5. Gangs—Illinois—Chicago—Comic books, strips, etc. 6. Violence—Illinois—Chicago—Comic books,
strips, etc. 7. Chicago (Ill.)—Social conditions—Comic books, strips, etc. 8. Chicago (Ill.)—Biography—
Comic books, strips, etc. 9. Graphic novels. I. DuBurke, Randy. II. Title.
F548.9.N4N47 2010
305.896'073077311092—dc22
[B]   2006017771

Robert "Yummy" Sandifer was a real person. He was born in 1983 and lived in the Roseland area of Chicago. At just eleven years old, Yummy became a poster child for youth gang violence in America after a series of tragic events led to his appearance on the cover of *TIME* magazine in September 1994. The essence of Yummy's story presented in this book has been re-created based on public records, media reports, and personal accounts. A certain amount of fictionalization was necessary to fill in gaps, condense events, and represent what Yummy might have been feeling. Roger, the narrator of this story, was invented to guide us, a means of trying to make sense of the madness that hit Roseland in the summer of 1994. I invite you, like Roger, to sort through all the opinions that poured in from the community, media, and politicians, and discover your own truth about Yummy.

—G.N.

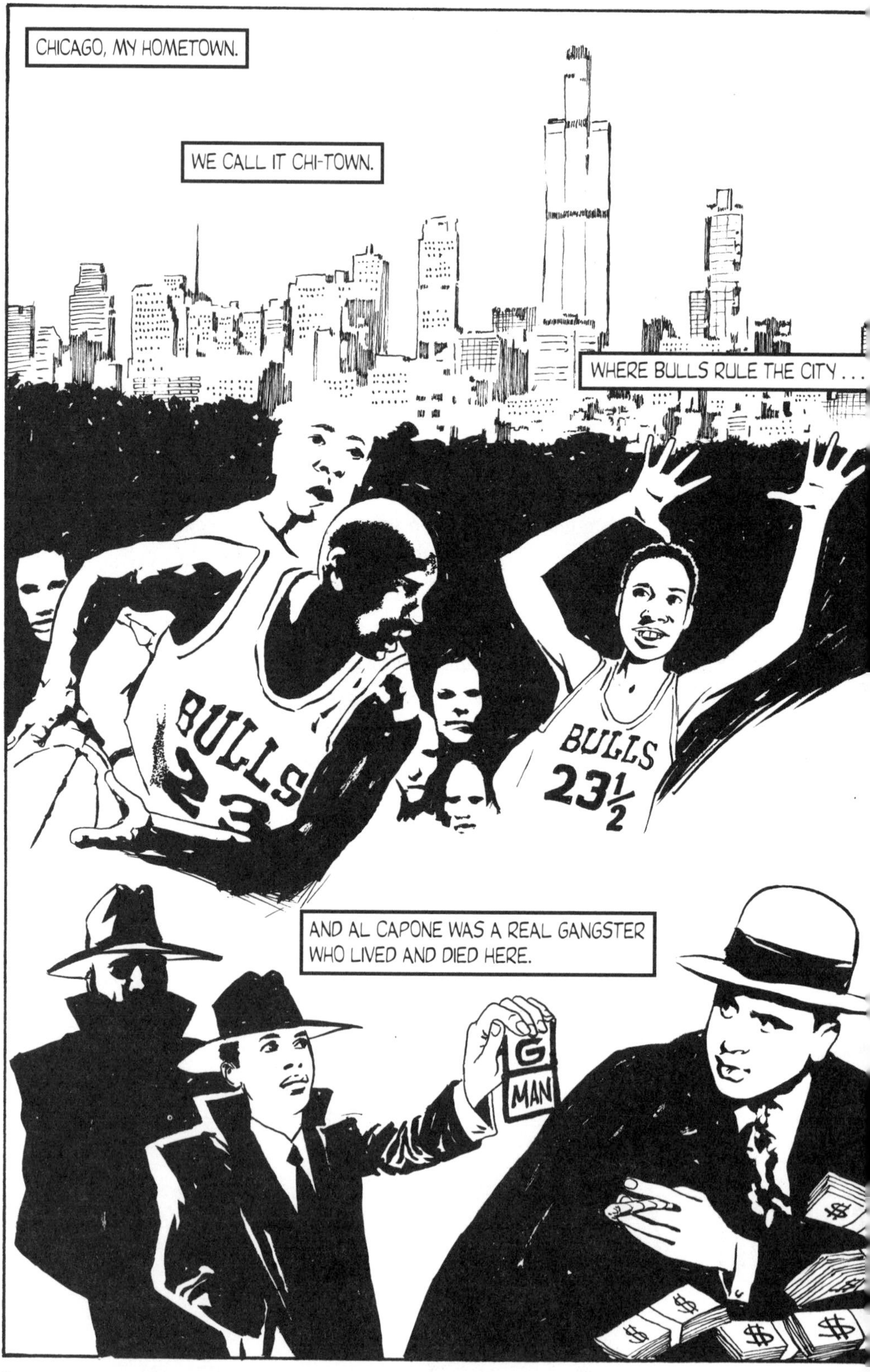
CHICAGO, MY HOMETOWN.
WE CALL IT CHI-TOWN.
WHERE BULLS RULE THE CITY . . .
BULLS
23
BULLS
23½
AND AL CAPONE WAS A REAL GANGSTER WHO LIVED AND DIED HERE.
G MAN

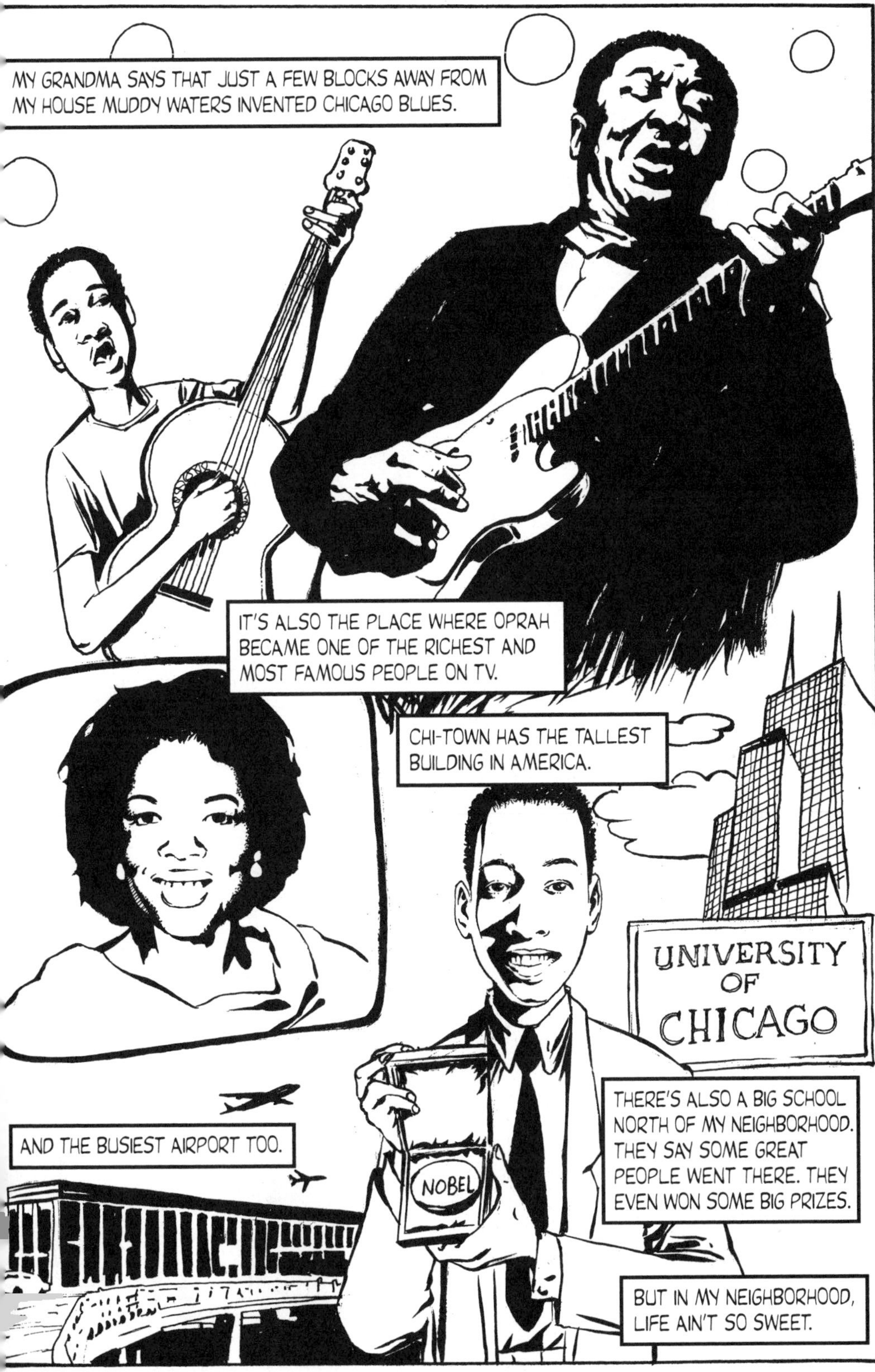
MY GRANDMA SAYS THAT JUST A FEW BLOCKS AWAY FROM MY HOUSE MUDDY WATERS INVENTED CHICAGO BLUES.
IT'S ALSO THE PLACE WHERE OPRAH BECAME ONE OF THE RICHEST AND MOST FAMOUS PEOPLE ON TV.
CHI-TOWN HAS THE TALLEST BUILDING IN AMERICA.
UNIVERSITY OF CHICAGO
AND THE BUSIEST AIRPORT TOO.
NOBEL
THERE'S ALSO A BIG SCHOOL NORTH OF MY NEIGHBORHOOD. THEY SAY SOME GREAT PEOPLE WENT THERE. THEY EVEN WON SOME BIG PRIZES.
BUT IN MY NEIGHBORHOOD, LIFE AIN'T SO SWEET.

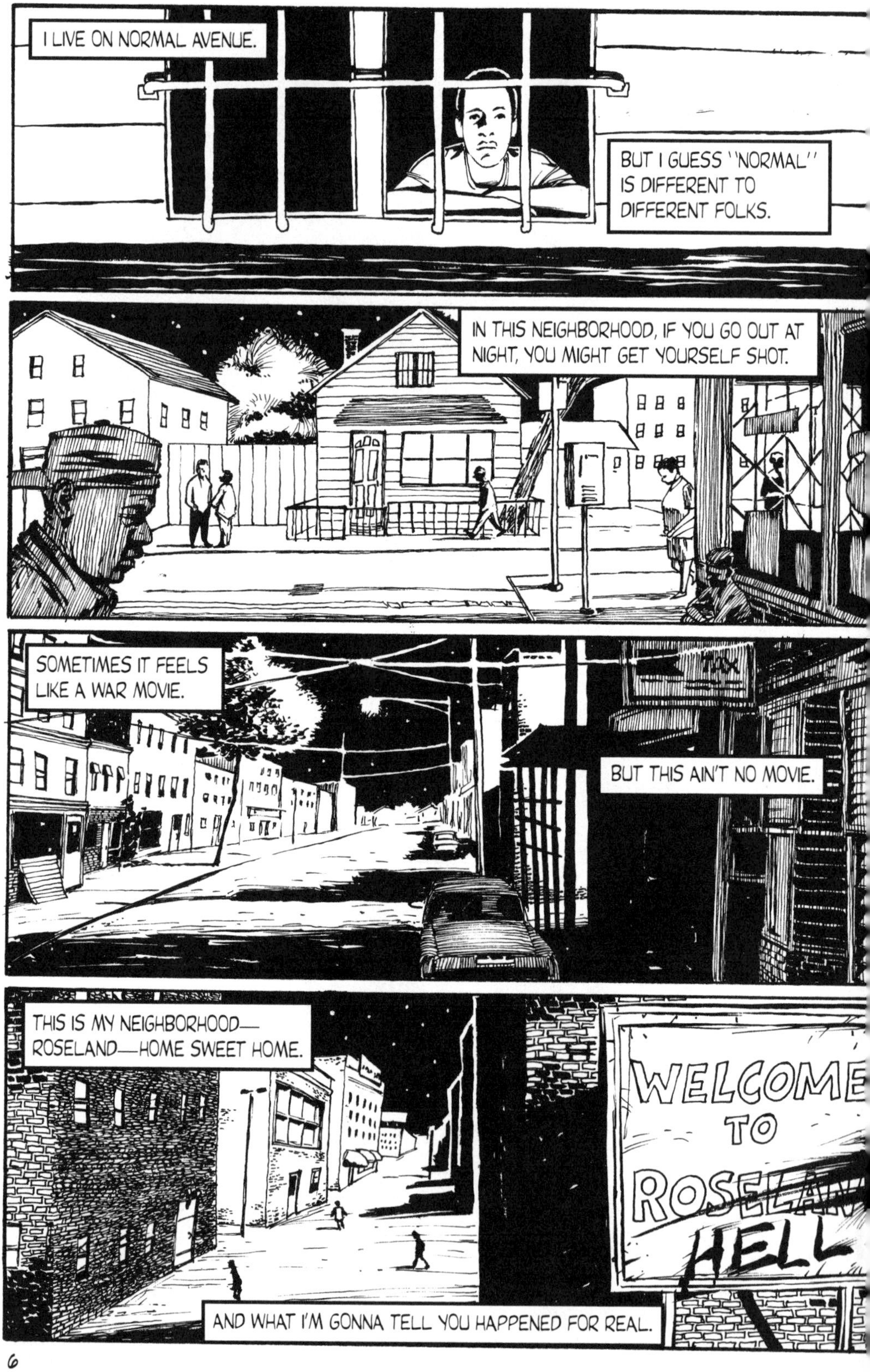

I LIVE ON NORMAL AVENUE.
BUT I GUESS "NORMAL" IS DIFFERENT TO DIFFERENT FOLKS.
IN THIS NEIGHBORHOOD, IF YOU GO OUT AT NIGHT, YOU MIGHT GET YOURSELF SHOT.
SOMETIMES IT FEELS LIKE A WAR MOVIE.
BUT THIS AIN'T NO MOVIE.
THIS IS MY NEIGHBORHOOD—ROSELAND—HOME SWEET HOME.
WELCOME TO ROSELAN
HELL
AND WHAT I'M GONNA TELL YOU HAPPENED FOR REAL.

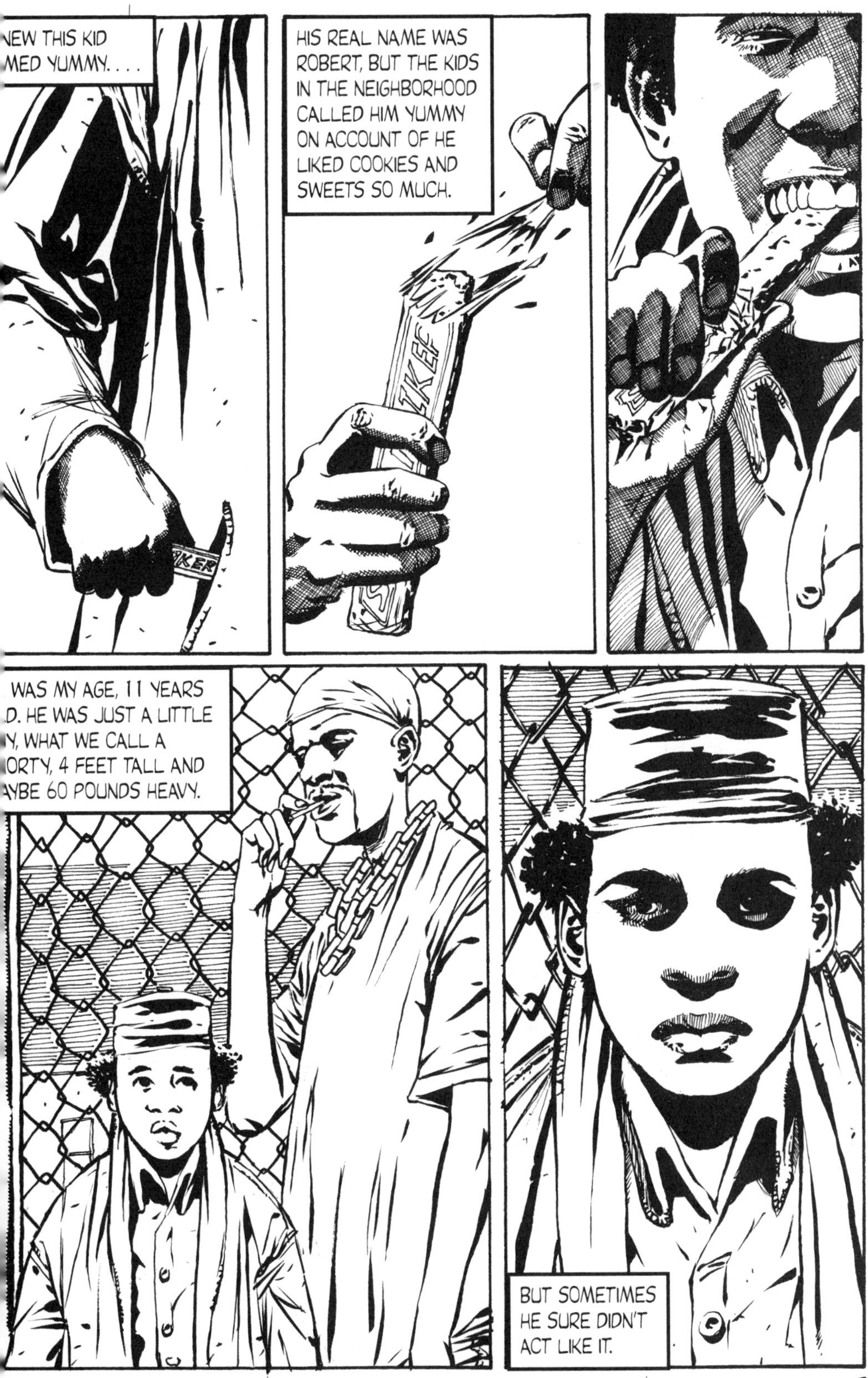
NEW THIS KID
MED YUMMY. . . .
HIS REAL NAME WAS ROBERT, BUT THE KIDS IN THE NEIGHBORHOOD CALLED HIM YUMMY ON ACCOUNT OF HE LIKED COOKIES AND SWEETS SO MUCH.
WAS MY AGE, 11 YEARS
D. HE WAS JUST A LITTLE
Y, WHAT WE CALL A
ORTY, 4 FEET TALL AND
YBE 60 POUNDS HEAVY.
BUT SOMETIMES HE SURE DIDN'T ACT LIKE IT.

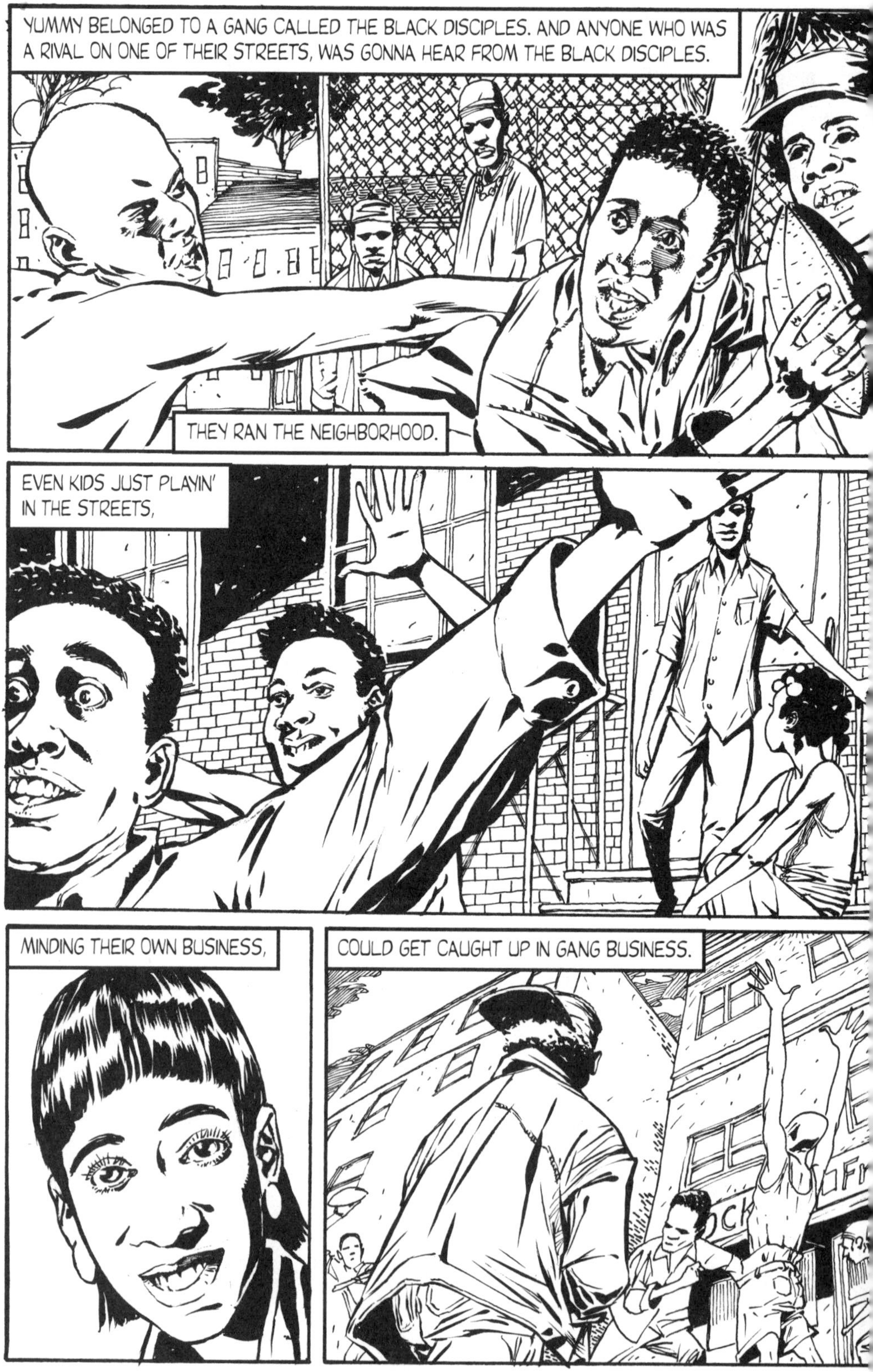
YUMMY BELONGED TO A GANG CALLED THE BLACK DISCIPLES. AND ANYONE WHO WAS A RIVAL ON ONE OF THEIR STREETS, WAS GONNA HEAR FROM THE BLACK DISCIPLES.
THEY RAN THE NEIGHBORHOOD.
EVEN KIDS JUST PLAYIN' IN THE STREETS,
MINDING THEIR OWN BUSINESS,
COULD GET CAUGHT UP IN GANG BUSINESS.

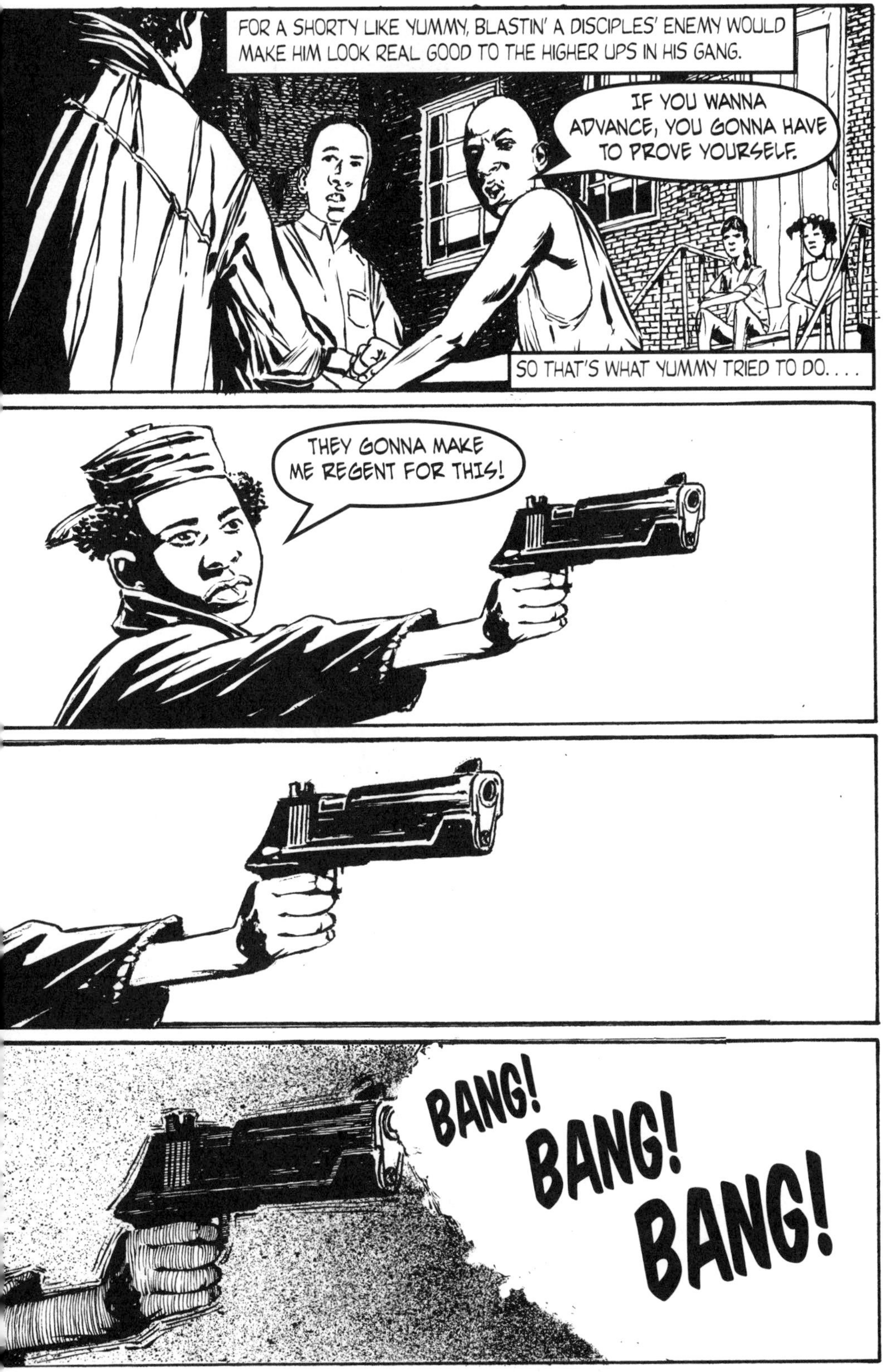
FOR A SHORTY LIKE YUMMY, BLASTIN' A DISCIPLES' ENEMY WOULD MAKE HIM LOOK REAL GOOD TO THE HIGHER UPS IN HIS GANG.
IF YOU WANNA ADVANCE, YOU GONNA HAVE TO PROVE YOURSELF.
SO THAT'S WHAT YUMMY TRIED TO DO. . . .
THEY GONNA MAKE ME REGENT FOR THIS!
BANG!
BANG!
BANG!

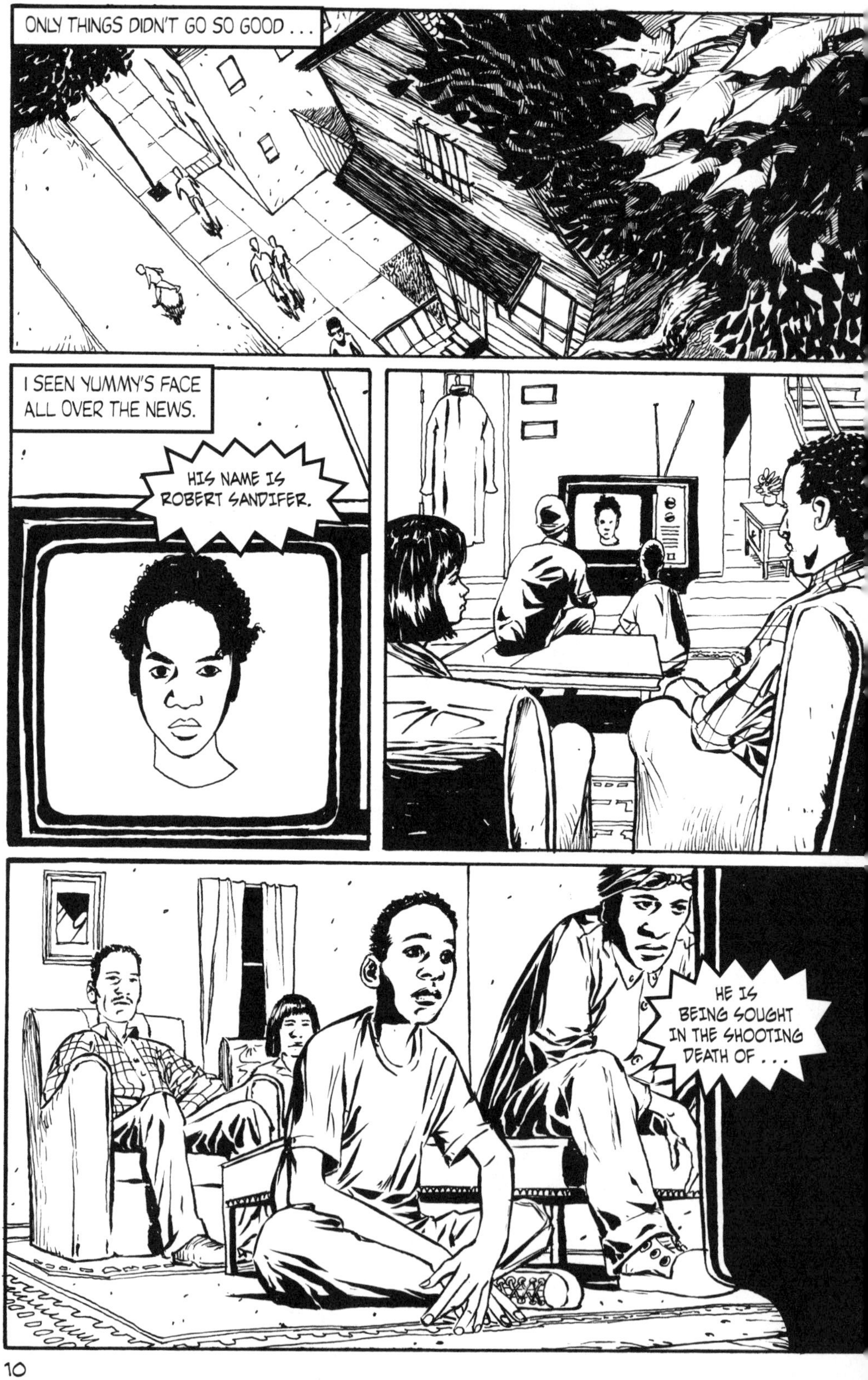

ONLY THINGS DIDN'T GO SO GOOD . . .
I SEEN YUMMY'S FACE ALL OVER THE NEWS.
HIS NAME IS ROBERT SANDIFER.
HE IS BEING SOUGHT IN THE SHOOTING DEATH OF . . .

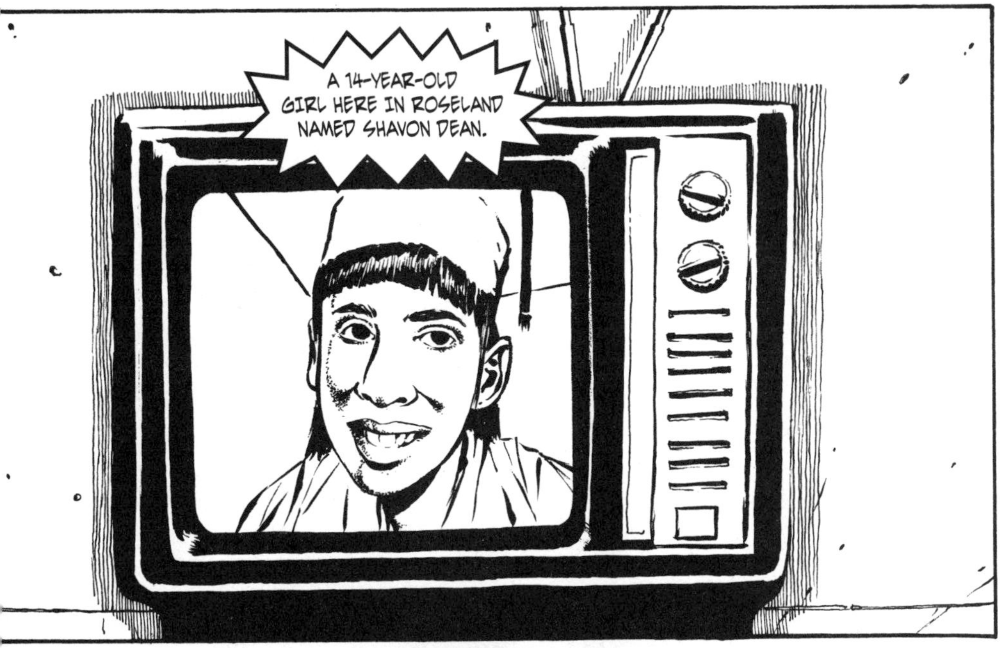
A 14-YEAR-OLD GIRL HERE IN ROSELAND NAMED SHAVON DEAN.

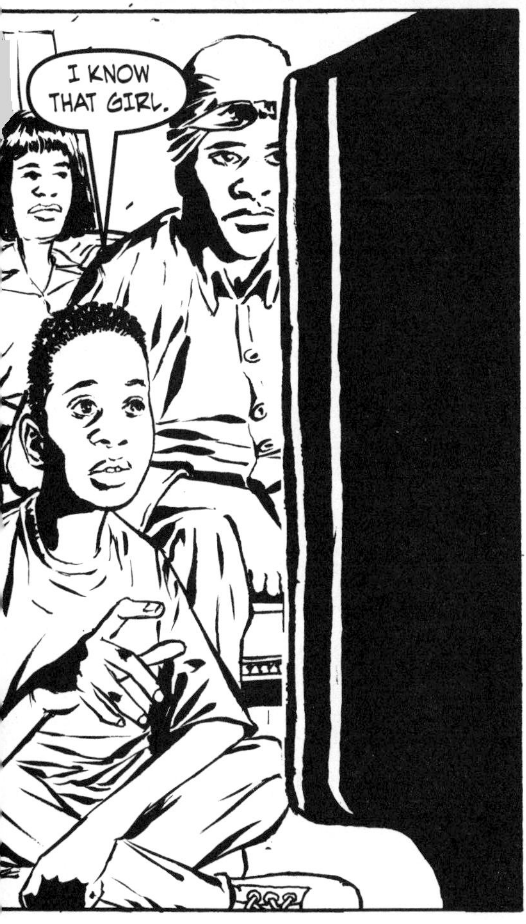
I KNOW THAT GIRL.

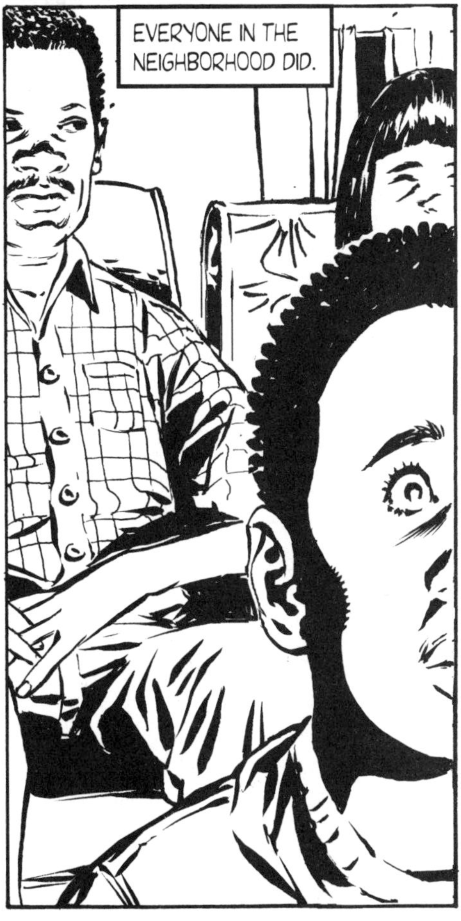
EVERYONE IN THE NEIGHBORHOOD DID.

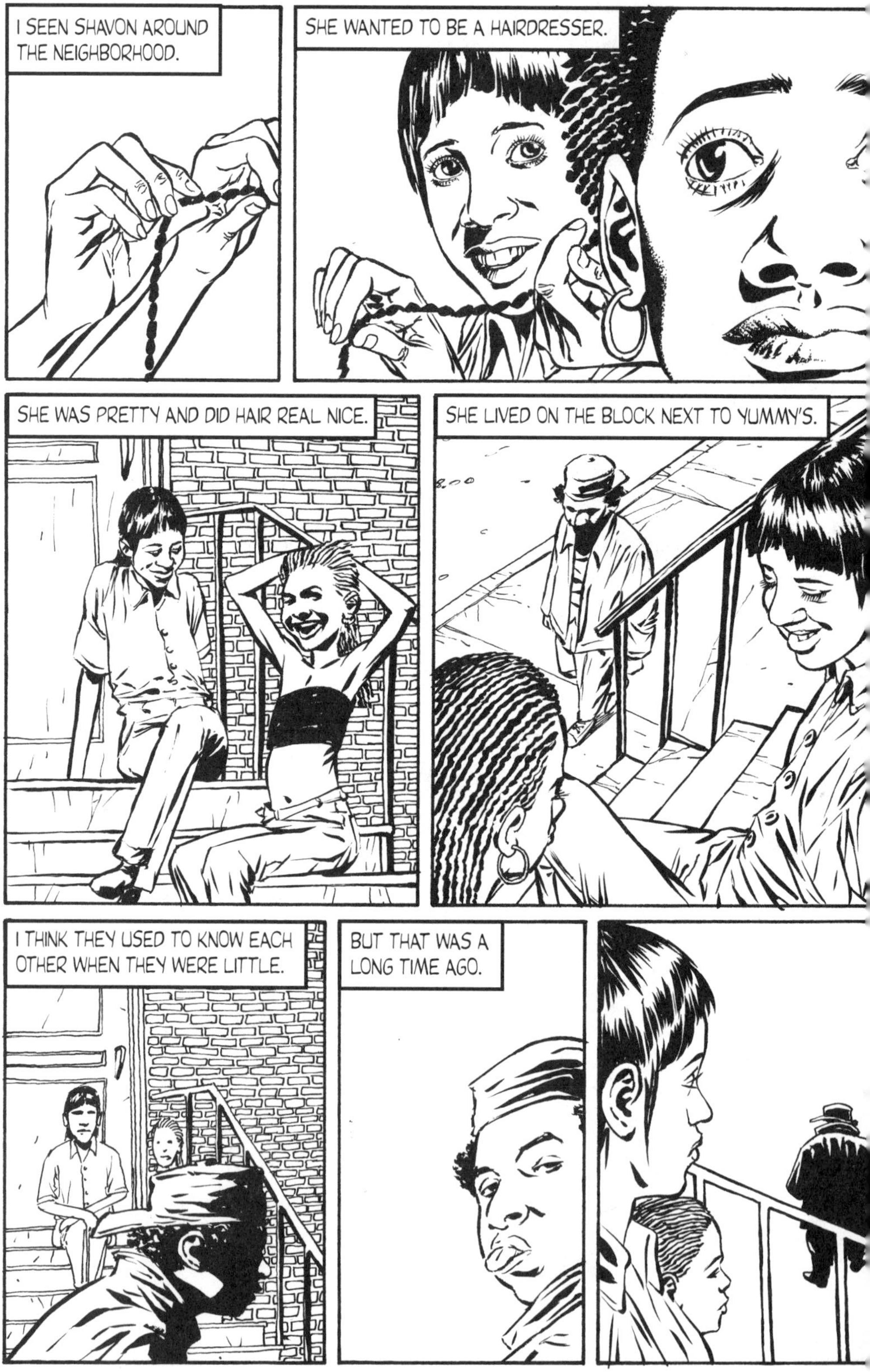
I SEEN SHAVON AROUND THE NEIGHBORHOOD.
SHE WANTED TO BE A HAIRDRESSER.
SHE WAS PRETTY AND DID HAIR REAL NICE.
SHE LIVED ON THE BLOCK NEXT TO YUMMY'S.
I THINK THEY USED TO KNOW EACH OTHER WHEN THEY WERE LITTLE.
BUT THAT WAS A LONG TIME AGO.

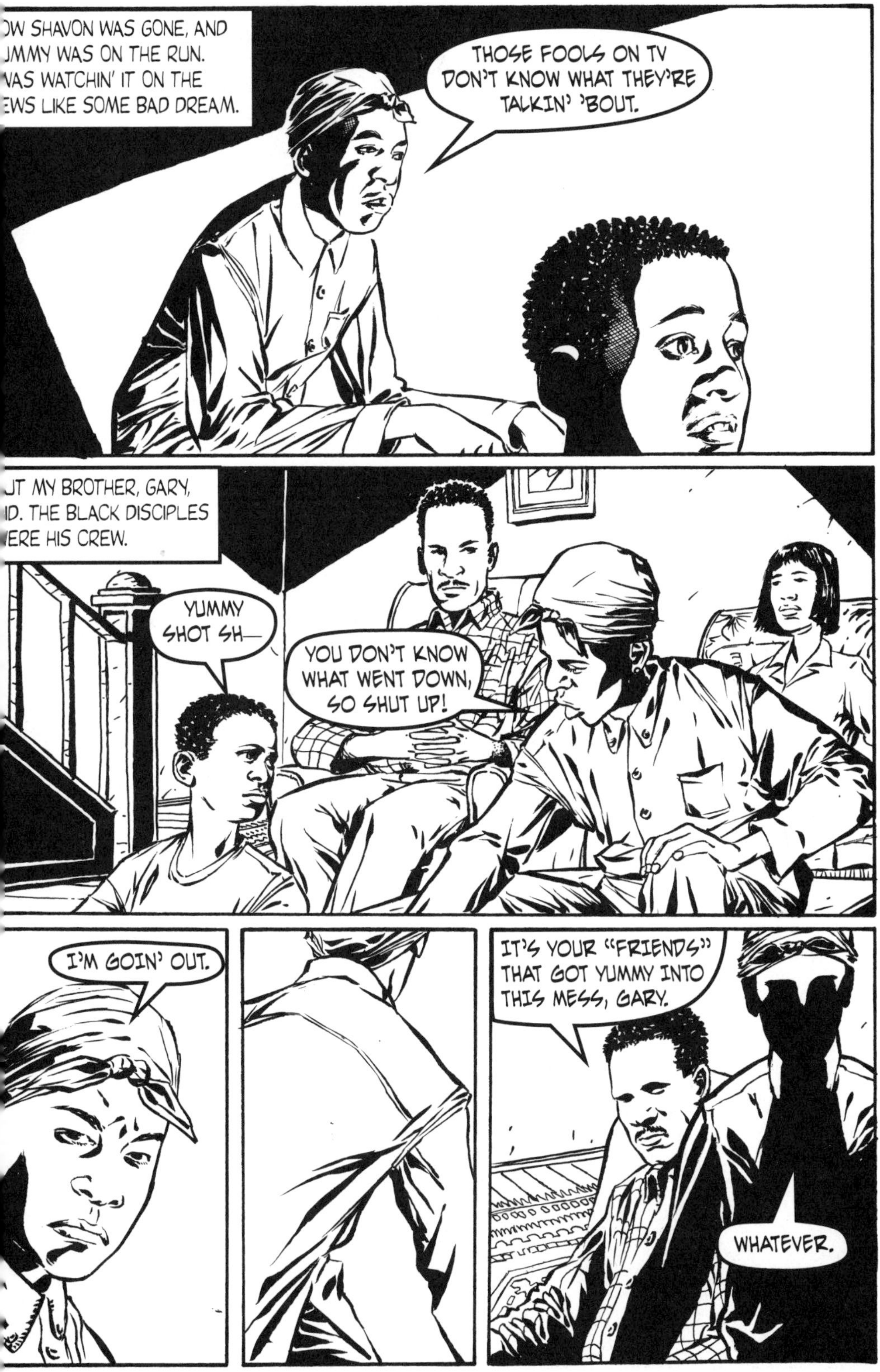

OW SHAVON WAS GONE, AND UMMY WAS ON THE RUN. VAS WATCHIN' IT ON THE EWS LIKE SOME BAD DREAM.
THOSE FOOLS ON TV DON'T KNOW WHAT THEY'RE TALKIN' 'BOUT.
UT MY BROTHER, GARY, ID. THE BLACK DISCIPLES VERE HIS CREW.
YUMMY SHOT SH—
YOU DON'T KNOW WHAT WENT DOWN, SO SHUT UP!
I'M GOIN' OUT.
IT'S YOUR "FRIENDS" THAT GOT YUMMY INTO THIS MESS, GARY.
WHATEVER.

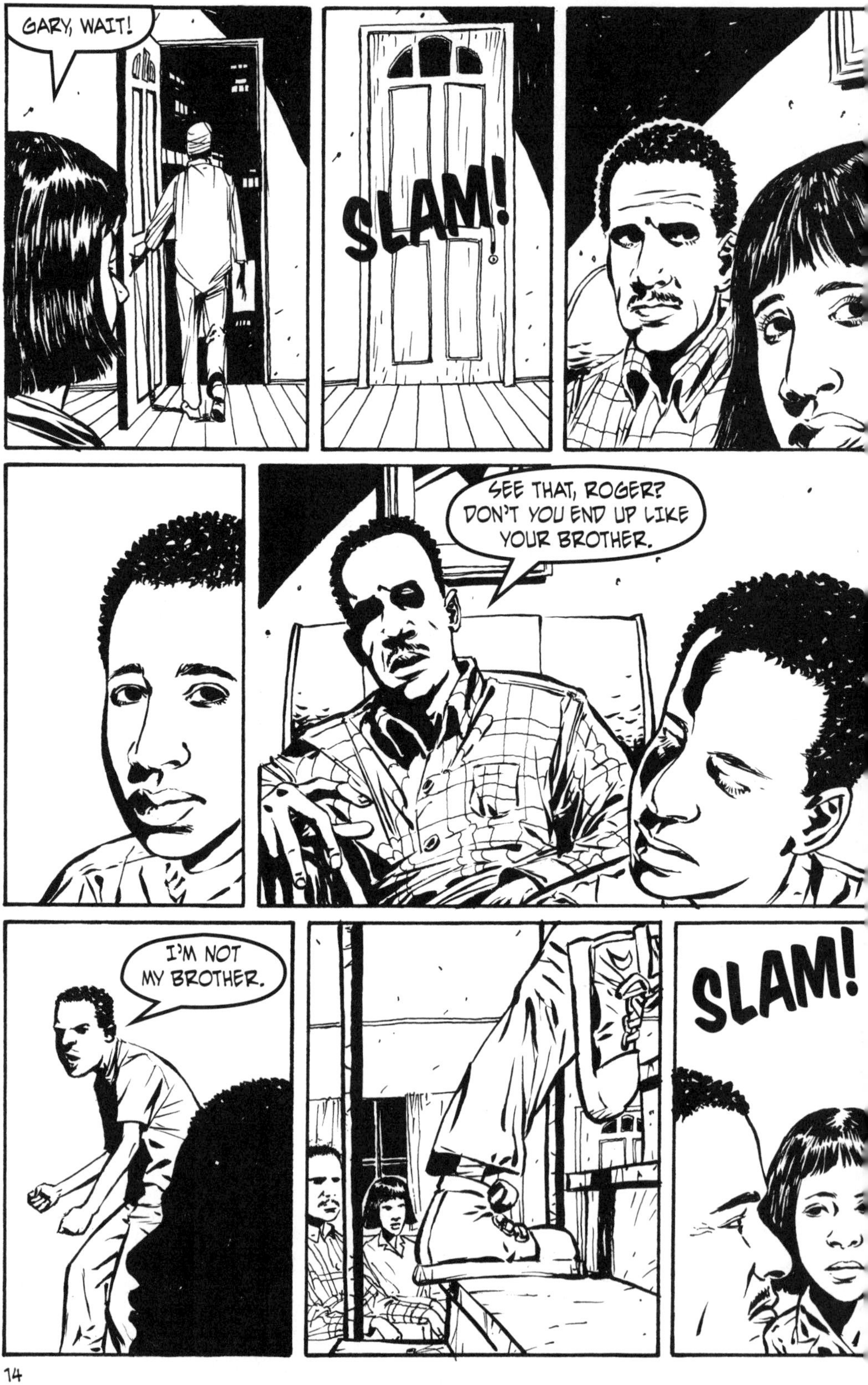
GARY, WAIT!
SLAM!
SEE THAT, ROGER? DON'T YOU END UP LIKE YOUR BROTHER.
I'M NOT MY BROTHER.
SLAM!

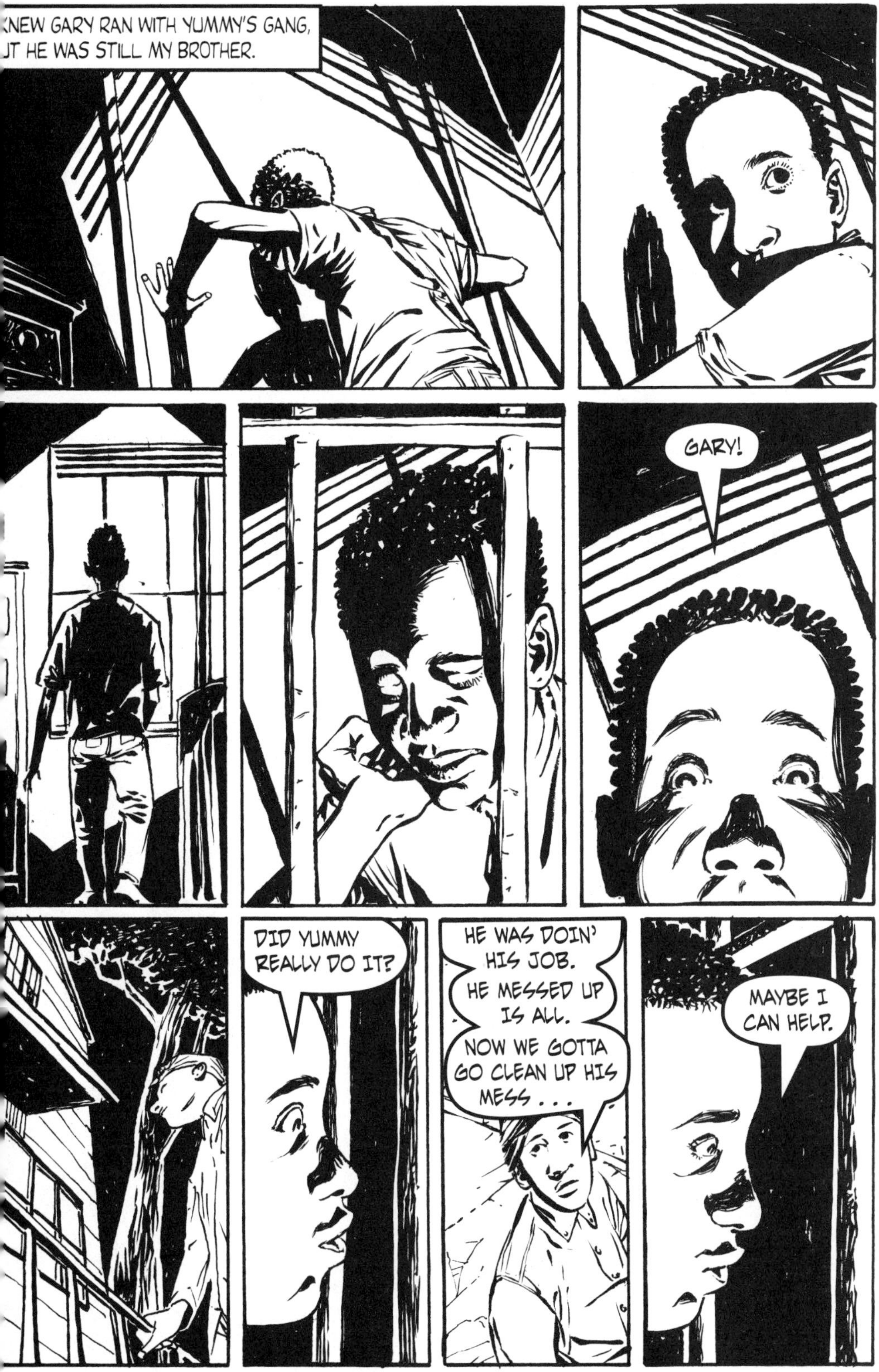
KNEW GARY RAN WITH YUMMY'S GANG, UT HE WAS STILL MY BROTHER.
GARY!
DID YUMMY REALLY DO IT?
HE WAS DOIN' HIS JOB.
HE MESSED UP IS ALL.
NOW WE GOTTA GO CLEAN UP HIS MESS . . .
MAYBE I CAN HELP.

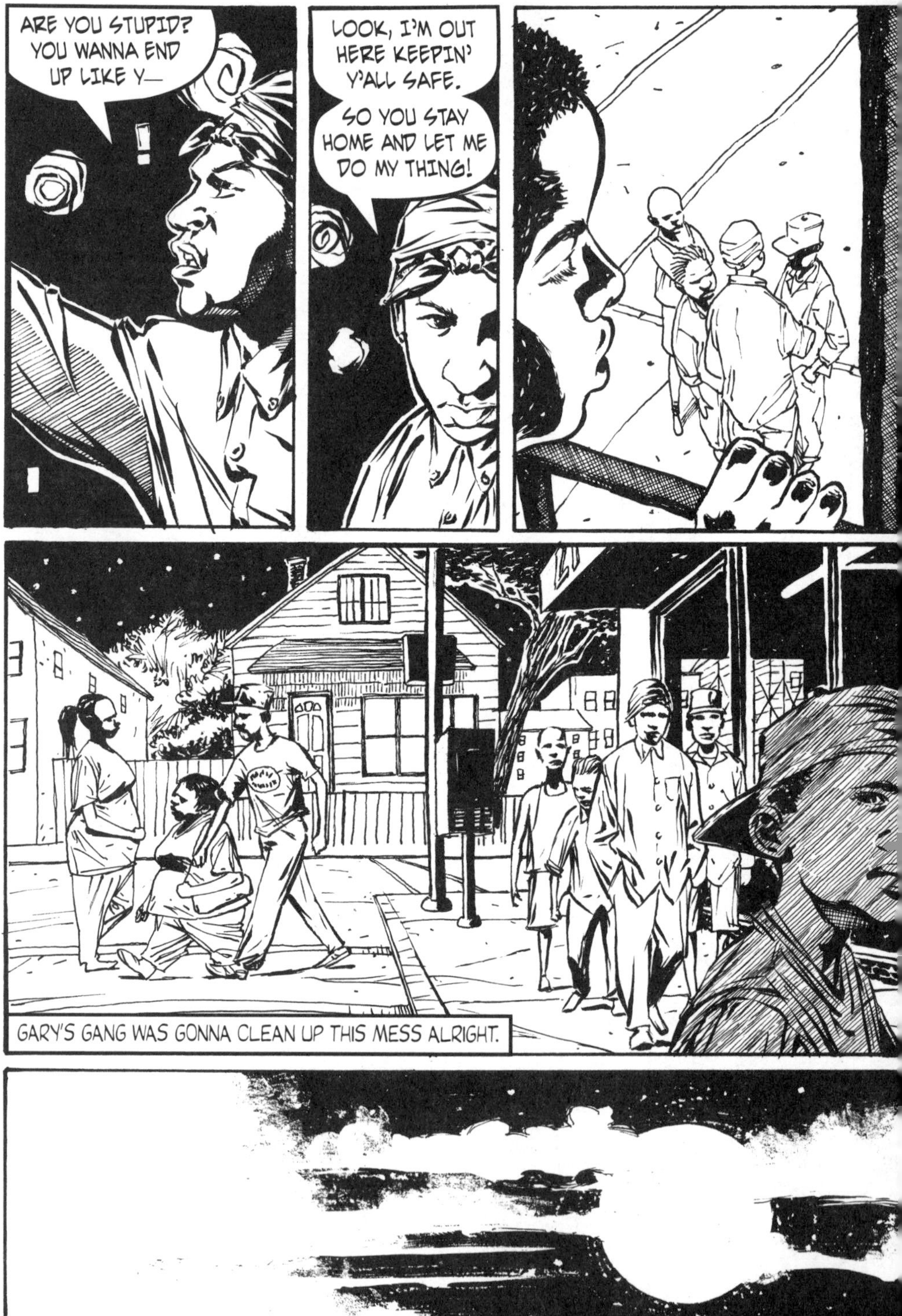
ARE YOU STUPID? YOU WANNA END UP LIKE Y—
!
LOOK, I'M OUT HERE KEEPIN' Y'ALL SAFE.
SO YOU STAY HOME AND LET ME DO MY THING!
GARY'S GANG WAS GONNA CLEAN UP THIS MESS ALRIGHT.
BUT I KNEW MORE TROUBLE WAS ON THE WAY . . .

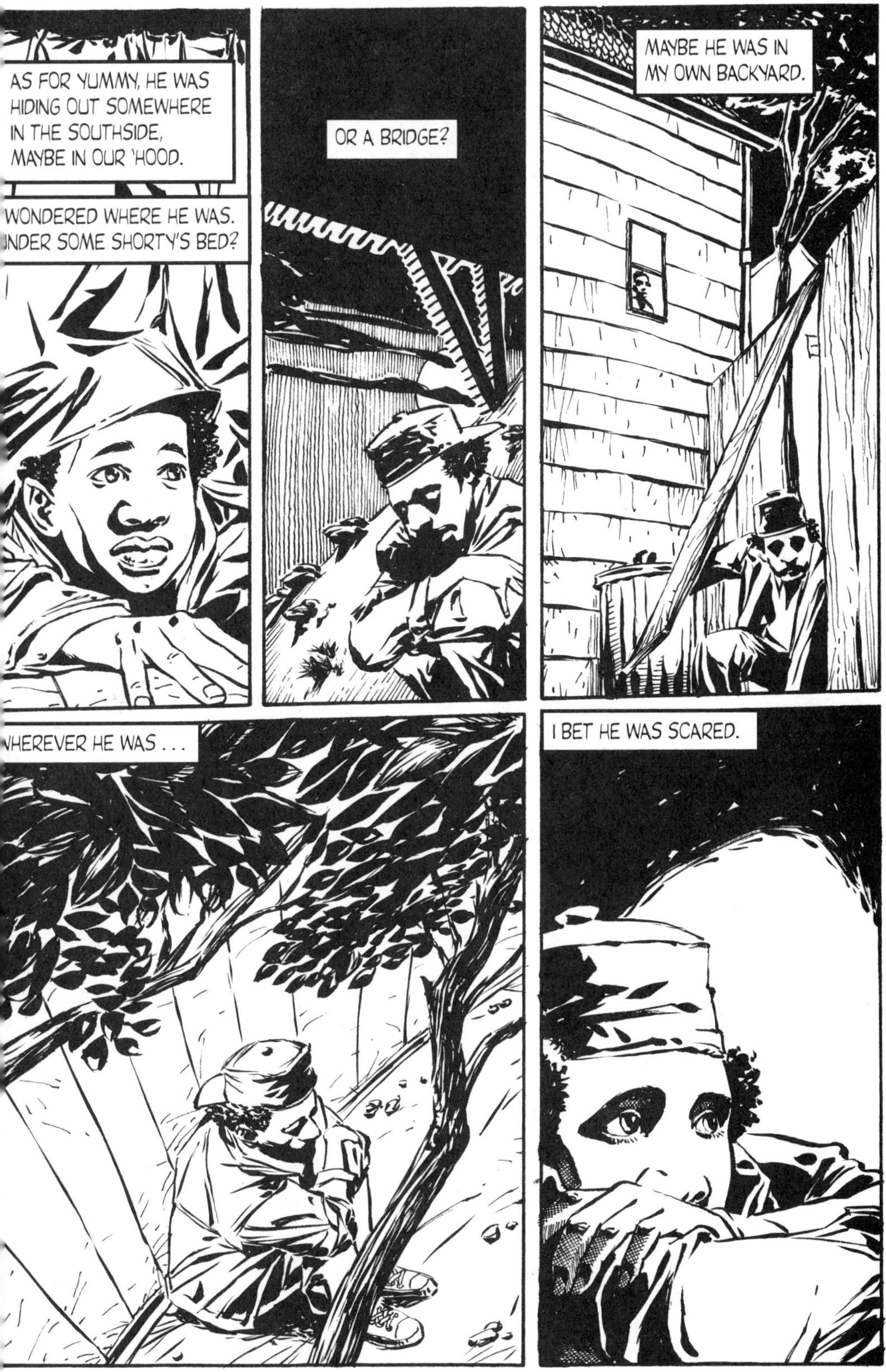
AS FOR YUMMY, HE WAS HIDING OUT SOMEWHERE IN THE SOUTHSIDE, MAYBE IN OUR 'HOOD.
WONDERED WHERE HE WAS. UNDER SOME SHORTY'S BED?
OR A BRIDGE?
MAYBE HE WAS IN MY OWN BACKYARD.
WHEREVER HE WAS . . .
I BET HE WAS SCARED.

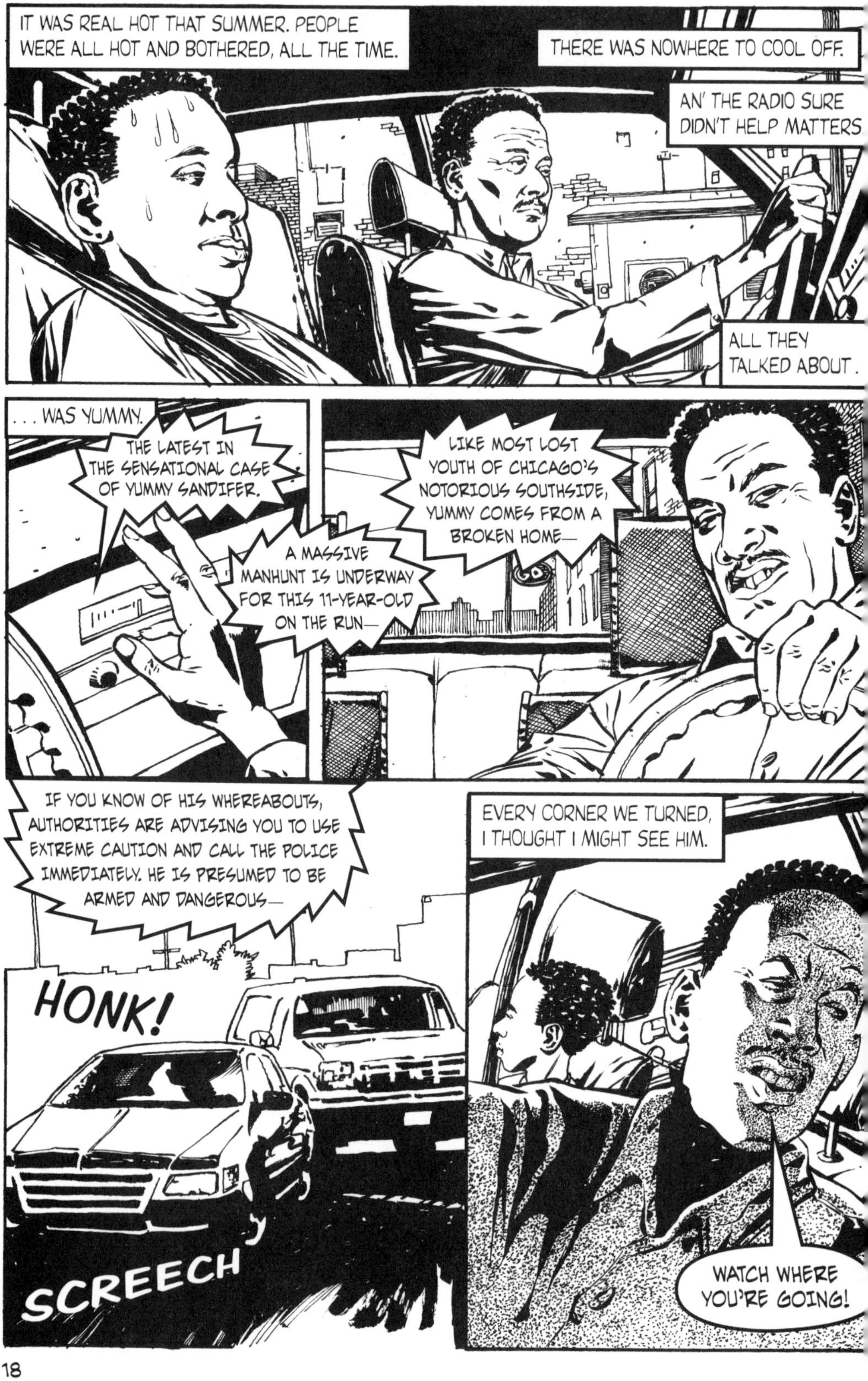
IT WAS REAL HOT THAT SUMMER. PEOPLE WERE ALL HOT AND BOTHERED, ALL THE TIME.
THERE WAS NOWHERE TO COOL OFF.
AN' THE RADIO SURE DIDN'T HELP MATTERS.
ALL THEY TALKED ABOUT . . .
. . . WAS YUMMY.
THE LATEST IN THE SENSATIONAL CASE OF YUMMY SANDIFER.
A MASSIVE MANHUNT IS UNDERWAY FOR THIS 11-YEAR-OLD ON THE RUN—
LIKE MOST LOST YOUTH OF CHICAGO'S NOTORIOUS SOUTHSIDE, YUMMY COMES FROM A BROKEN HOME—
IF YOU KNOW OF HIS WHEREABOUTS, AUTHORITIES ARE ADVISING YOU TO USE EXTREME CAUTION AND CALL THE POLICE IMMEDIATELY. HE IS PRESUMED TO BE ARMED AND DANGEROUS—
HONK!
SCREECH
EVERY CORNER WE TURNED, I THOUGHT I MIGHT SEE HIM.
WATCH WHERE YOU'RE GOING!

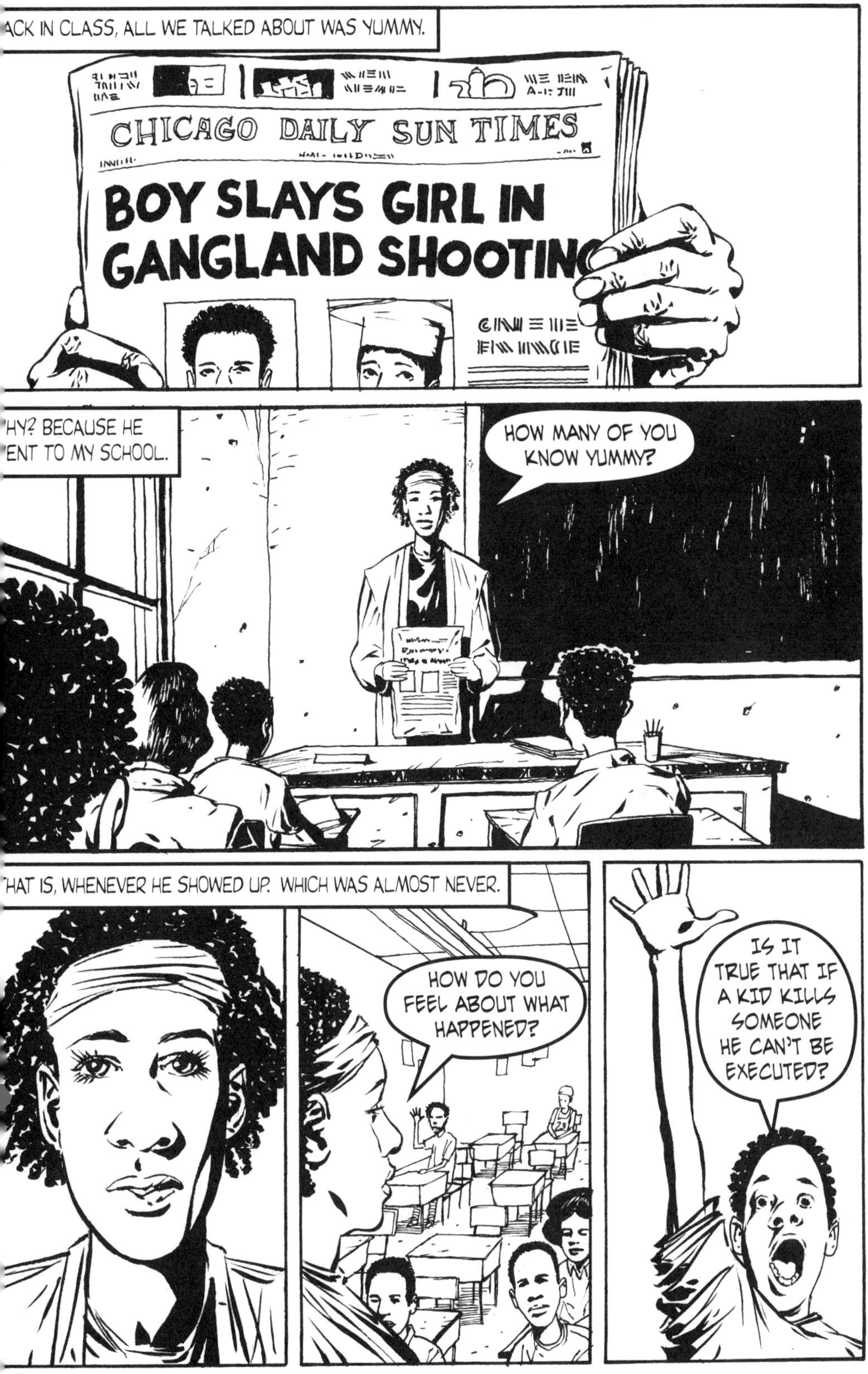
ACK IN CLASS, ALL WE TALKED ABOUT WAS YUMMY.
CHICAGO DAILY SUN TIMES
BOY SLAYS GIRL IN GANGLAND SHOOTIN
HY? BECAUSE HE ENT TO MY SCHOOL.
HOW MANY OF YOU KNOW YUMMY?
HAT IS, WHENEVER HE SHOWED UP. WHICH WAS ALMOST NEVER.
HOW DO YOU FEEL ABOUT WHAT HAPPENED?
IS IT TRUE THAT IF A KID KILLS SOMEONE HE CAN'T BE EXECUTED?

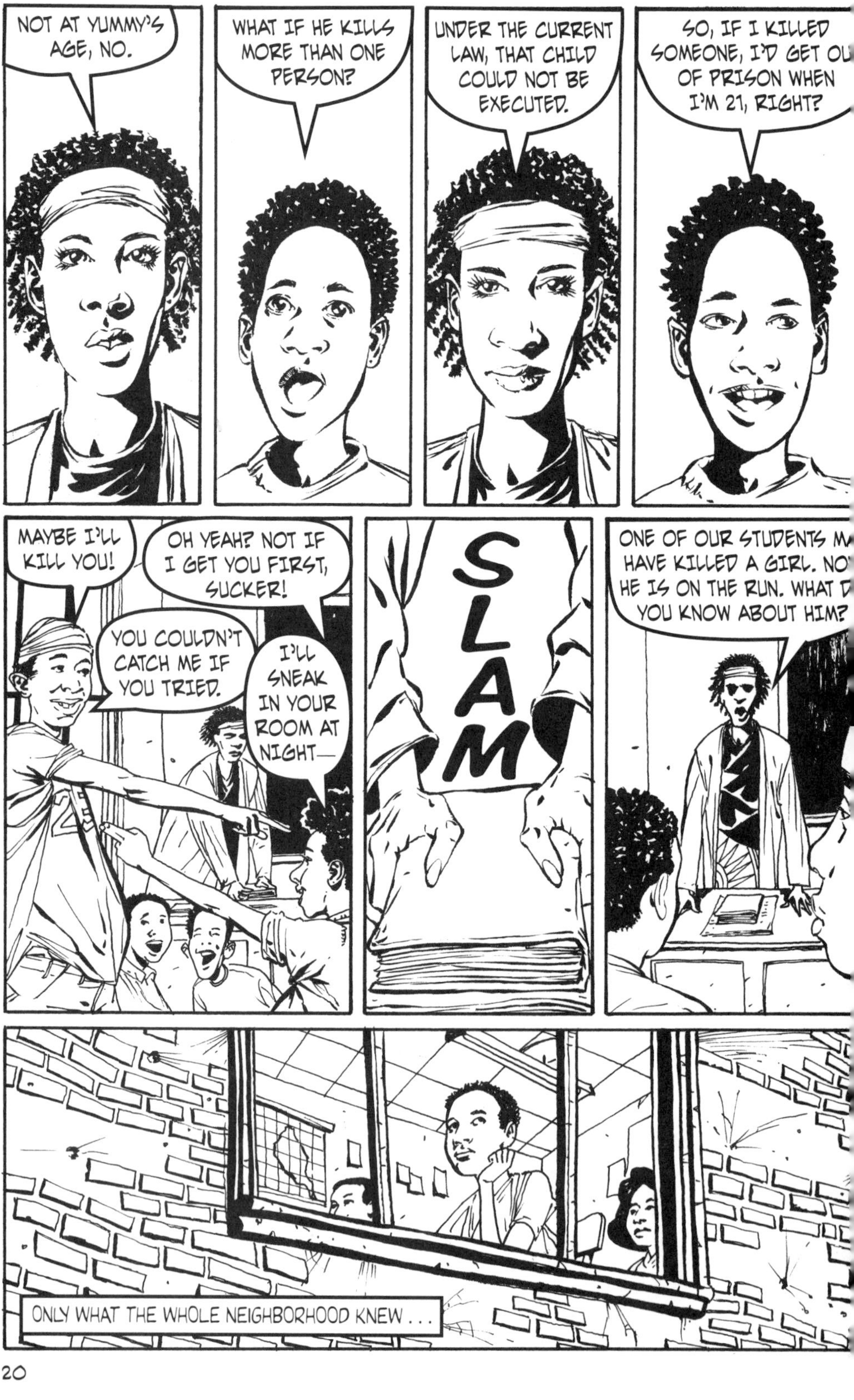
NOT AT YUMMY'S AGE, NO.
WHAT IF HE KILLS MORE THAN ONE PERSON?
UNDER THE CURRENT LAW, THAT CHILD COULD NOT BE EXECUTED.
SO, IF I KILLED SOMEONE, I'D GET OU OF PRISON WHEN I'M 21, RIGHT?
MAYBE I'LL KILL YOU!
OH YEAH? NOT IF I GET YOU FIRST, SUCKER!
YOU COULDN'T CATCH ME IF YOU TRIED.
I'LL SNEAK IN YOUR ROOM AT NIGHT—
SLAM
ONE OF OUR STUDENTS M HAVE KILLED A GIRL. NO HE IS ON THE RUN. WHAT D YOU KNOW ABOUT HIM?
ONLY WHAT THE WHOLE NEIGHBORHOOD KNEW . . .

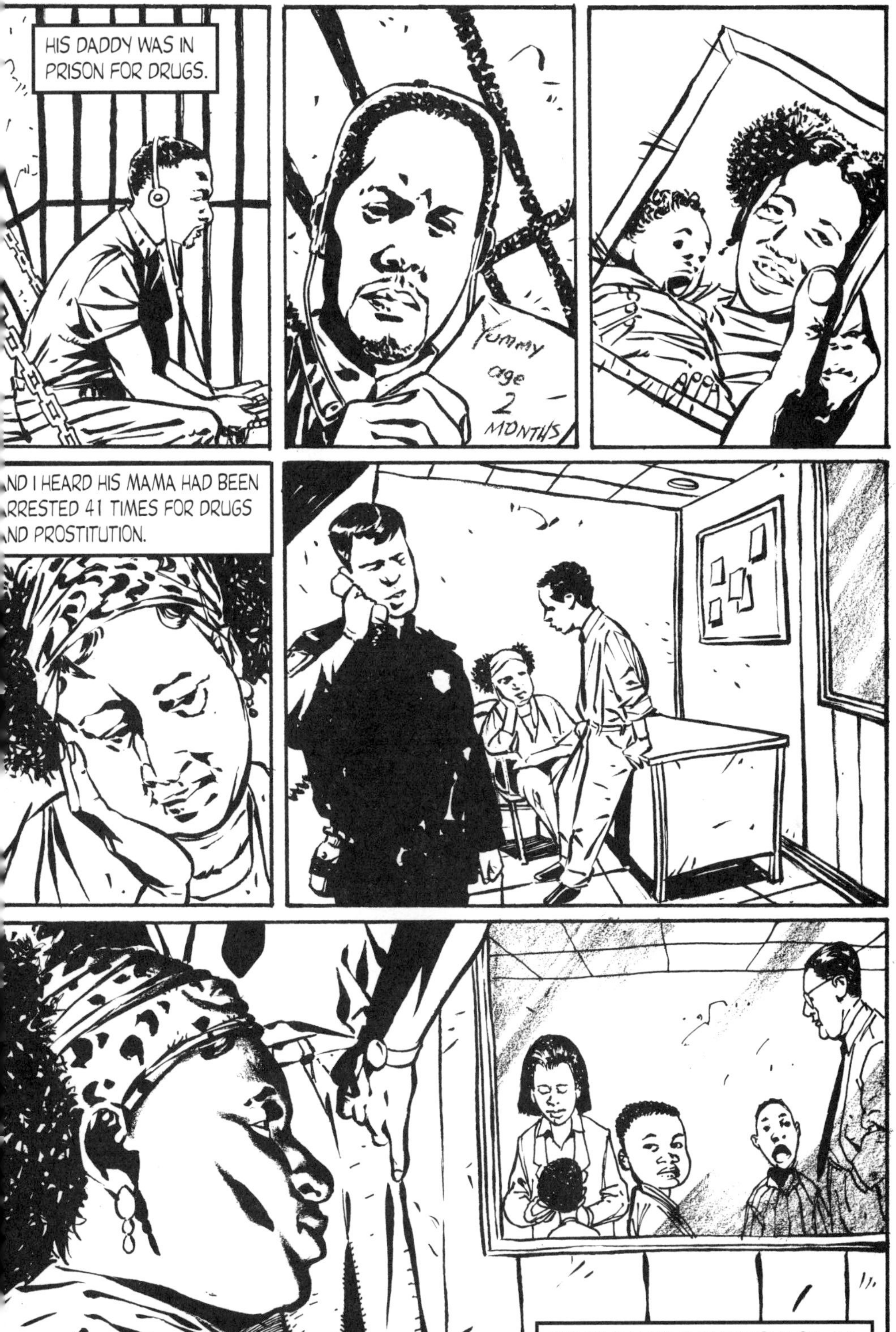
HIS DADDY WAS IN PRISON FOR DRUGS.
Yummy age 2 MONTHS
ND I HEARD HIS MAMA HAD BEEN
RRESTED 41 TIMES FOR DRUGS
ND PROSTITUTION.
SHE WAS ALWAYS IN AND OUT OF JAIL.

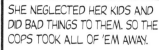
SHE NEGLECTED HER KIDS AND DID BAD THINGS TO THEM. SO THE COPS TOOK ALL OF 'EM AWAY.

AN' FOR GOOD REASON.

EVER SINCE I KNEW HIM, WHEN HE WAS LIKE 3, YUMMY HAD SCARS AND BURNS ALL OVER HIMSELF. HE USED TO SHOW THEM OFF TO US.

THIS ONE WAS FROM WHEN I GOT WHOOPED WITH A 'LECTRICAL CORD.

DANG, YUMMY, YOU ONE BAD BOY!

I THOUGHT THEY WERE UGLY.

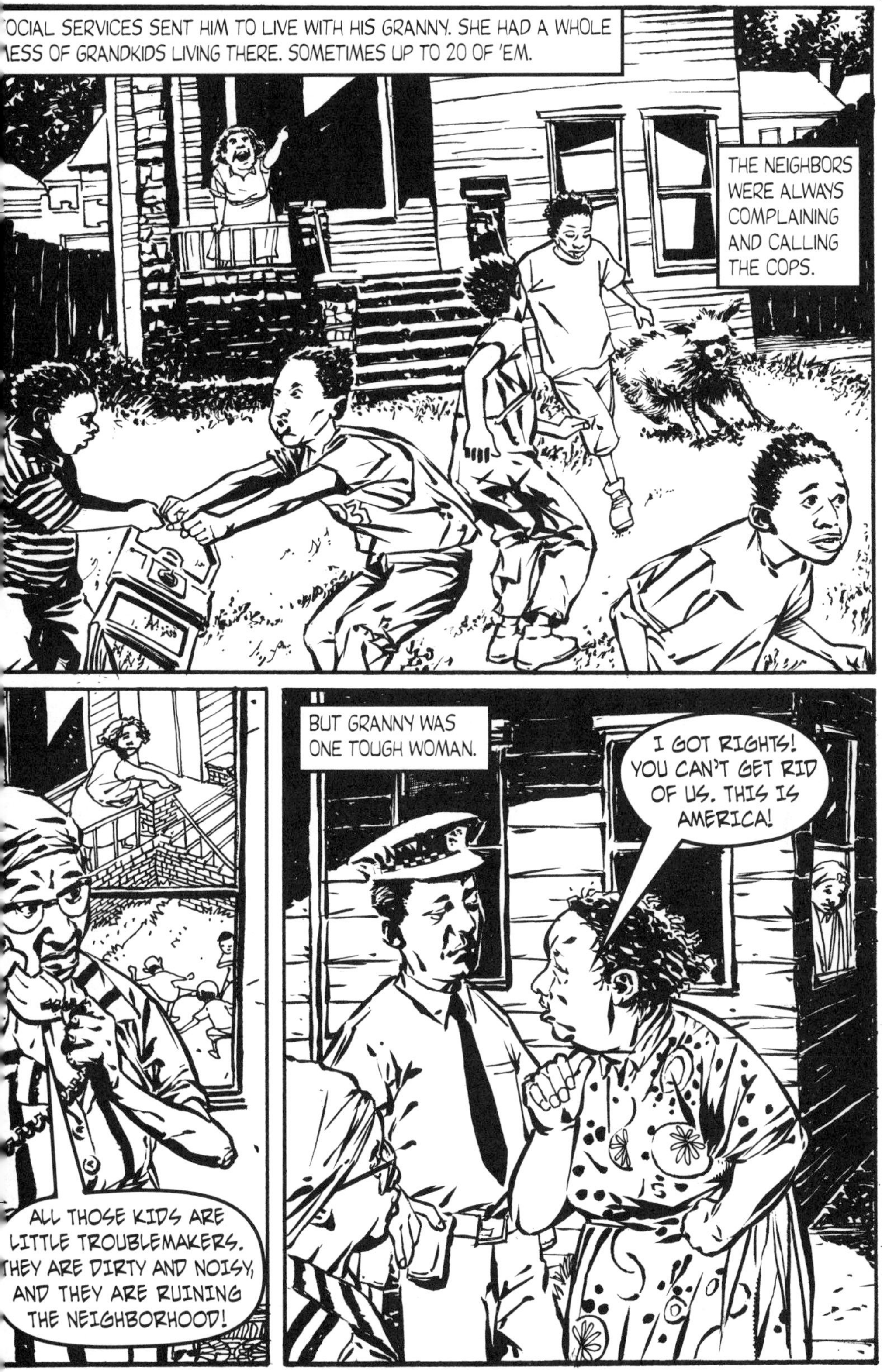
OCIAL SERVICES SENT HIM TO LIVE WITH HIS GRANNY. SHE HAD A WHOLE
ESS OF GRANDKIDS LIVING THERE. SOMETIMES UP TO 20 OF 'EM.
THE NEIGHBORS WERE ALWAYS COMPLAINING AND CALLING THE COPS.
ALL THOSE KIDS ARE LITTLE TROUBLEMAKERS. HEY ARE DIRTY AND NOISY, AND THEY ARE RUINING THE NEIGHBORHOOD!
BUT GRANNY WAS ONE TOUGH WOMAN.
I GOT RIGHTS! YOU CAN'T GET RID OF US. THIS IS AMERICA!

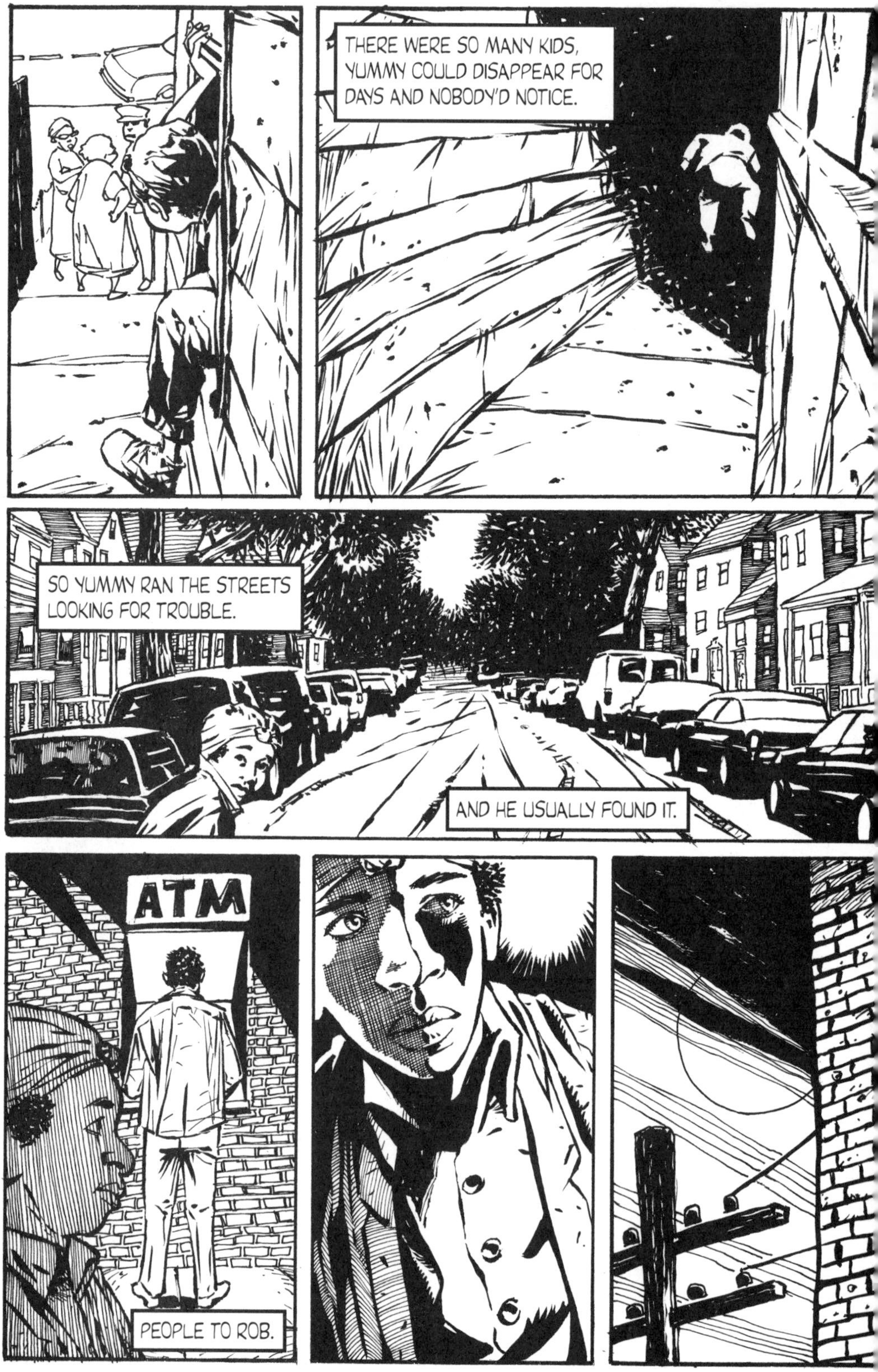
THERE WERE SO MANY KIDS, YUMMY COULD DISAPPEAR FOR DAYS AND NOBODY'D NOTICE.
SO YUMMY RAN THE STREETS LOOKING FOR TROUBLE.
AND HE USUALLY FOUND IT.
ATM
PEOPLE TO ROB.

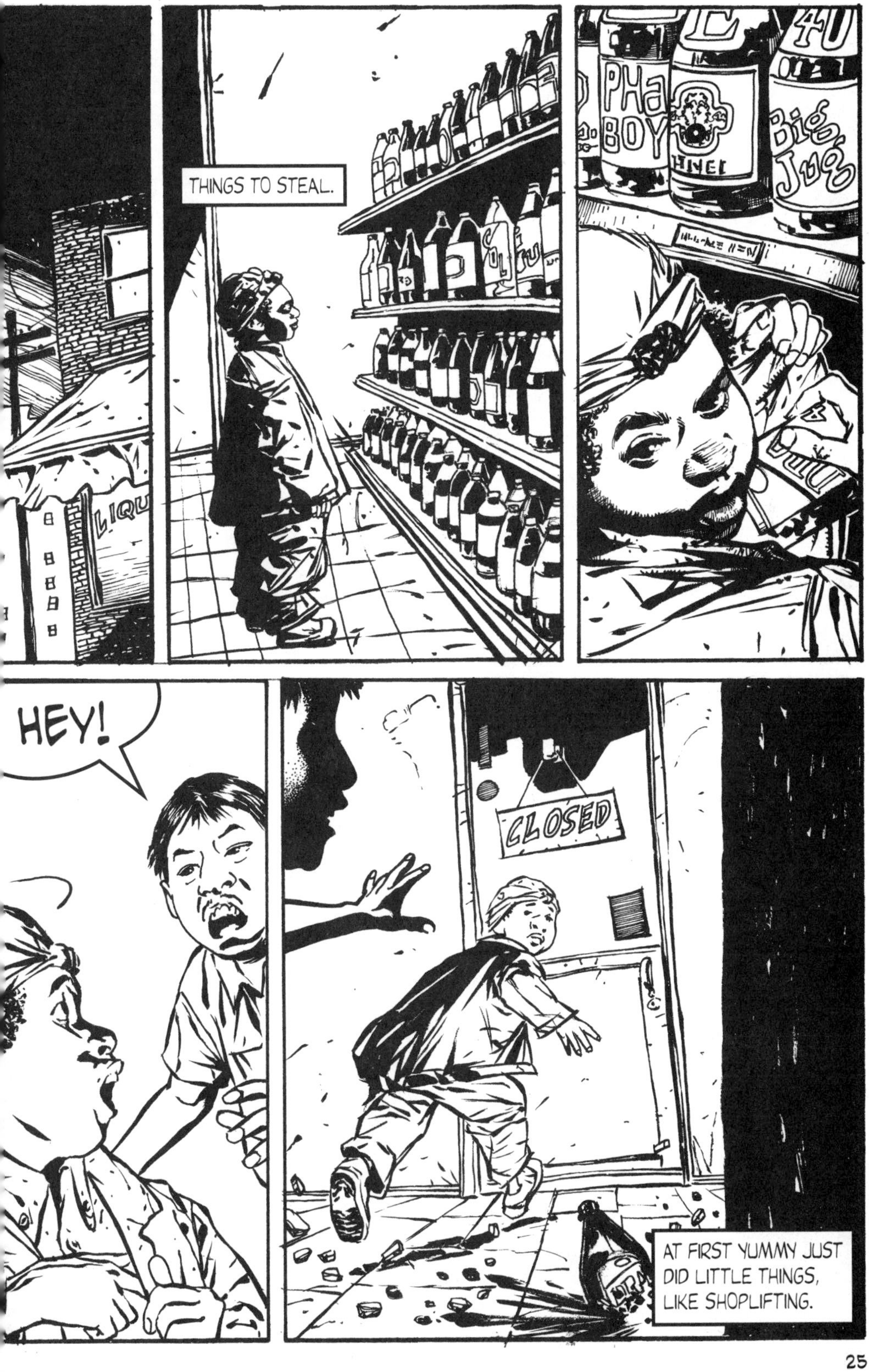
LIQU
THINGS TO STEAL.
PHA
BOY
40
Big
Jug
HEY!
CLOSED
AT FIRST YUMMY JUST DID LITTLE THINGS, LIKE SHOPLIFTING.

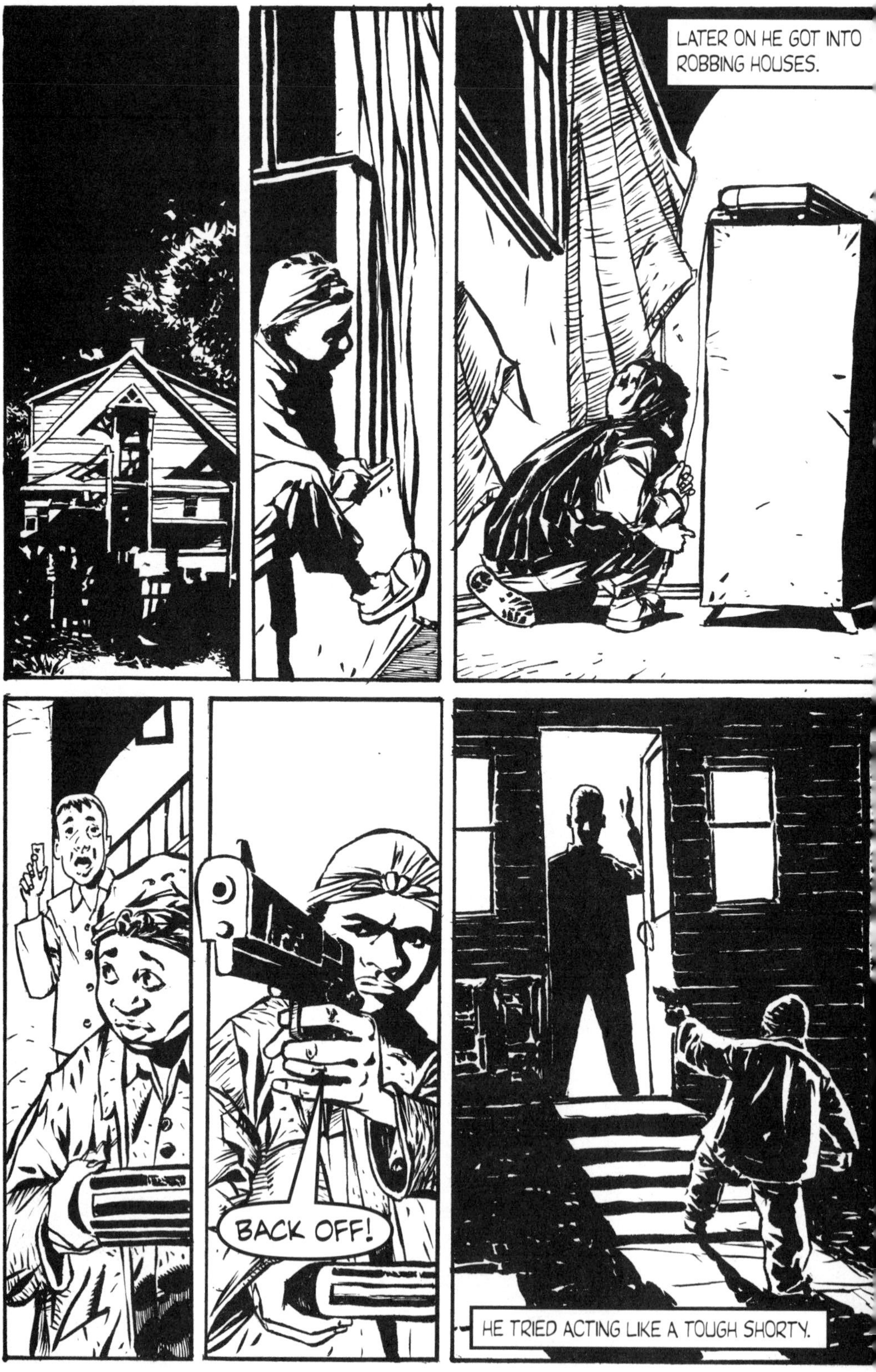
LATER ON HE GOT INTO ROBBING HOUSES.
BACK OFF!
HE TRIED ACTING LIKE A TOUGH SHORTY.

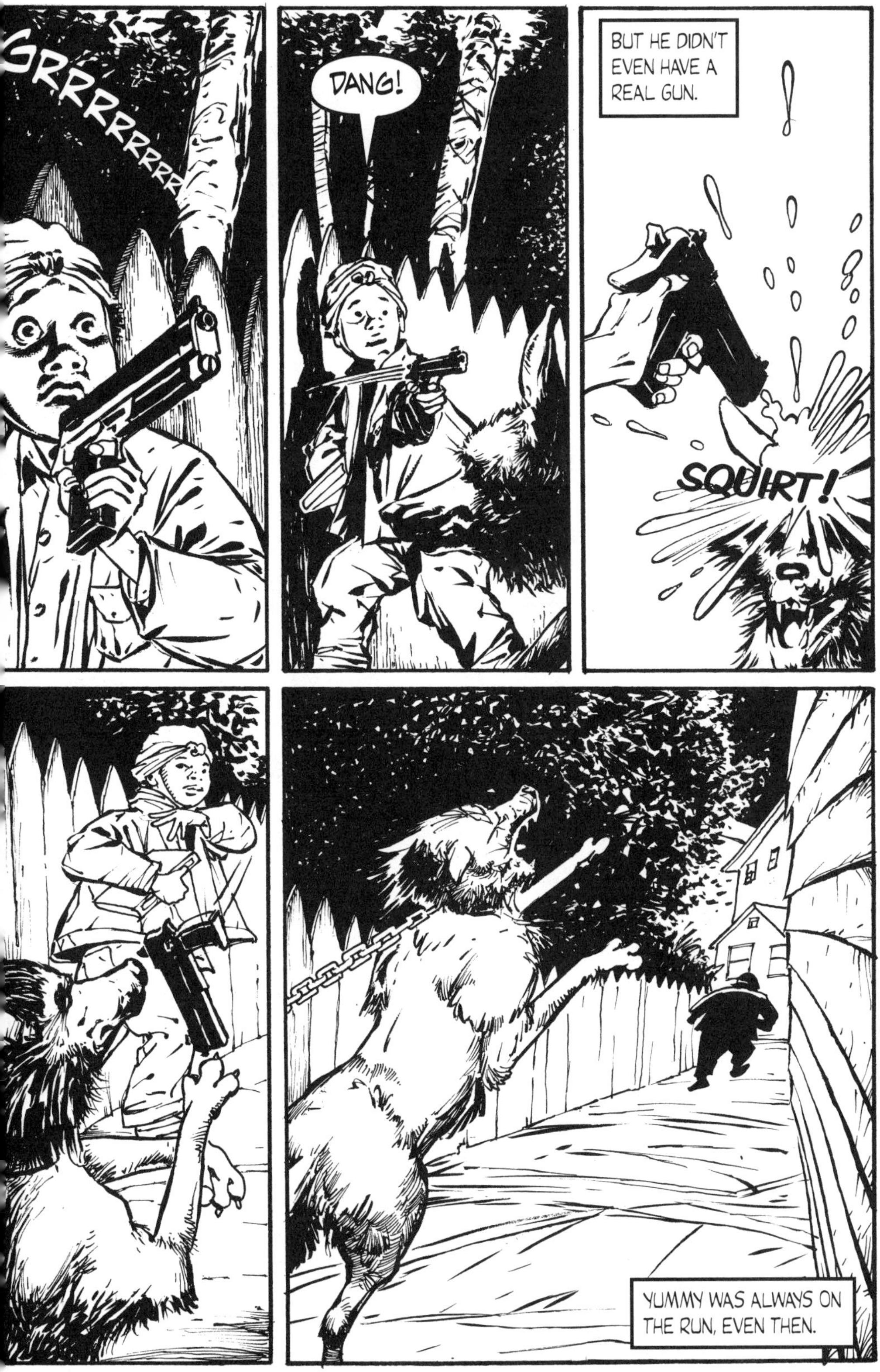
GRRRRRRRRR
DANG!
BUT HE DIDN'T EVEN HAVE A REAL GUN.
SQUIRT!
YUMMY WAS ALWAYS ON THE RUN, EVEN THEN.

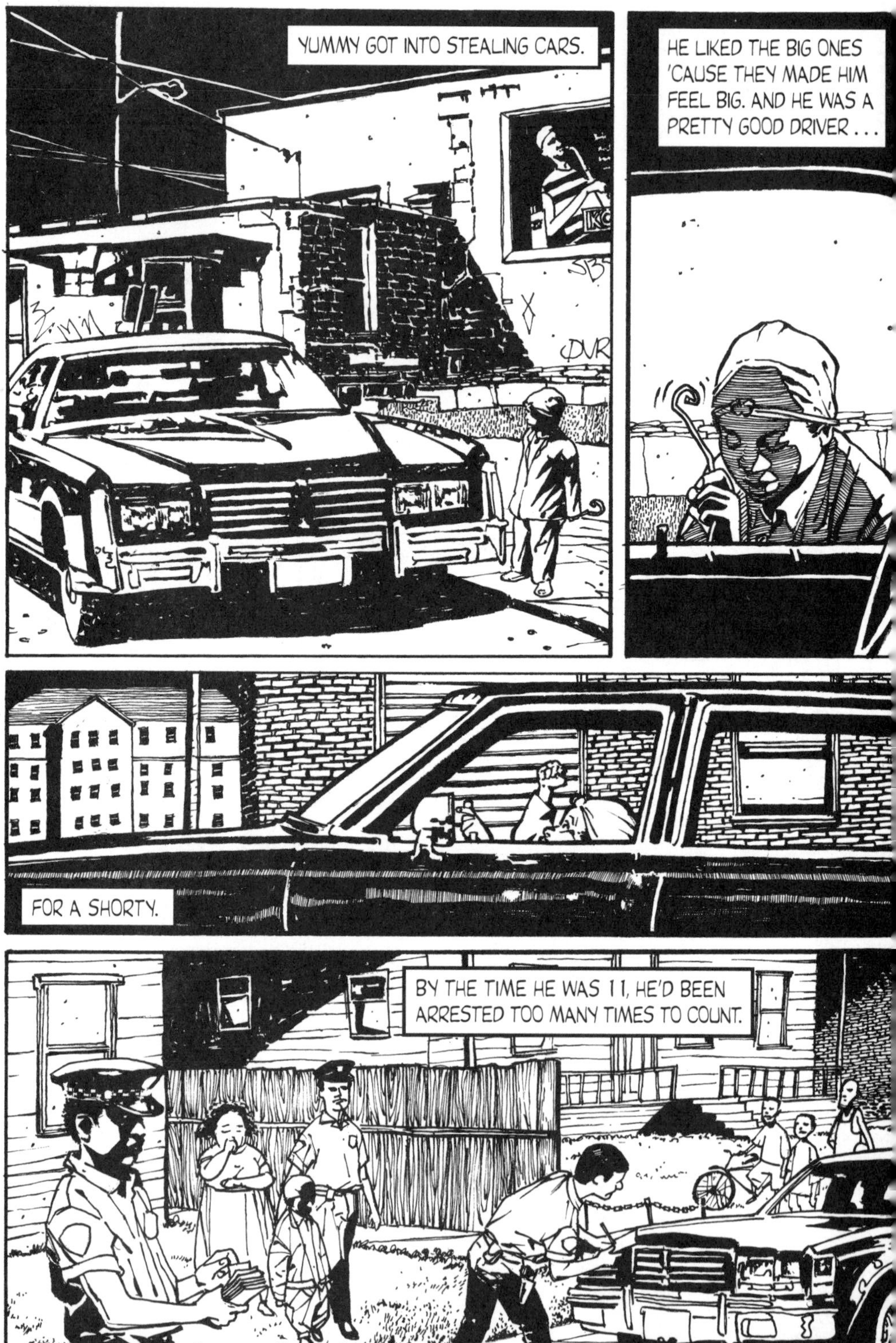
YUMMY GOT INTO STEALING CARS.
HE LIKED THE BIG ONES 'CAUSE THEY MADE HIM FEEL BIG. AND HE WAS A PRETTY GOOD DRIVER . . .
FOR A SHORTY.
BY THE TIME HE WAS 11, HE'D BEEN ARRESTED TOO MANY TIMES TO COUNT.

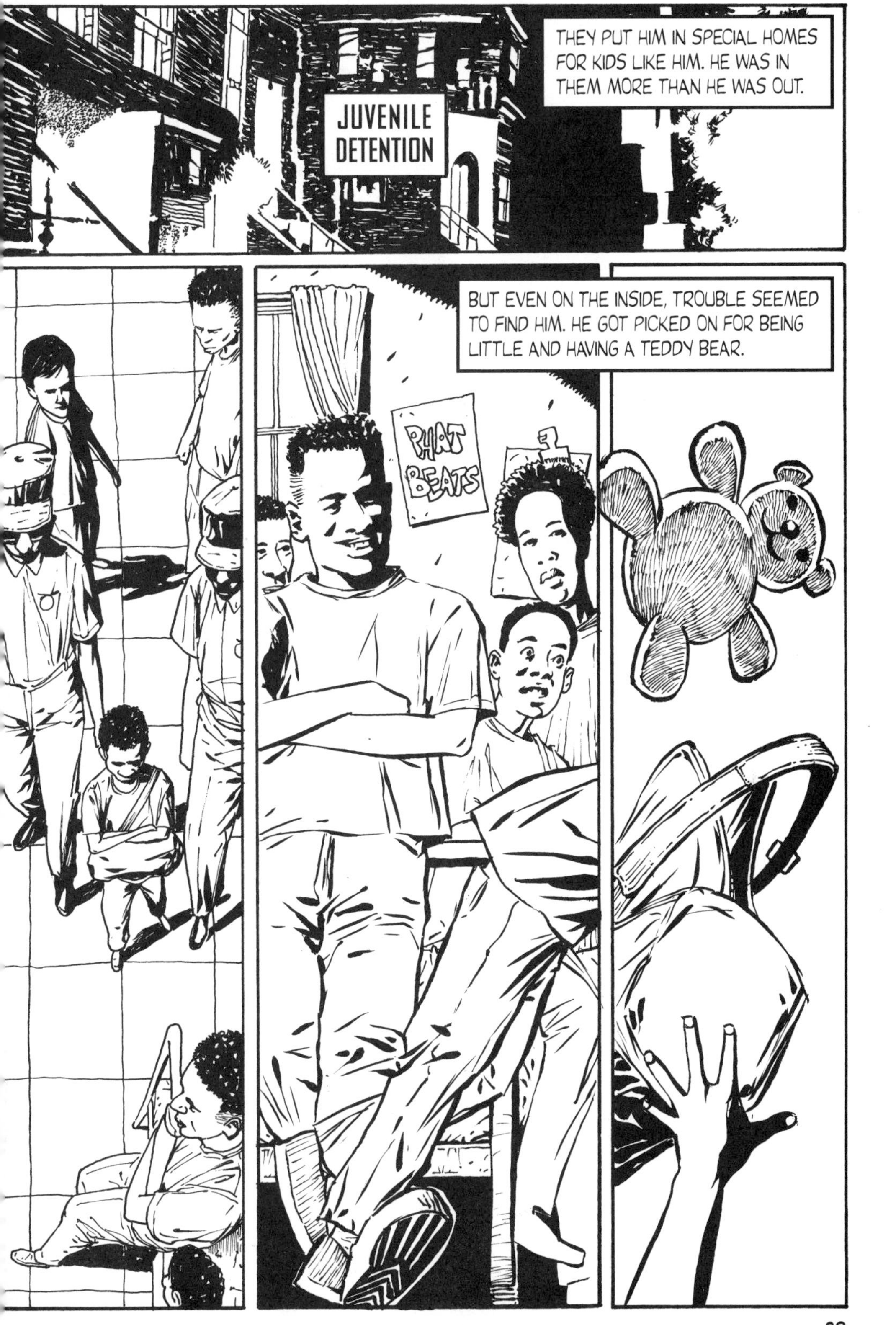
JUVENILE DETENTION
THEY PUT HIM IN SPECIAL HOMES FOR KIDS LIKE HIM. HE WAS IN THEM MORE THAN HE WAS OUT.
BUT EVEN ON THE INSIDE, TROUBLE SEEMED TO FIND HIM. HE GOT PICKED ON FOR BEING LITTLE AND HAVING A TEDDY BEAR.
PHAT BEATS

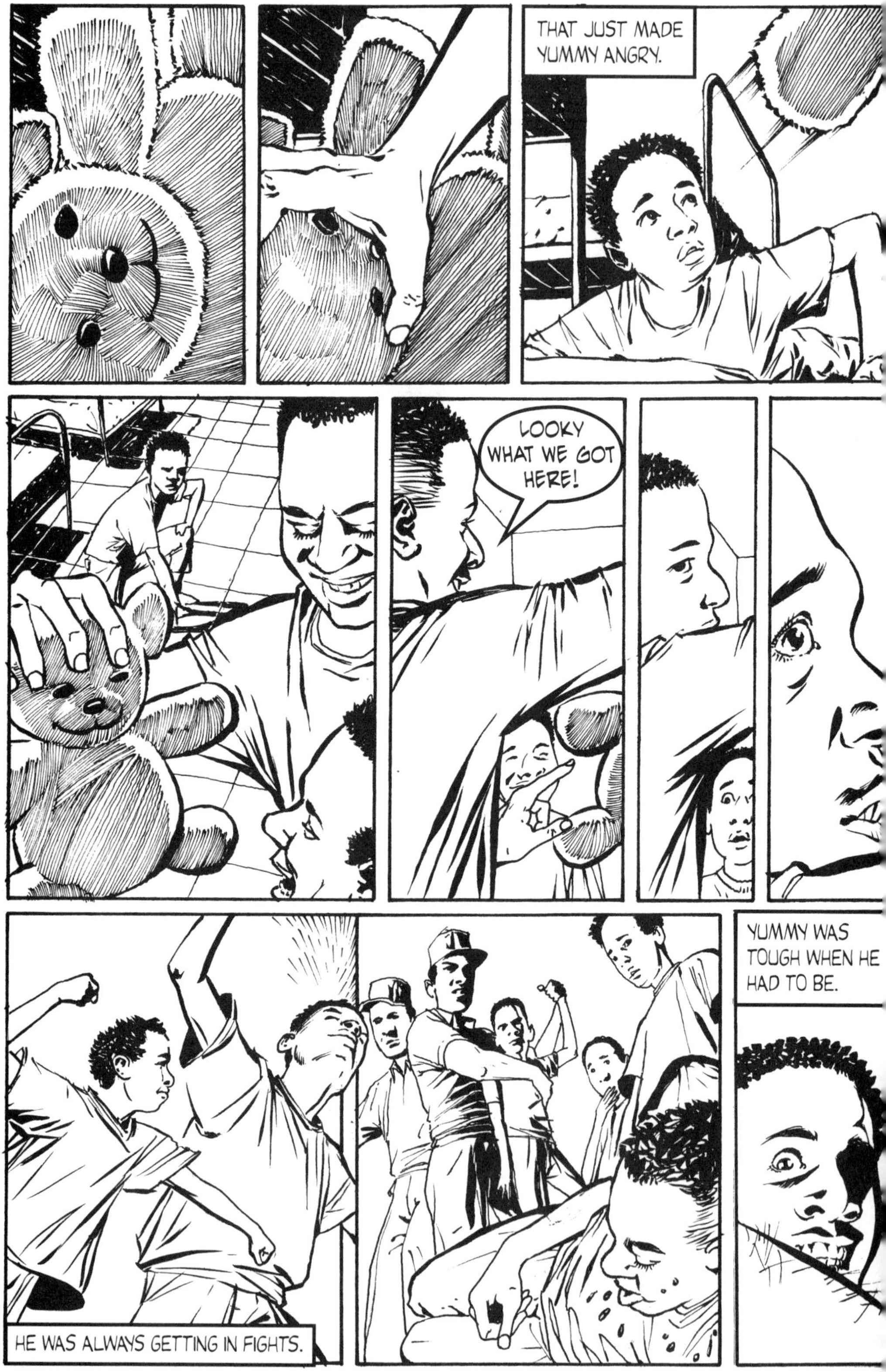
THAT JUST MADE YUMMY ANGRY.
LOOKY WHAT WE GOT HERE!
YUMMY WAS TOUGH WHEN HE HAD TO BE.
HE WAS ALWAYS GETTING IN FIGHTS.

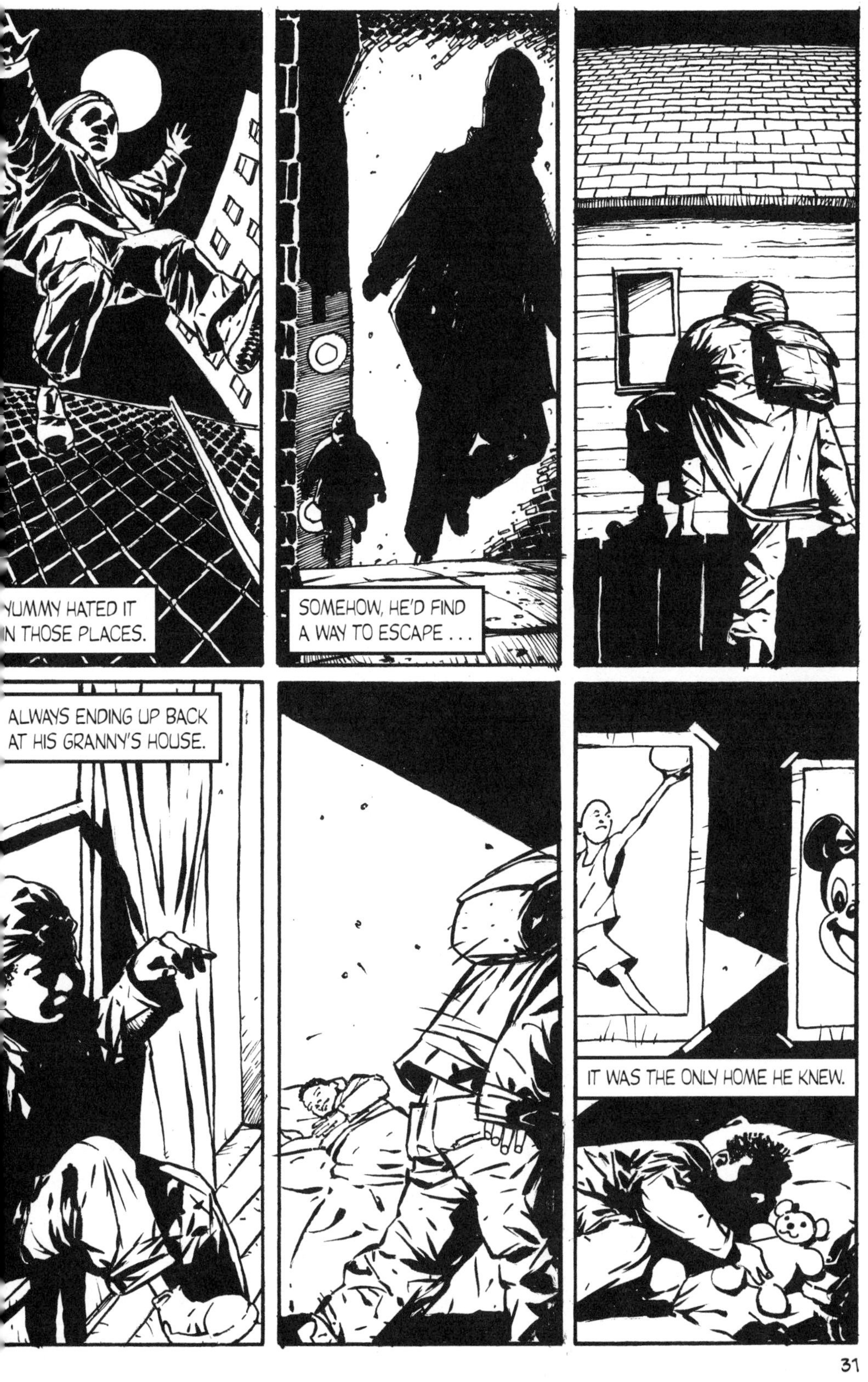
YUMMY HATED IT
IN THOSE PLACES.
SOMEHOW, HE'D FIND
A WAY TO ESCAPE . . .
ALWAYS ENDING UP BACK
AT HIS GRANNY'S HOUSE.
IT WAS THE ONLY HOME HE KNEW.

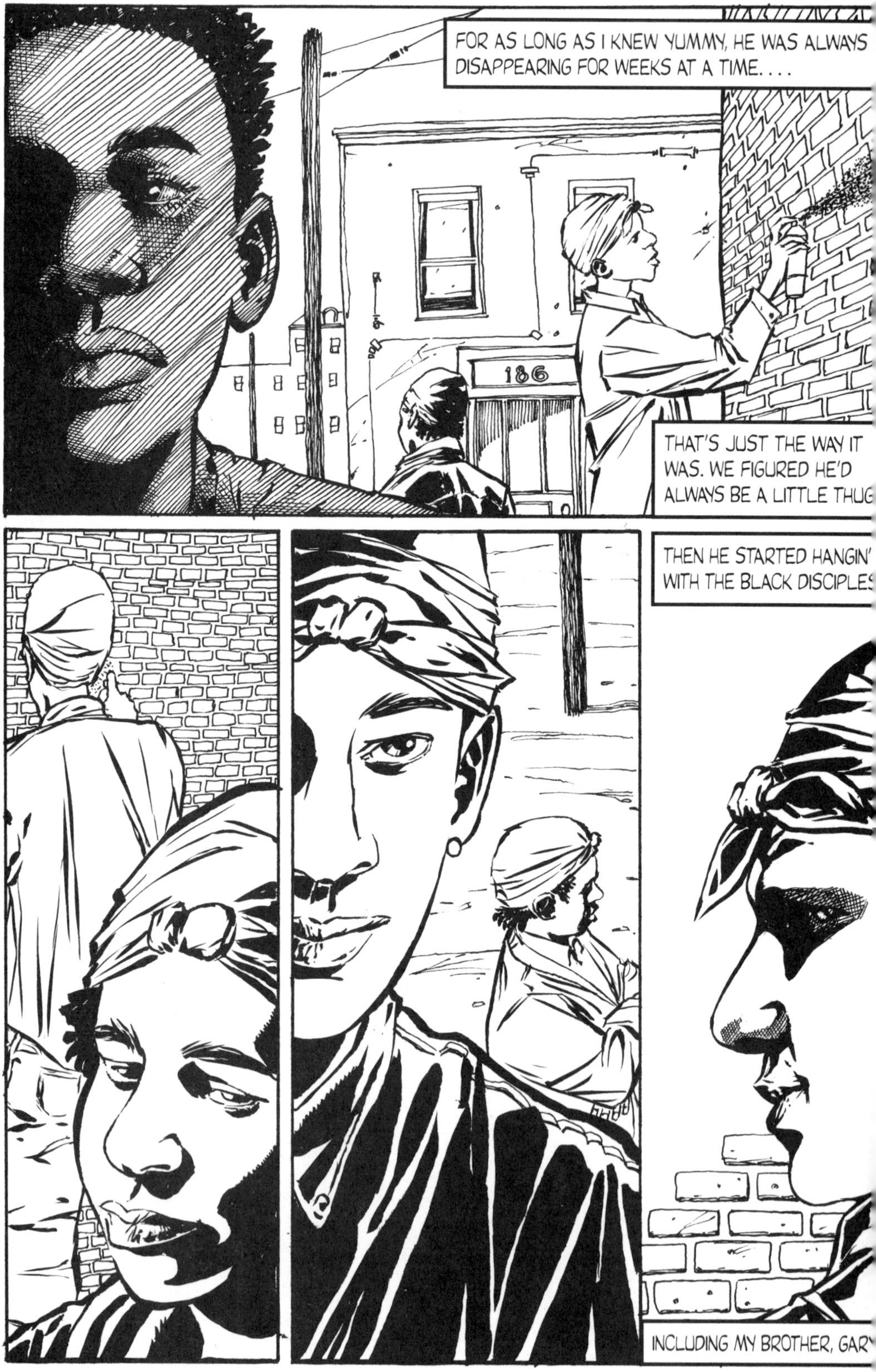

FOR AS LONG AS I KNEW YUMMY, HE WAS ALWAYS DISAPPEARING FOR WEEKS AT A TIME. . . .
186
THAT'S JUST THE WAY IT WAS. WE FIGURED HE'D ALWAYS BE A LITTLE THUG
THEN HE STARTED HANGIN' WITH THE BLACK DISCIPLES
INCLUDING MY BROTHER, GARY

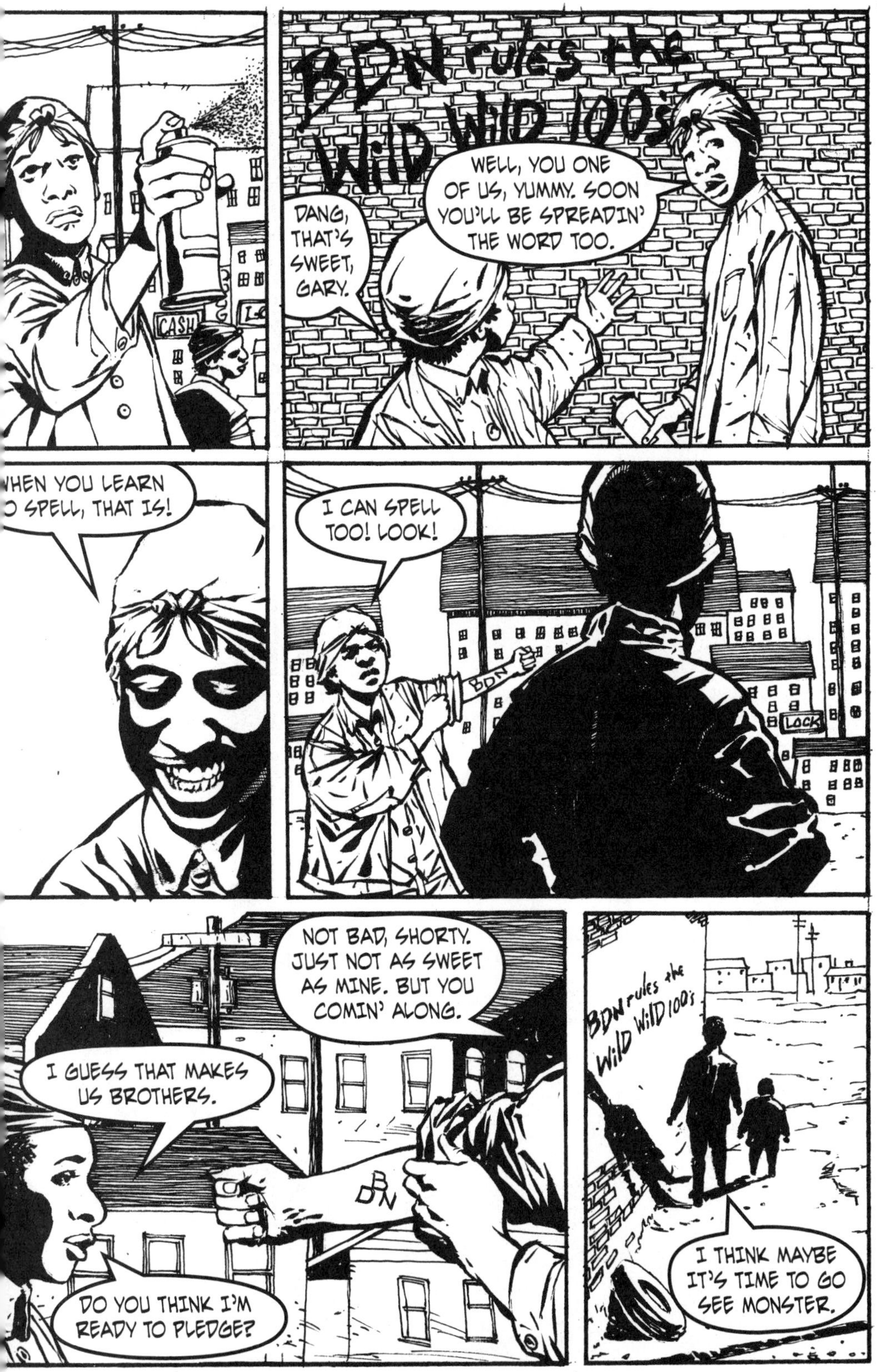
BDN rules the Wild Wild 100's
DANG, THAT'S SWEET, GARY.
WELL, YOU ONE OF US, YUMMY. SOON YOU'LL BE SPREADIN' THE WORD TOO.
CASH
WHEN YOU LEARN TO SPELL, THAT IS!
I CAN SPELL TOO! LOOK!
BDN
LOCK
I GUESS THAT MAKES US BROTHERS.
NOT BAD, SHORTY. JUST NOT AS SWEET AS MINE. BUT YOU COMIN' ALONG.
BDN
DO YOU THINK I'M READY TO PLEDGE?
BDN rules the Wild Wild 100's
I THINK MAYBE IT'S TIME TO GO SEE MONSTER.

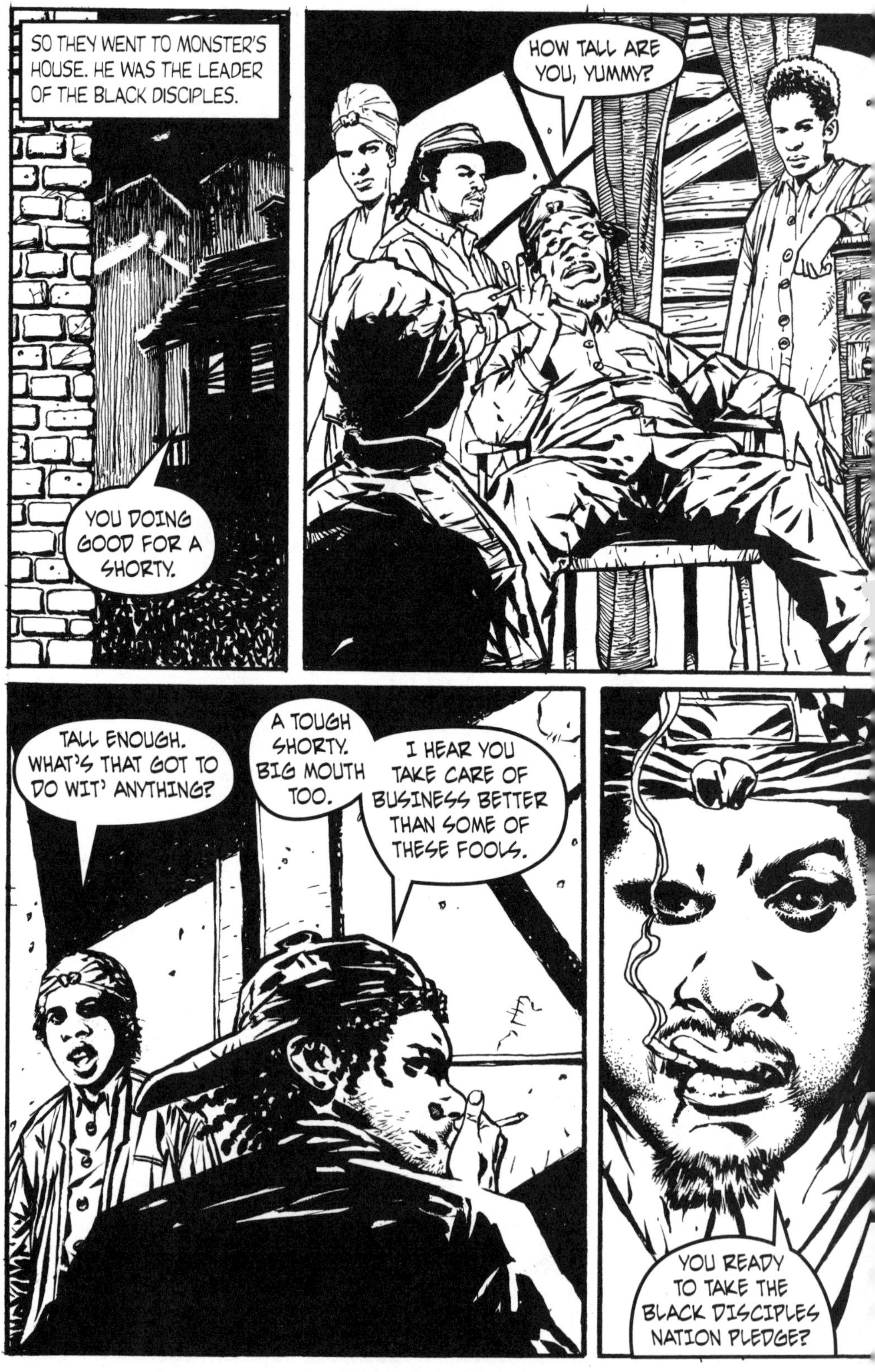

SO THEY WENT TO MONSTER'S HOUSE. HE WAS THE LEADER OF THE BLACK DISCIPLES.
YOU DOING GOOD FOR A SHORTY.
HOW TALL ARE YOU, YUMMY?
TALL ENOUGH. WHAT'S THAT GOT TO DO WIT' ANYTHING?
A TOUGH SHORTY. BIG MOUTH TOO.
I HEAR YOU TAKE CARE OF BUSINESS BETTER THAN SOME OF THESE FOOLS.
YOU READY TO TAKE THE BLACK DISCIPLES NATION PLEDGE?

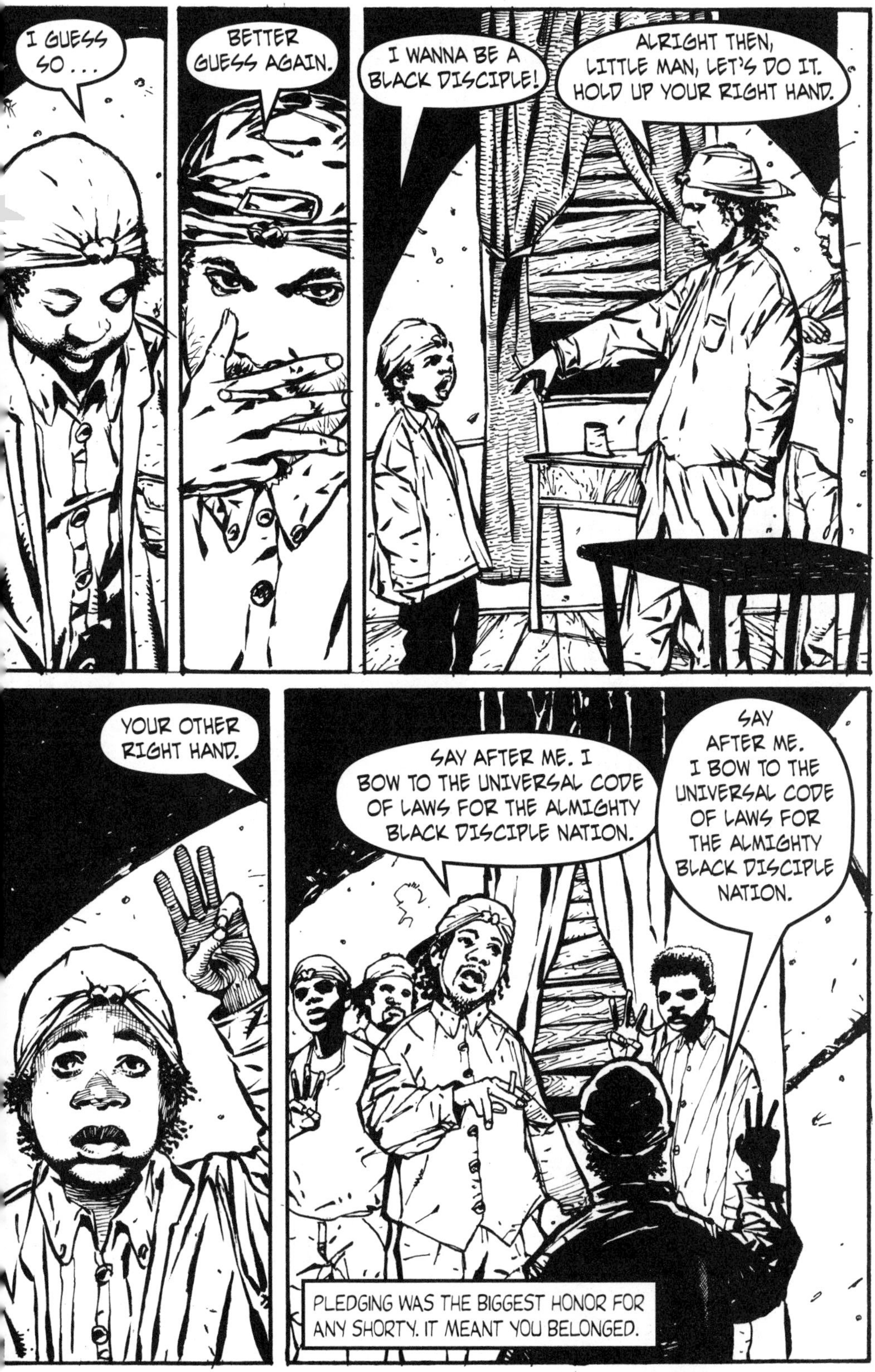
I GUESS SO . . .
BETTER GUESS AGAIN.
I WANNA BE A BLACK DISCIPLE!
ALRIGHT THEN, LITTLE MAN, LET'S DO IT. HOLD UP YOUR RIGHT HAND.
YOUR OTHER RIGHT HAND.
SAY AFTER ME. I BOW TO THE UNIVERSAL CODE OF LAWS FOR THE ALMIGHTY BLACK DISCIPLE NATION.
SAY AFTER ME. I BOW TO THE UNIVERSAL CODE OF LAWS FOR THE ALMIGHTY BLACK DISCIPLE NATION.
PLEDGING WAS THE BIGGEST HONOR FOR ANY SHORTY. IT MEANT YOU BELONGED.

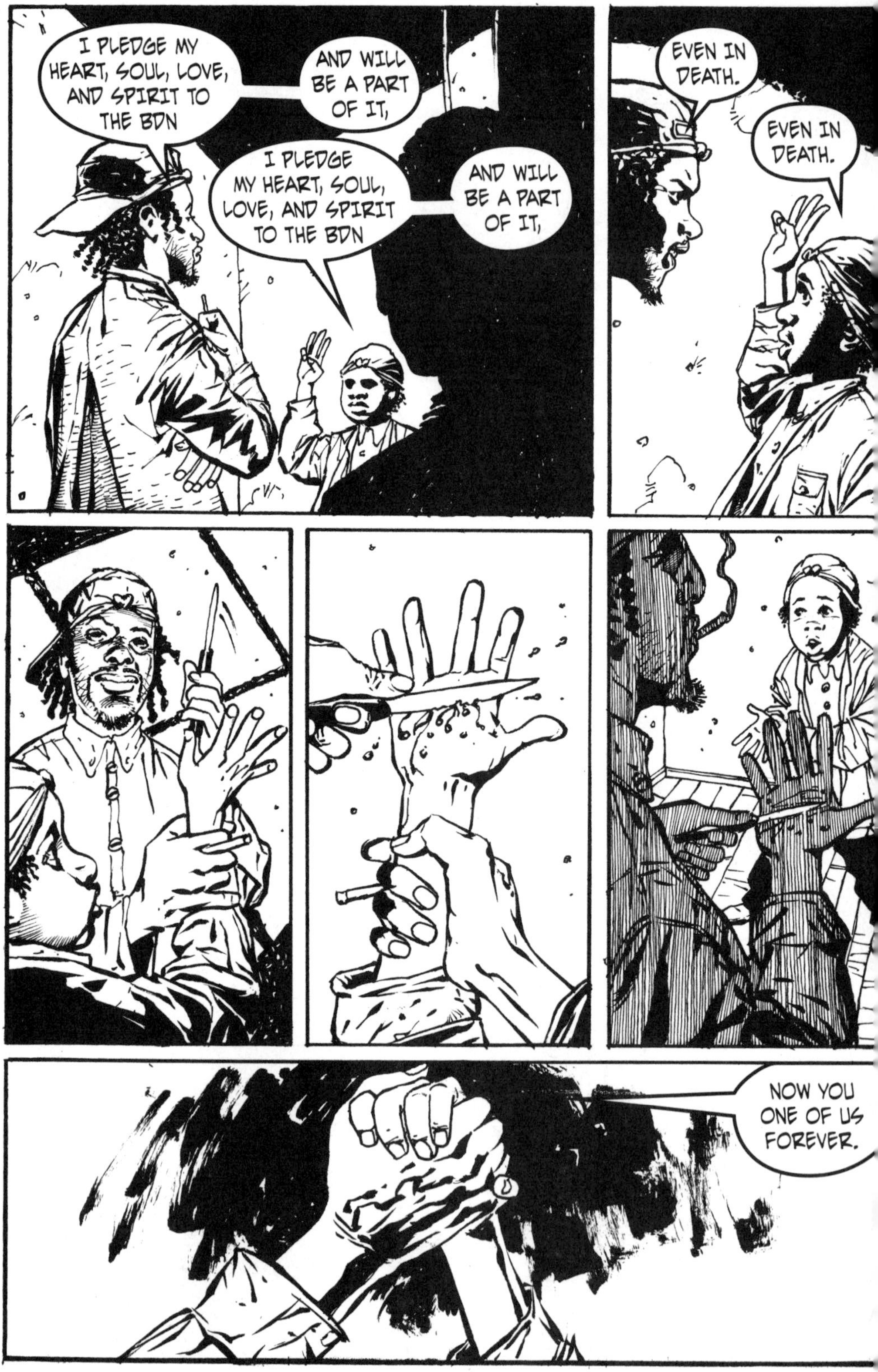
I PLEDGE MY HEART, SOUL, LOVE, AND SPIRIT TO THE BDN
AND WILL BE A PART OF IT,
I PLEDGE MY HEART, SOUL, LOVE, AND SPIRIT TO THE BDN
AND WILL BE A PART OF IT,
EVEN IN DEATH.
EVEN IN DEATH.
NOW YOU ONE OF US FOREVER.

NOW WE FAMILY. YOU WORK FOR US.

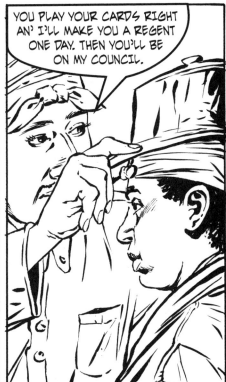

YOU PLAY YOUR CARDS RIGHT AN' I'LL MAKE YOU A REGENT ONE DAY. THEN YOU'LL BE ON MY COUNCIL.

THANKS, MONSTER.

GOT YOU A PRESENT.

NOBODY NEVER GAVE ME NOTHIN' BEFORE.

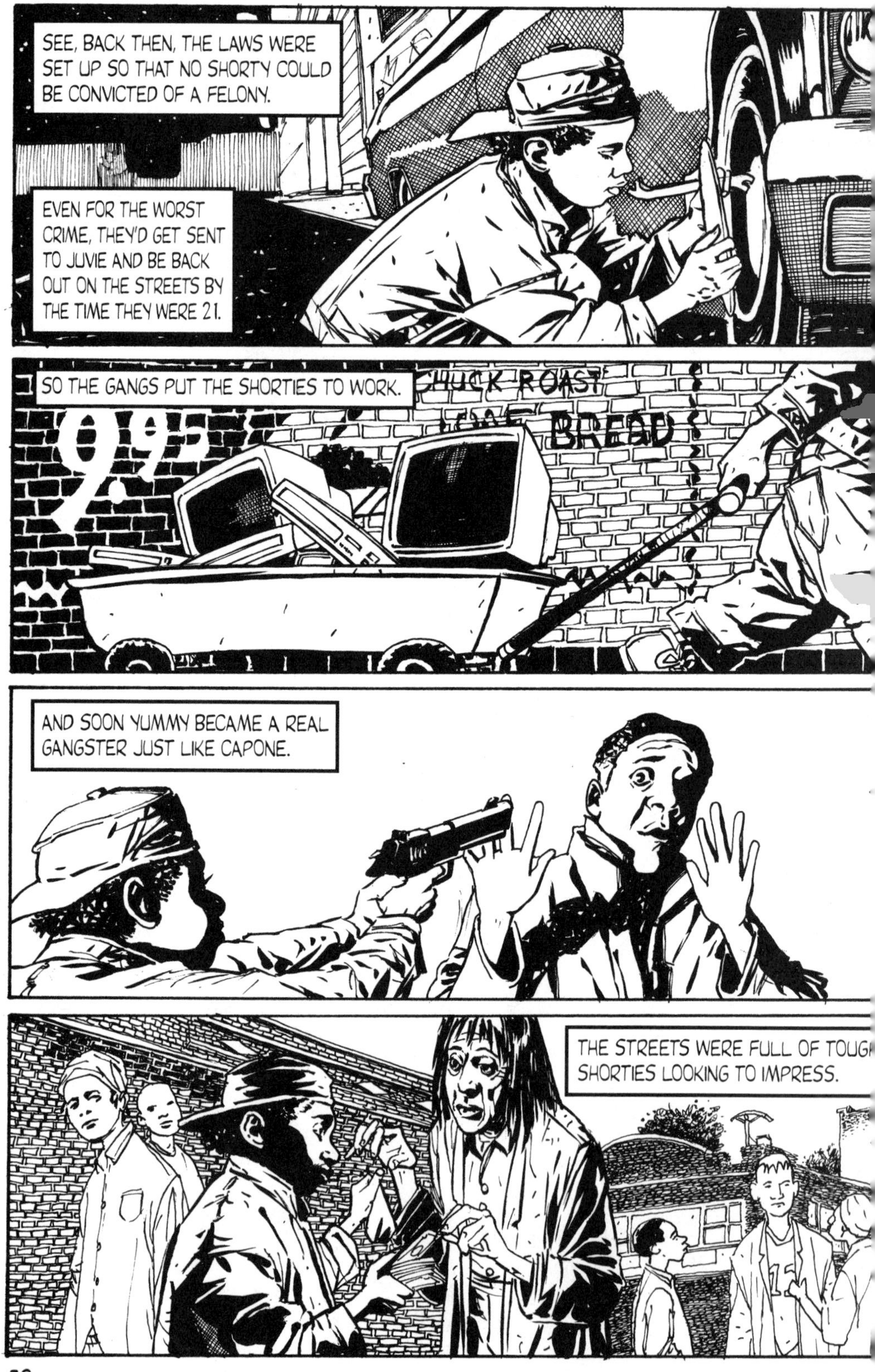
SEE, BACK THEN, THE LAWS WERE SET UP SO THAT NO SHORTY COULD BE CONVICTED OF A FELONY.
EVEN FOR THE WORST CRIME, THEY'D GET SENT TO JUVIE AND BE BACK OUT ON THE STREETS BY THE TIME THEY WERE 21.
SO THE GANGS PUT THE SHORTIES TO WORK.
BREAD
AND SOON YUMMY BECAME A REAL GANGSTER JUST LIKE CAPONE.
THE STREETS WERE FULL OF TOUG
SHORTIES LOOKING TO IMPRESS.

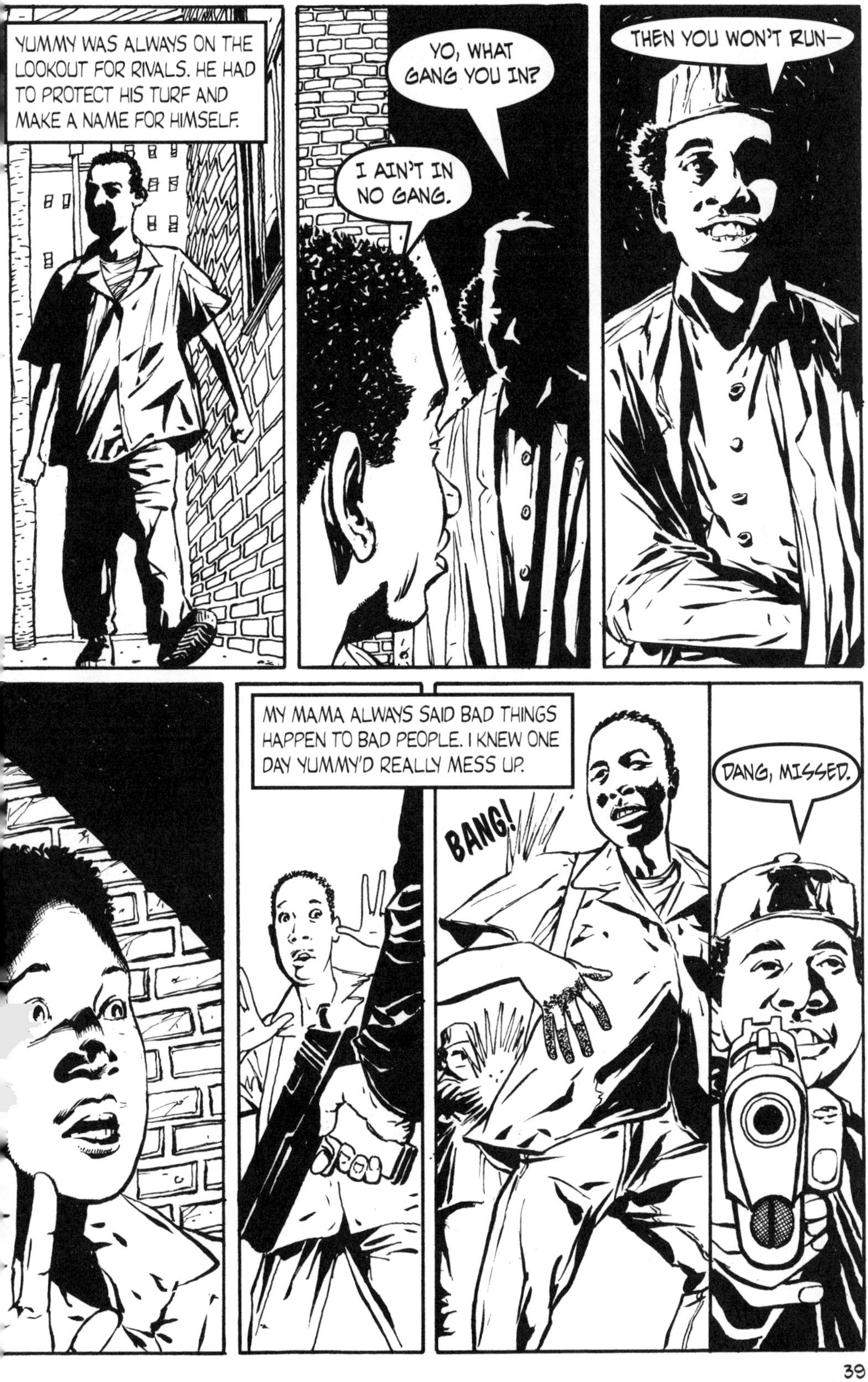
YUMMY WAS ALWAYS ON THE LOOKOUT FOR RIVALS. HE HAD TO PROTECT HIS TURF AND MAKE A NAME FOR HIMSELF.
YO, WHAT GANG YOU IN?
I AIN'T IN NO GANG.
THEN YOU WON'T RUN—
MY MAMA ALWAYS SAID BAD THINGS HAPPEN TO BAD PEOPLE. I KNEW ONE DAY YUMMY'D REALLY MESS UP.
BANG!
DANG, MISSED.

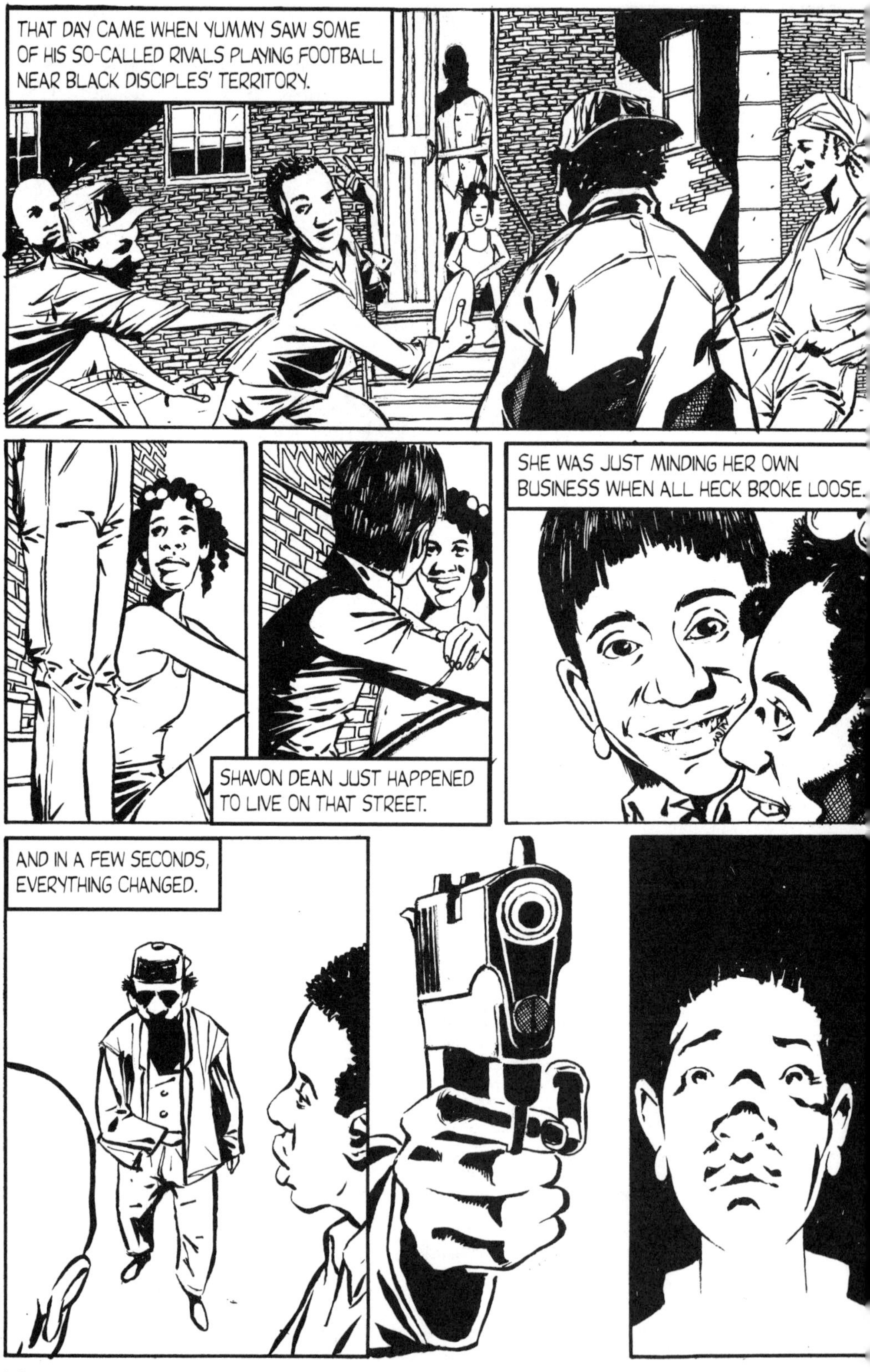
THAT DAY CAME WHEN YUMMY SAW SOME OF HIS SO-CALLED RIVALS PLAYING FOOTBALL NEAR BLACK DISCIPLES' TERRITORY.
SHAVON DEAN JUST HAPPENED TO LIVE ON THAT STREET.
SHE WAS JUST MINDING HER OWN BUSINESS WHEN ALL HECK BROKE LOOSE.
AND IN A FEW SECONDS, EVERYTHING CHANGED.

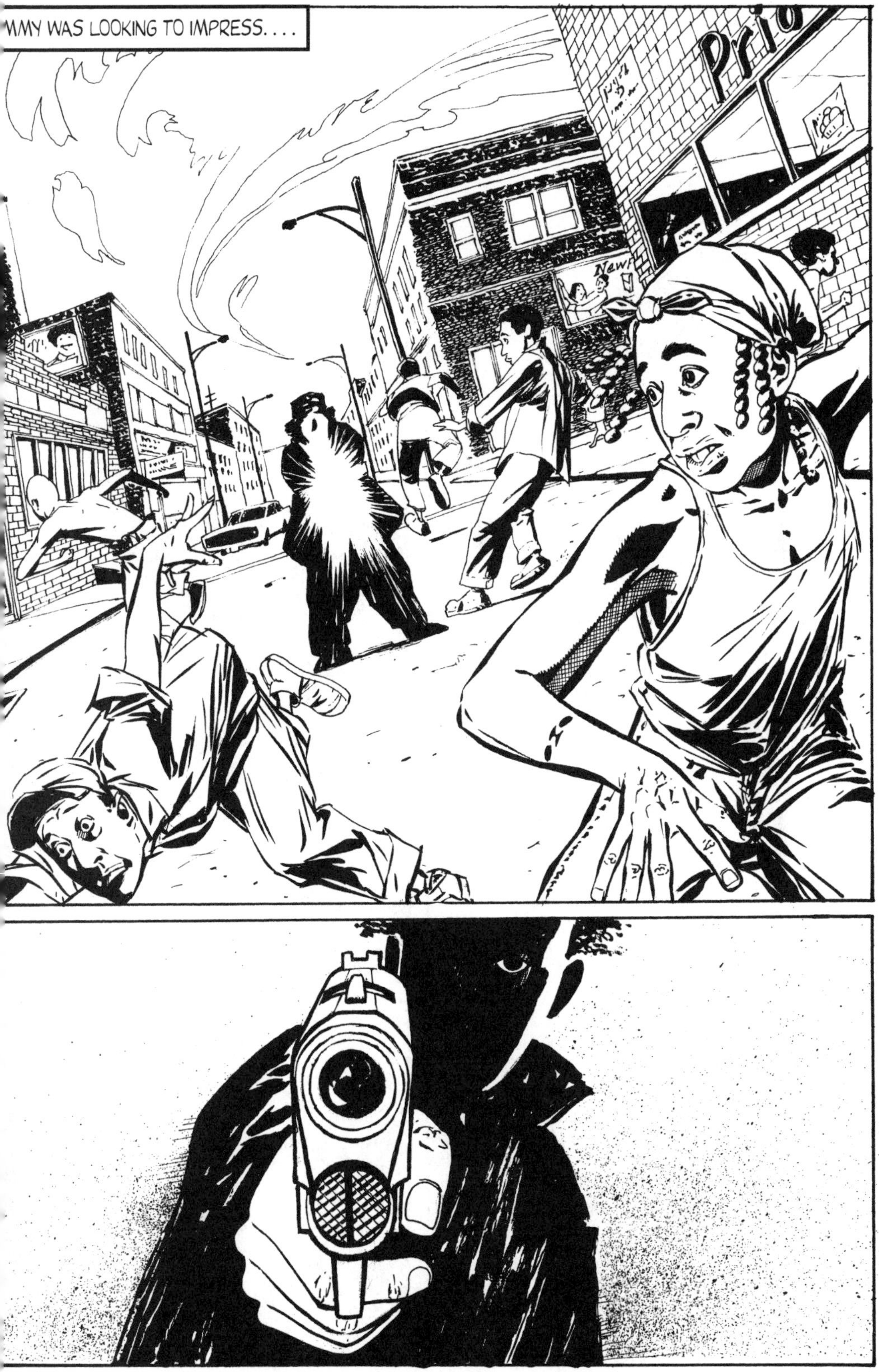
MMY WAS LOOKING TO IMPRESS. . . .
Prio
News

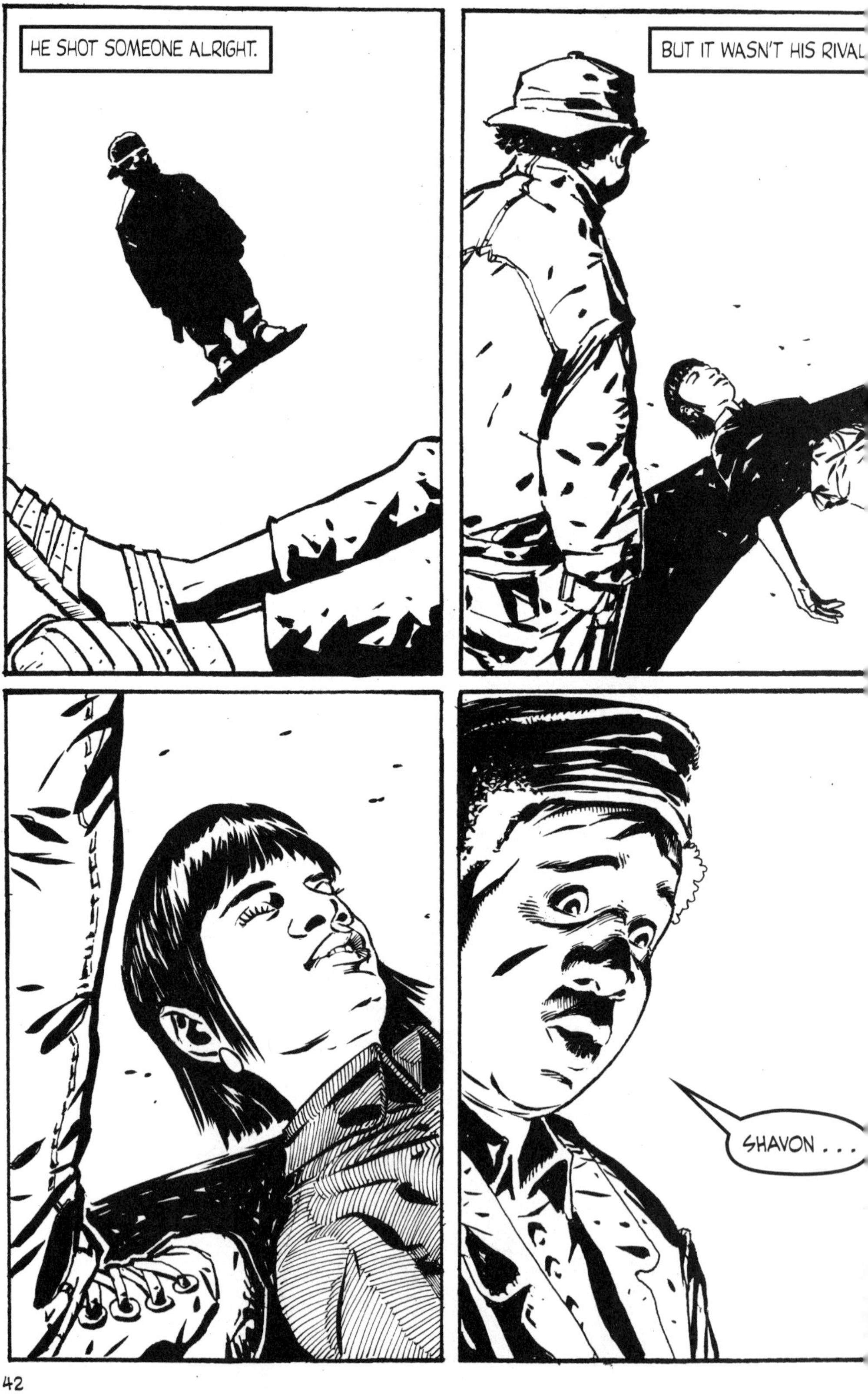
HE SHOT SOMEONE ALRIGHT.
BUT IT WASN'T HIS RIVAL
SHAVON . . .

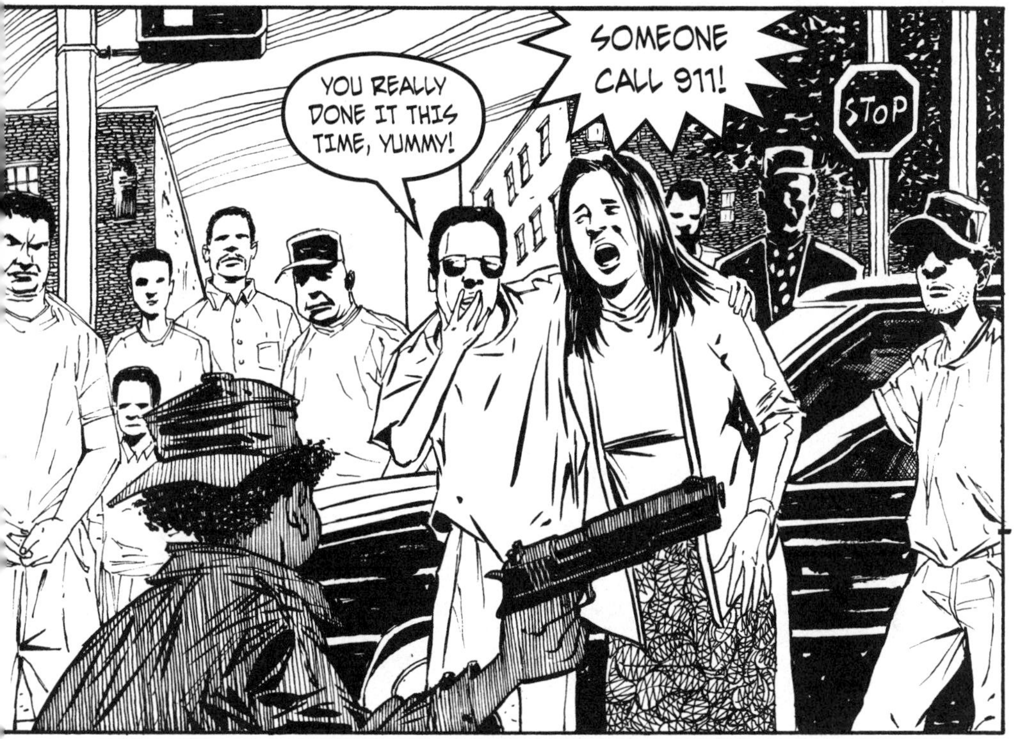
YOU REALLY DONE IT THIS TIME, YUMMY!
SOMEONE CALL 911!
STOP

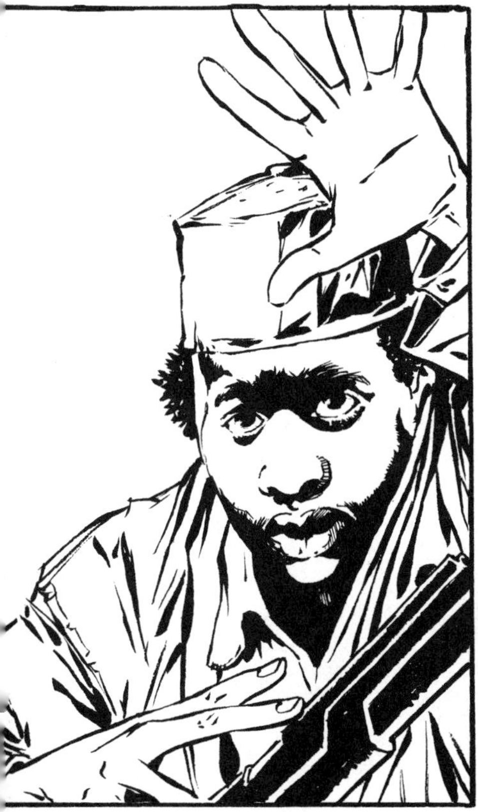

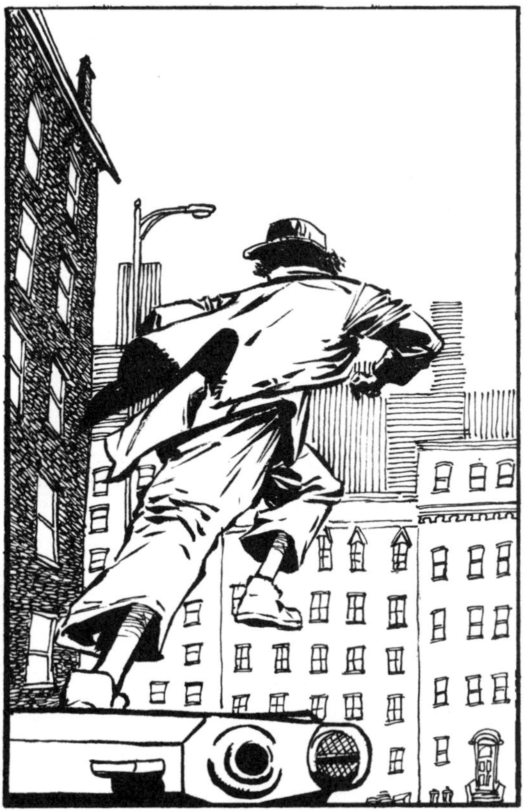

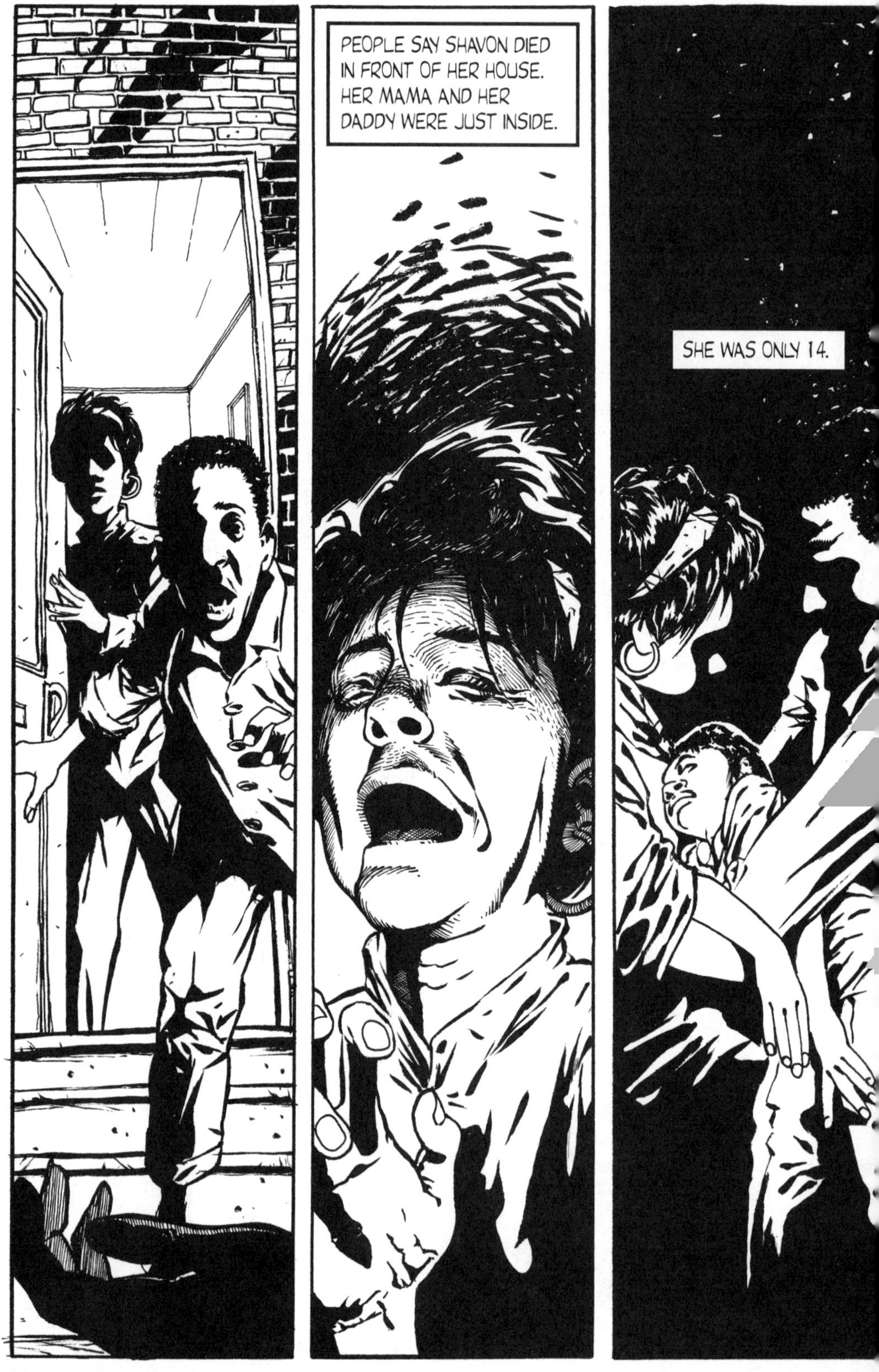
PEOPLE SAY SHAVON DIED IN FRONT OF HER HOUSE. HER MAMA AND HER DADDY WERE JUST INSIDE.
SHE WAS ONLY 14.

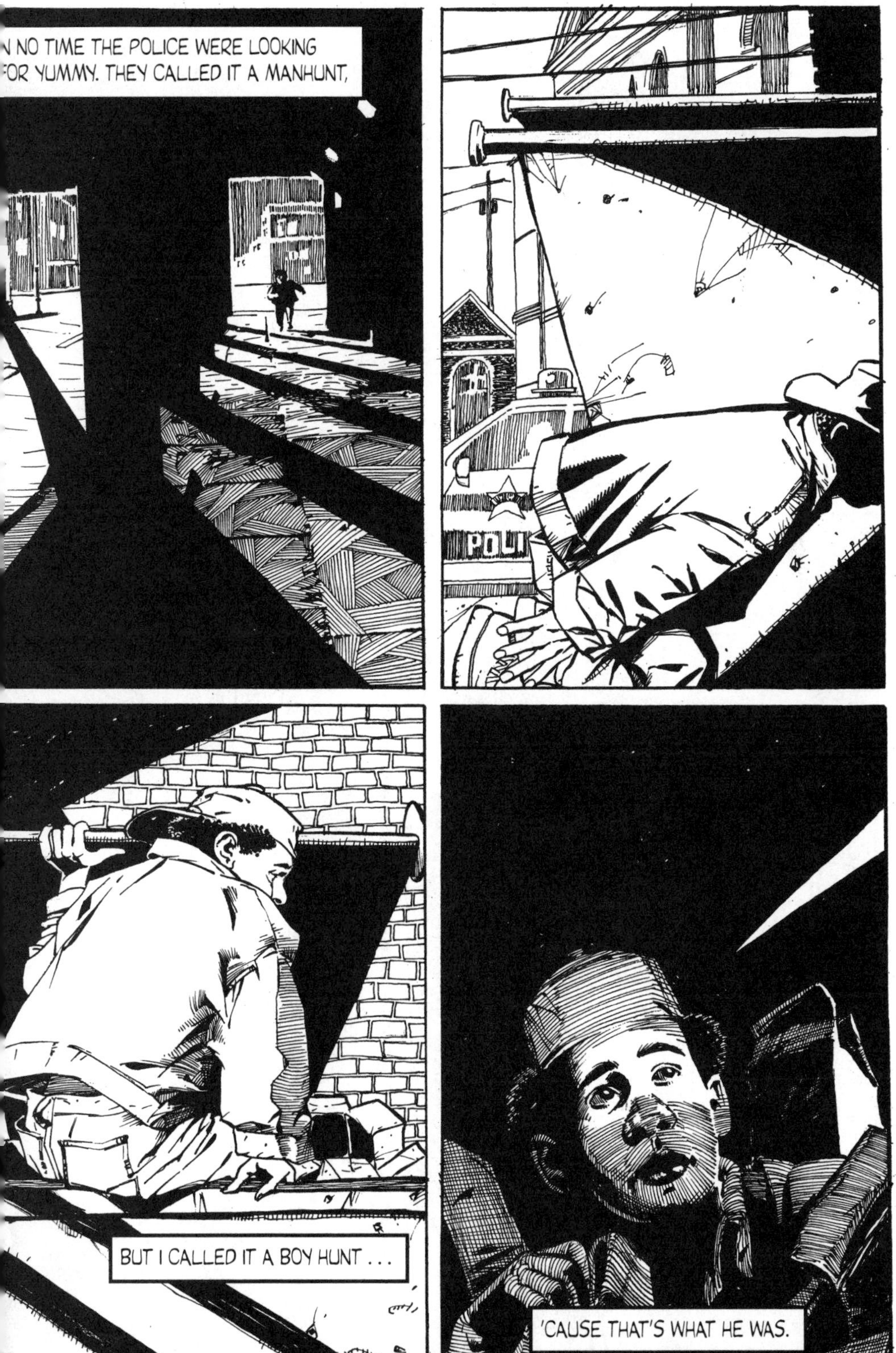
N NO TIME THE POLICE WERE LOOKING FOR YUMMY. THEY CALLED IT A MANHUNT,
POLI
BUT I CALLED IT A BOY HUNT . . .
'CAUSE THAT'S WHAT HE WAS.

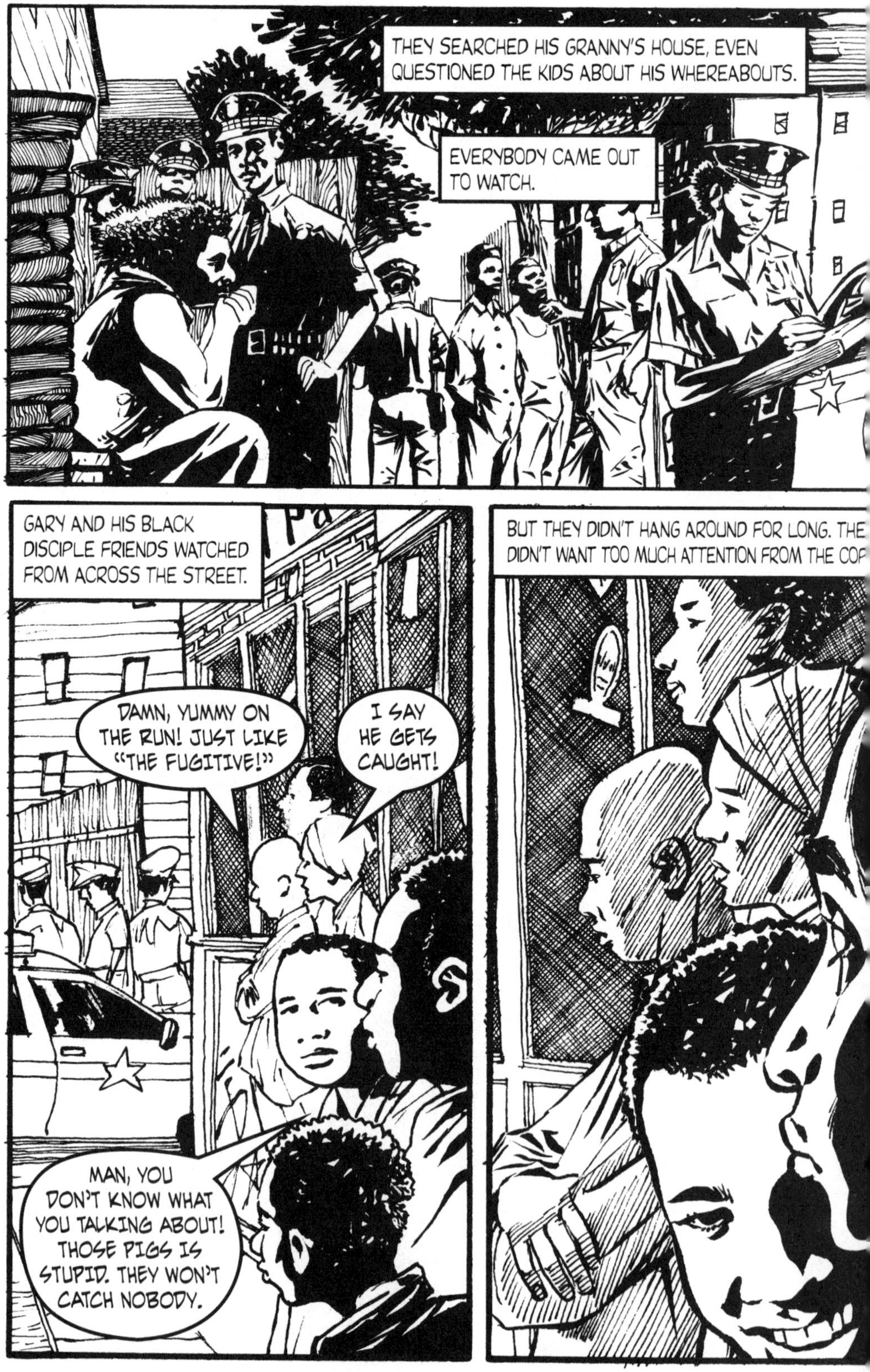
THEY SEARCHED HIS GRANNY'S HOUSE, EVEN QUESTIONED THE KIDS ABOUT HIS WHEREABOUTS.
EVERYBODY CAME OUT TO WATCH.
GARY AND HIS BLACK DISCIPLE FRIENDS WATCHED FROM ACROSS THE STREET.
DAMN, YUMMY ON THE RUN! JUST LIKE "THE FUGITIVE!"
I SAY HE GETS CAUGHT!
MAN, YOU DON'T KNOW WHAT YOU TALKING ABOUT! THOSE PIGS IS STUPID. THEY WON'T CATCH NOBODY.
BUT THEY DIDN'T HANG AROUND FOR LONG. THE
DIDN'T WANT TOO MUCH ATTENTION FROM THE COP

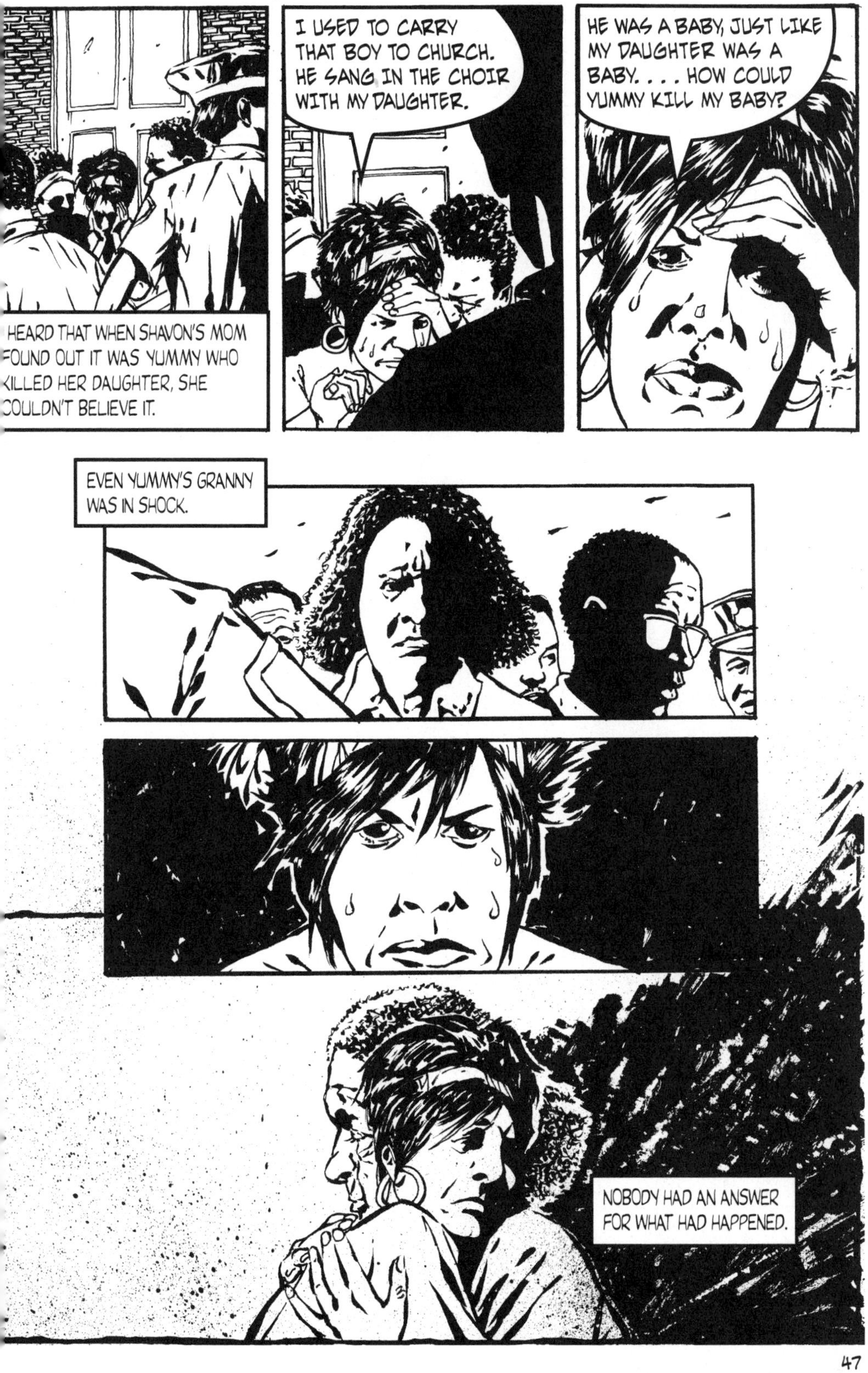
HEARD THAT WHEN SHAVON'S MOM FOUND OUT IT WAS YUMMY WHO KILLED HER DAUGHTER, SHE COULDN'T BELIEVE IT.
I USED TO CARRY THAT BOY TO CHURCH. HE SANG IN THE CHOIR WITH MY DAUGHTER.
HE WAS A BABY, JUST LIKE MY DAUGHTER WAS A BABY. . . . HOW COULD YUMMY KILL MY BABY?
EVEN YUMMY'S GRANNY WAS IN SHOCK.
NOBODY HAD AN ANSWER FOR WHAT HAD HAPPENED.

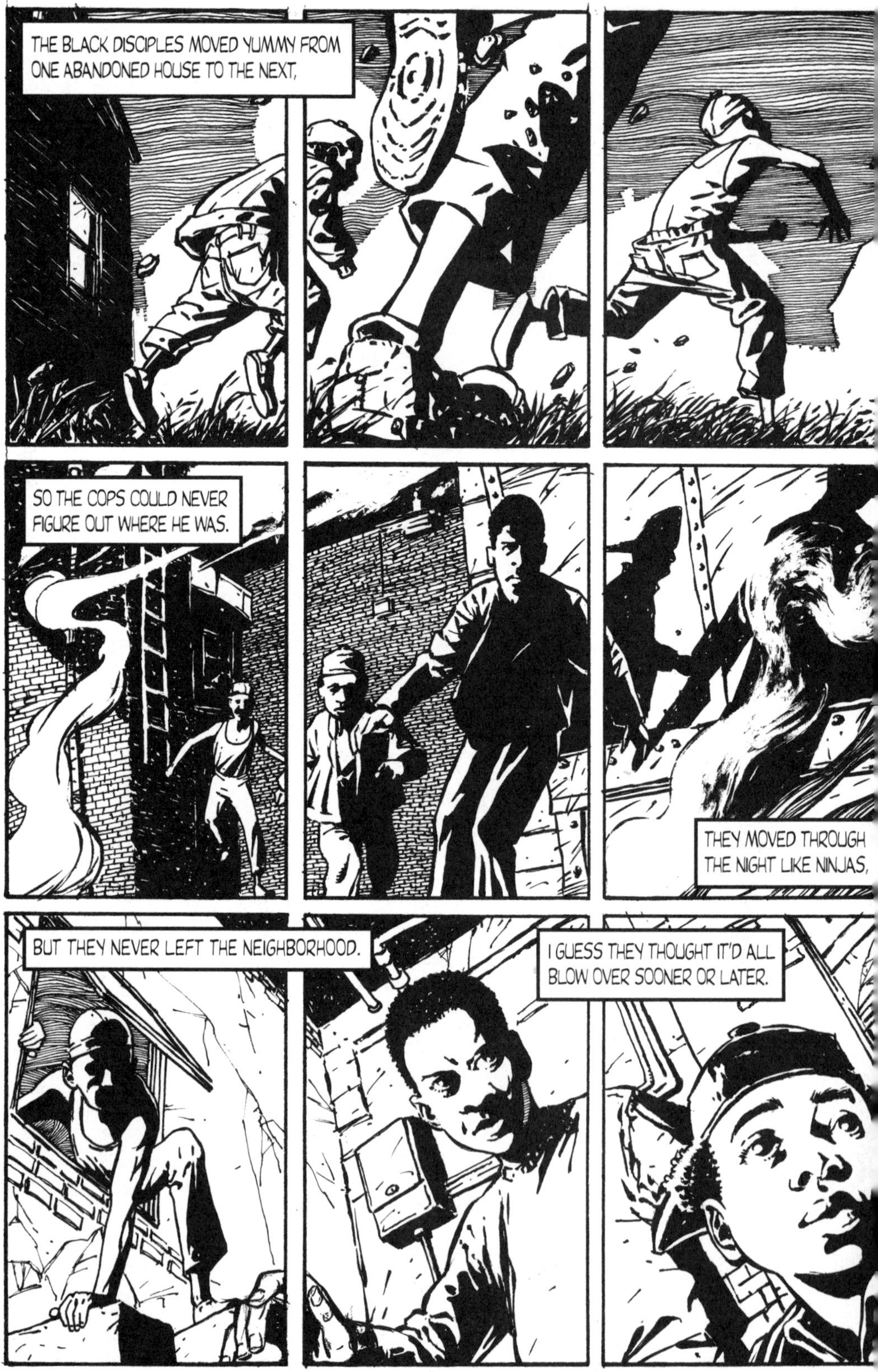
THE BLACK DISCIPLES MOVED YUMMY FROM ONE ABANDONED HOUSE TO THE NEXT,
SO THE COPS COULD NEVER FIGURE OUT WHERE HE WAS.
THEY MOVED THROUGH THE NIGHT LIKE NINJAS,
BUT THEY NEVER LEFT THE NEIGHBORHOOD.
I GUESS THEY THOUGHT IT'D ALL BLOW OVER SOONER OR LATER.

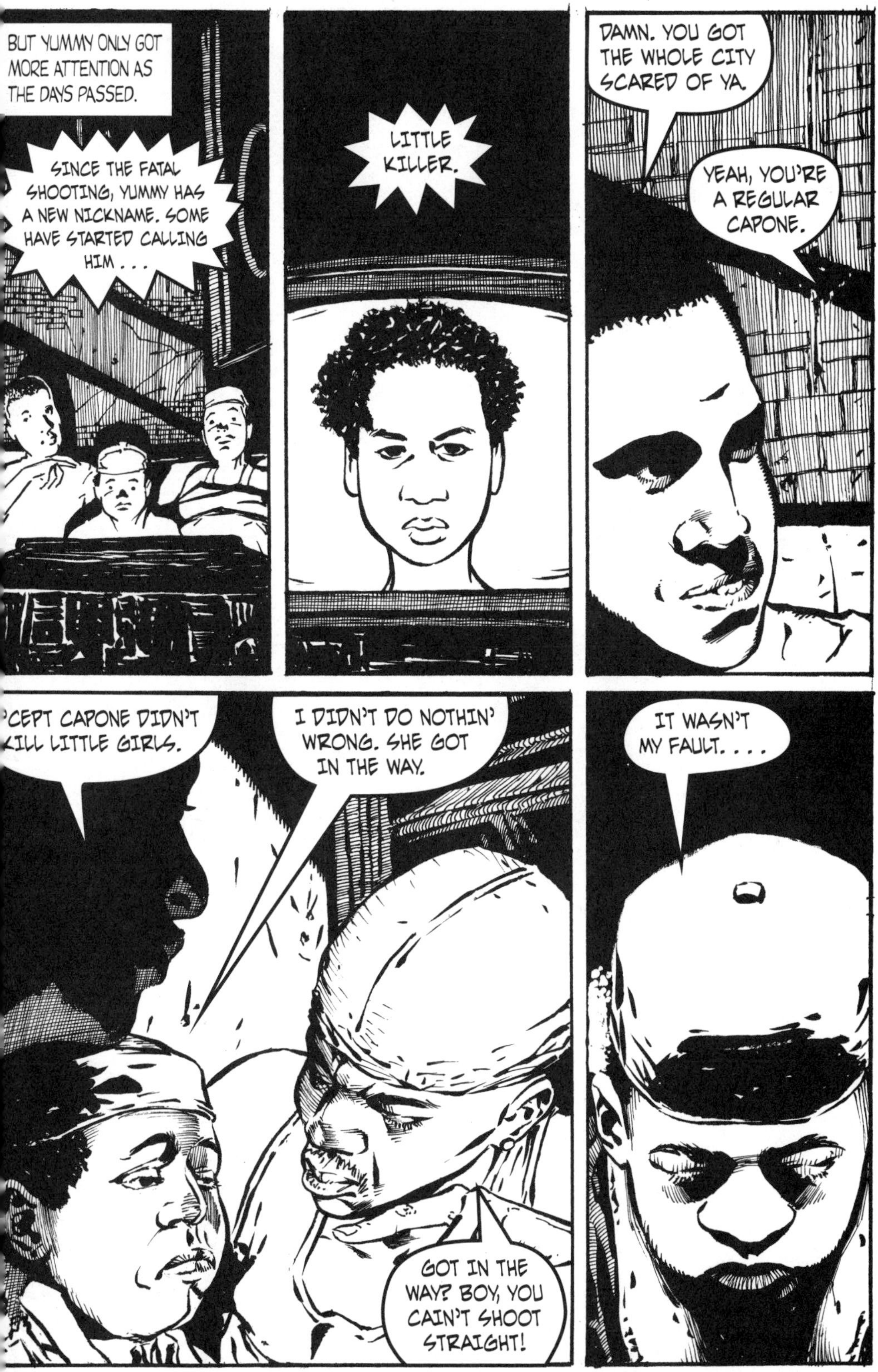

BUT YUMMY ONLY GOT MORE ATTENTION AS THE DAYS PASSED.
SINCE THE FATAL SHOOTING, YUMMY HAS A NEW NICKNAME. SOME HAVE STARTED CALLING HIM . . .
LITTLE KILLER.
DAMN. YOU GOT THE WHOLE CITY SCARED OF YA.
YEAH, YOU'RE A REGULAR CAPONE.
'CEPT CAPONE DIDN'T KILL LITTLE GIRLS.
I DIDN'T DO NOTHIN' WRONG. SHE GOT IN THE WAY.
GOT IN THE WAY? BOY, YOU CAIN'T SHOOT STRAIGHT!
IT WASN'T MY FAULT. . . .

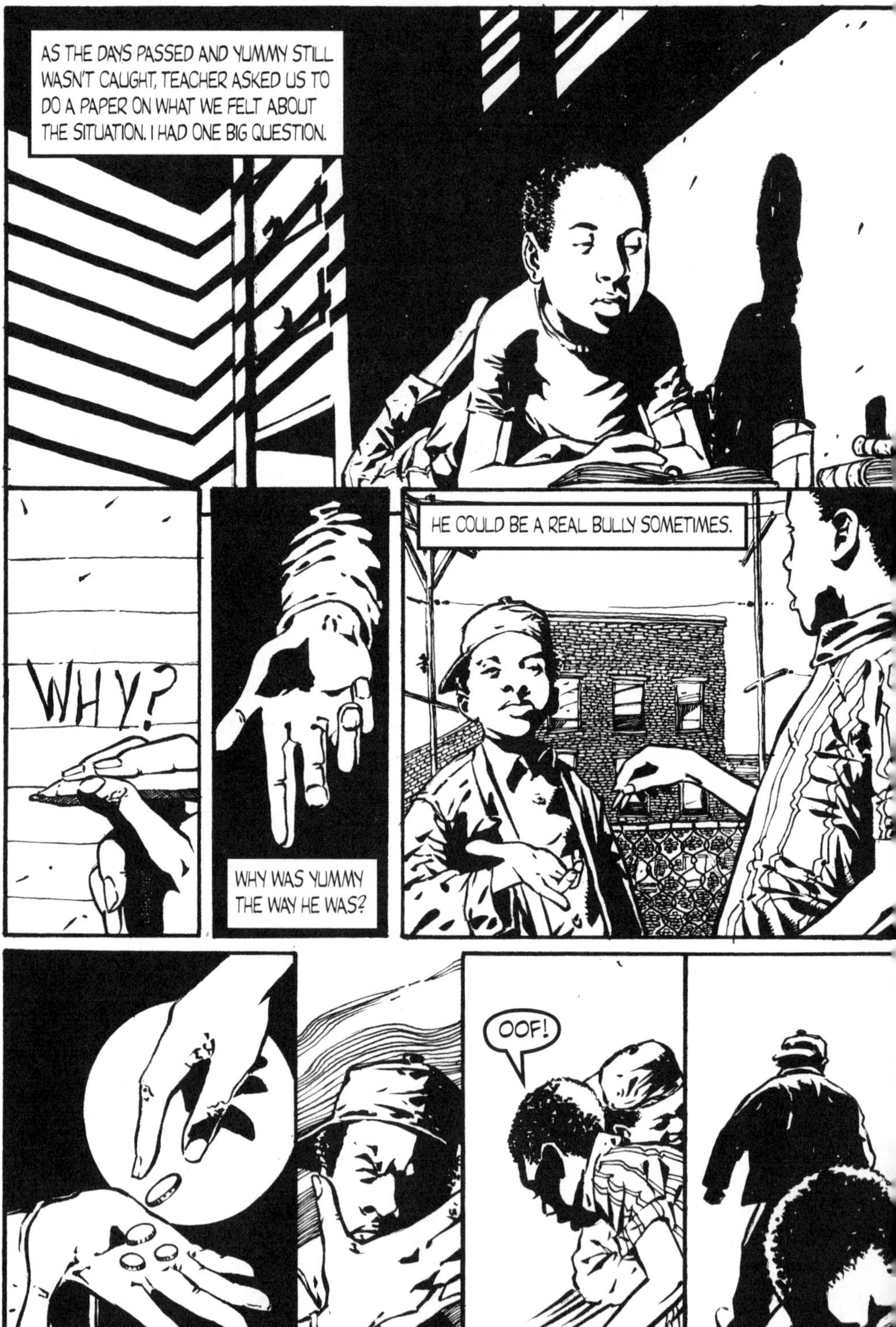
AS THE DAYS PASSED AND YUMMY STILL WASN'T CAUGHT, TEACHER ASKED US TO DO A PAPER ON WHAT WE FELT ABOUT THE SITUATION. I HAD ONE BIG QUESTION.
WHY?
WHY WAS YUMMY THE WAY HE WAS?
HE COULD BE A REAL BULLY SOMETIMES.
HE STOLE LUNCH MONEY FROM OTHER KIDS, INCLUDING ME.
OOF!

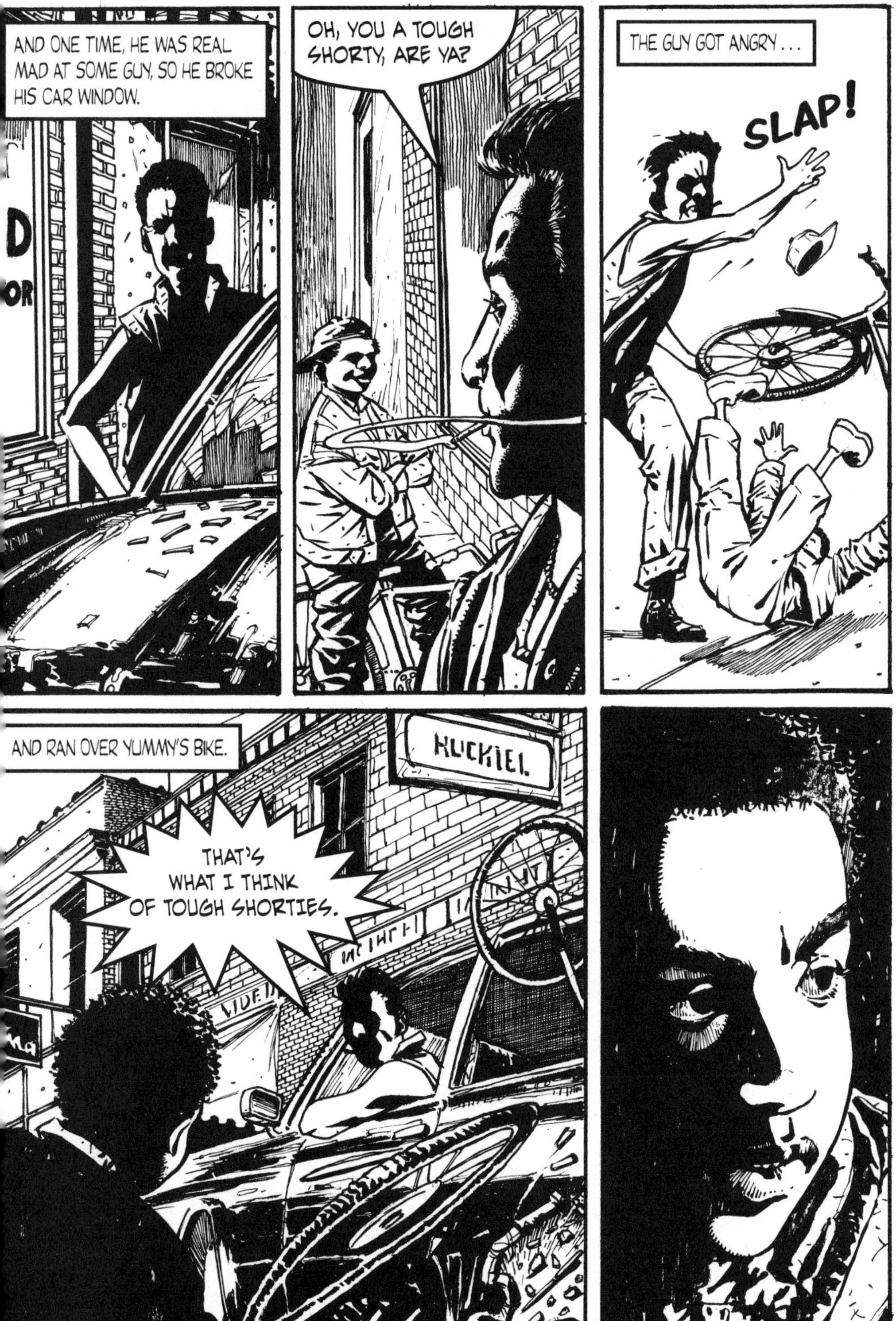
AND ONE TIME, HE WAS REAL MAD AT SOME GUY, SO HE BROKE HIS CAR WINDOW.
OH, YOU A TOUGH SHORTY, ARE YA?
THE GUY GOT ANGRY . . .
SLAP!
AND RAN OVER YUMMY'S BIKE.
THAT'S WHAT I THINK OF TOUGH SHORTIES.
THAT JUST MADE YUMMY MADDER.

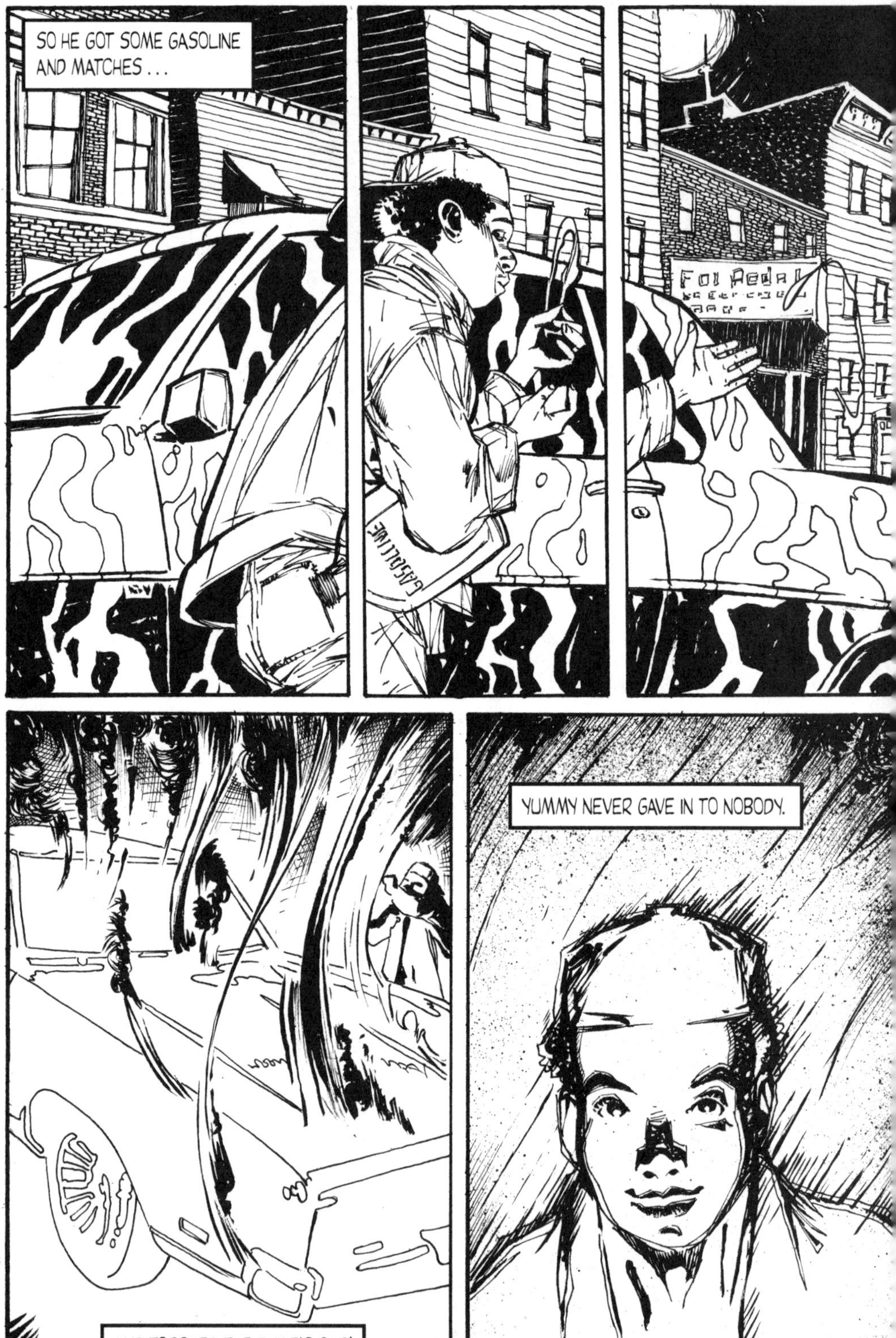
SO HE GOT SOME GASOLINE AND MATCHES . . .
AND TORCHED THE DUDE'S CAR!
YUMMY NEVER GAVE IN TO NOBODY.

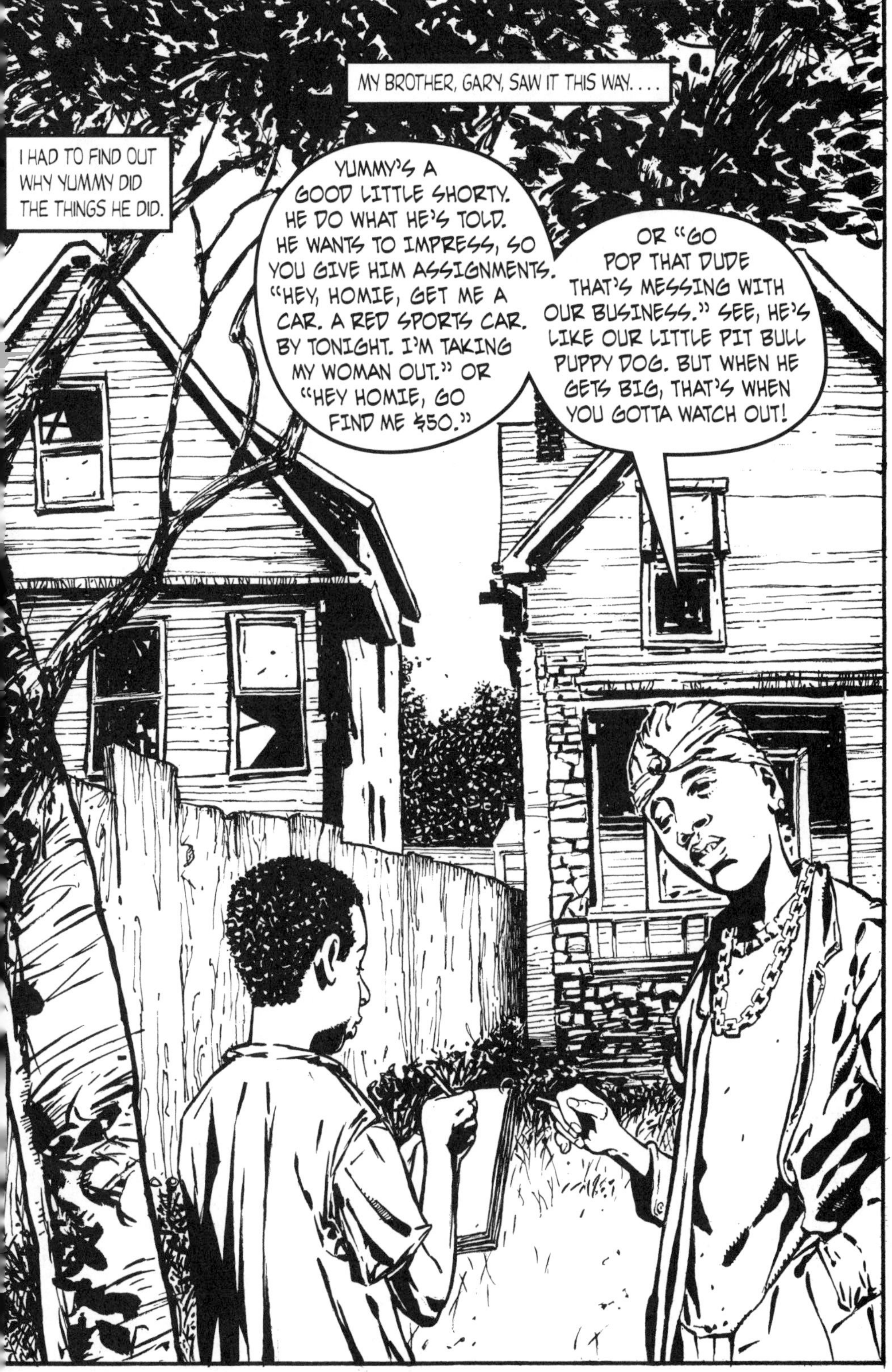
MY BROTHER, GARY, SAW IT THIS WAY. . . .
I HAD TO FIND OUT WHY YUMMY DID THE THINGS HE DID.
YUMMY'S A GOOD LITTLE SHORTY. HE DO WHAT HE'S TOLD. HE WANTS TO IMPRESS, SO YOU GIVE HIM ASSIGNMENTS. "HEY, HOMIE, GET ME A CAR. A RED SPORTS CAR. BY TONIGHT. I'M TAKING MY WOMAN OUT." OR "HEY HOMIE, GO FIND ME $50."
OR "GO POP THAT DUDE THAT'S MESSING WITH OUR BUSINESS." SEE, HE'S LIKE OUR LITTLE PIT BULL PUPPY DOG. BUT WHEN HE GETS BIG, THAT'S WHEN YOU GOTTA WATCH OUT!

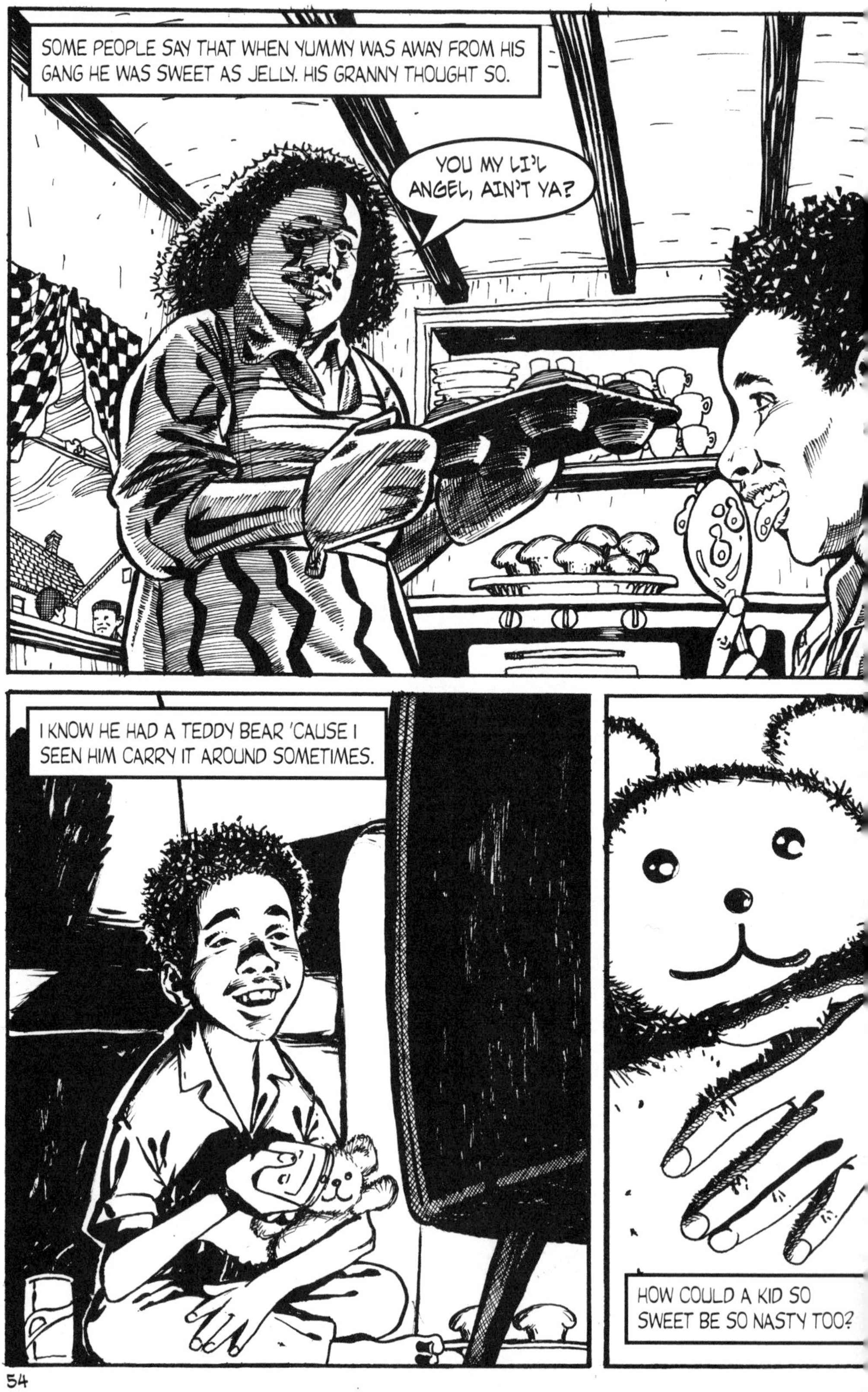
SOME PEOPLE SAY THAT WHEN YUMMY WAS AWAY FROM HIS GANG HE WAS SWEET AS JELLY. HIS GRANNY THOUGHT SO.
YOU MY LI'L ANGEL, AIN'T YA?
I KNOW HE HAD A TEDDY BEAR 'CAUSE I SEEN HIM CARRY IT AROUND SOMETIMES.
HOW COULD A KID SO SWEET BE SO NASTY TOO?

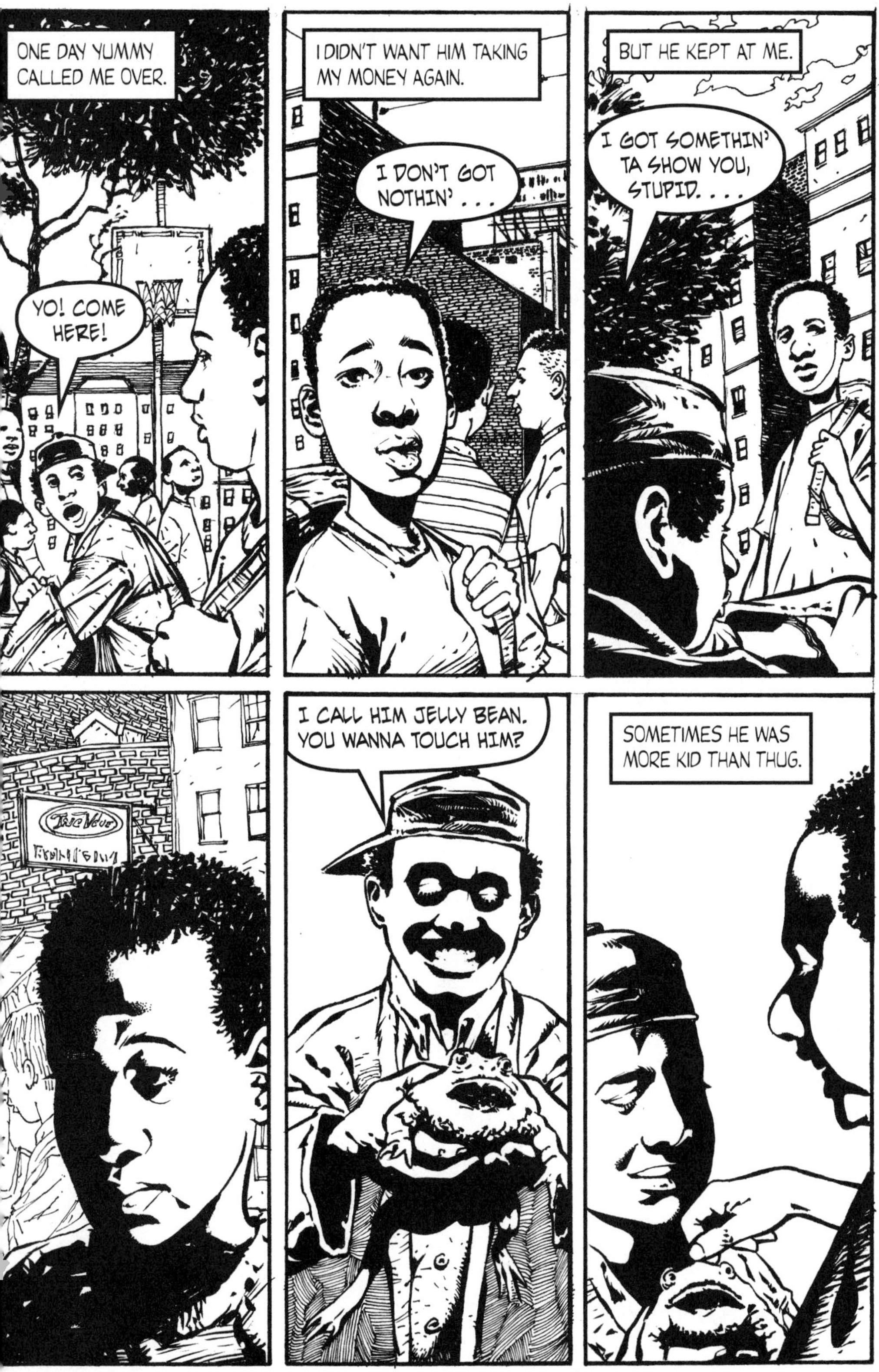
ONE DAY YUMMY CALLED ME OVER.
YO! COME HERE!
I DIDN'T WANT HIM TAKING MY MONEY AGAIN.
I DON'T GOT NOTHIN' . . .
BUT HE KEPT AT ME.
I GOT SOMETHIN' TA SHOW YOU, STUPID. . . .
I CALL HIM JELLY BEAN. YOU WANNA TOUCH HIM?
SOMETIMES HE WAS MORE KID THAN THUG.

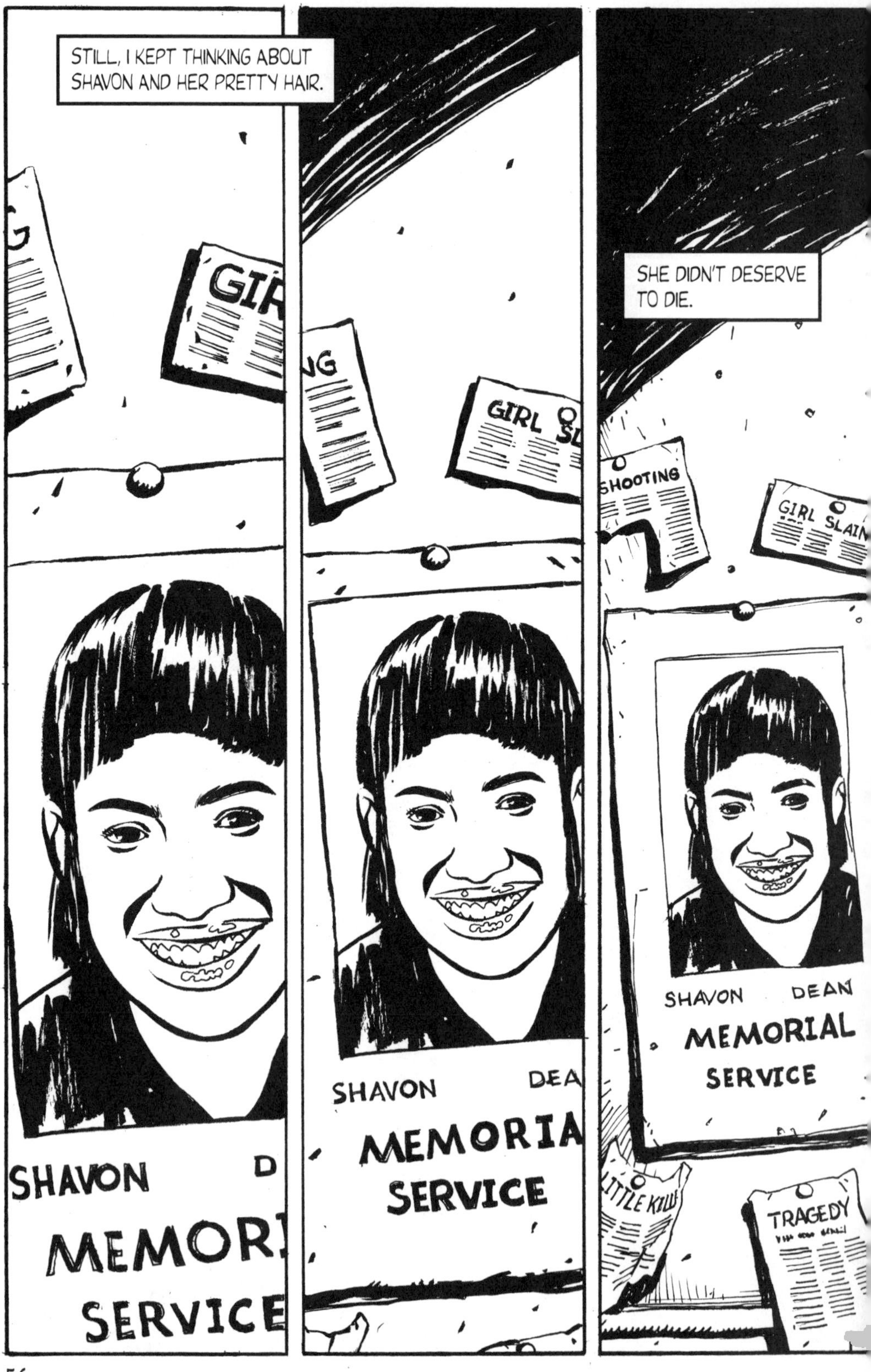
STILL, I KEPT THINKING ABOUT SHAVON AND HER PRETTY HAIR.
SHAVON
MEMORIAL SERVICE
GIRL
SHAVON
MEMORIA
SERVICE
SHE DIDN'T DESERVE TO DIE.
SHOOTING
GIRL SLAIN
SHAVON DEAN
MEMORIAL SERVICE
TRAGEDY

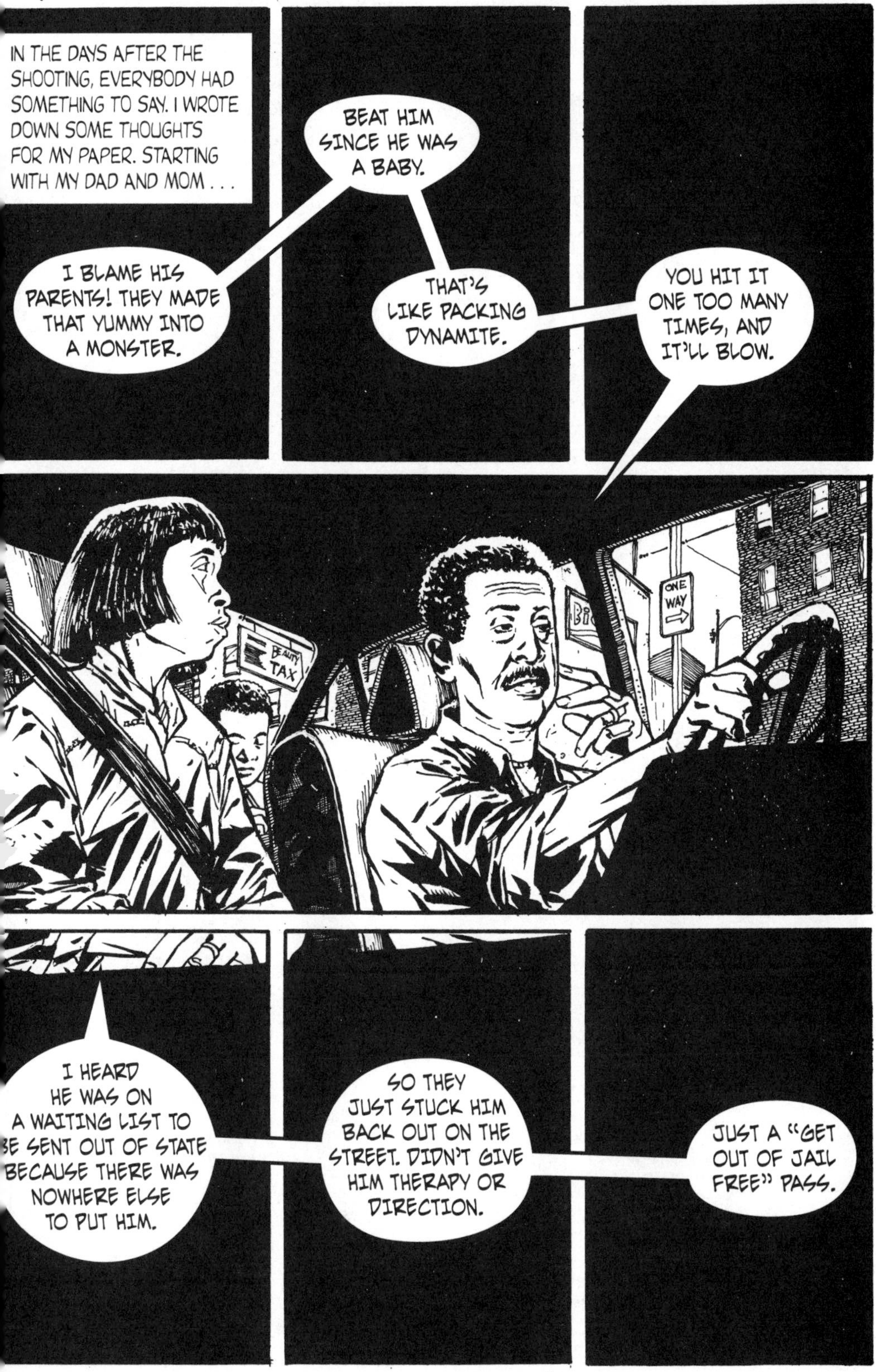
IN THE DAYS AFTER THE SHOOTING, EVERYBODY HAD SOMETHING TO SAY. I WROTE DOWN SOME THOUGHTS FOR MY PAPER. STARTING WITH MY DAD AND MOM . . .
I BLAME HIS PARENTS! THEY MADE THAT YUMMY INTO A MONSTER.
BEAT HIM SINCE HE WAS A BABY.
THAT'S LIKE PACKING DYNAMITE.
YOU HIT IT ONE TOO MANY TIMES, AND IT'LL BLOW.
BEAUTY TAX
ONE WAY
I HEARD HE WAS ON A WAITING LIST TO BE SENT OUT OF STATE BECAUSE THERE WAS NOWHERE ELSE TO PUT HIM.
SO THEY JUST STUCK HIM BACK OUT ON THE STREET. DIDN'T GIVE HIM THERAPY OR DIRECTION.
JUST A "GET OUT OF JAIL FREE" PASS.

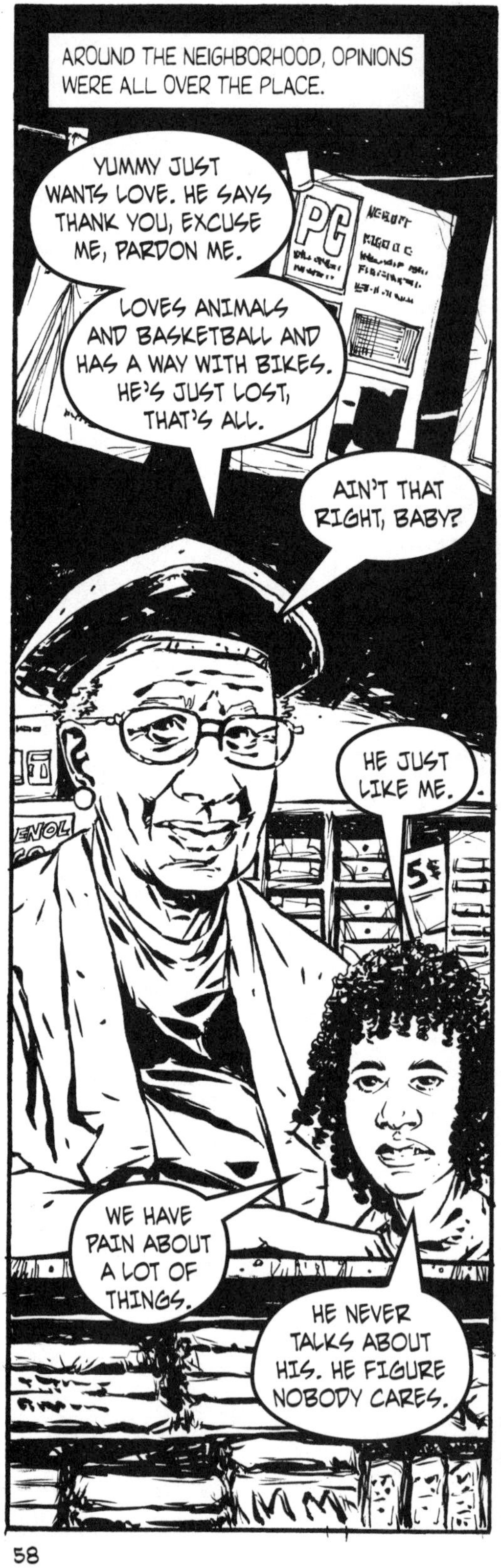
AROUND THE NEIGHBORHOOD, OPINIONS WERE ALL OVER THE PLACE.
YUMMY JUST WANTS LOVE. HE SAYS THANK YOU, EXCUSE ME, PARDON ME.
LOVES ANIMALS AND BASKETBALL AND HAS A WAY WITH BIKES. HE'S JUST LOST, THAT'S ALL.
AIN'T THAT RIGHT, BABY?
HE JUST LIKE ME.
WE HAVE PAIN ABOUT A LOT OF THINGS.
HE NEVER TALKS ABOUT HIS. HE FIGURE NOBODY CARES.
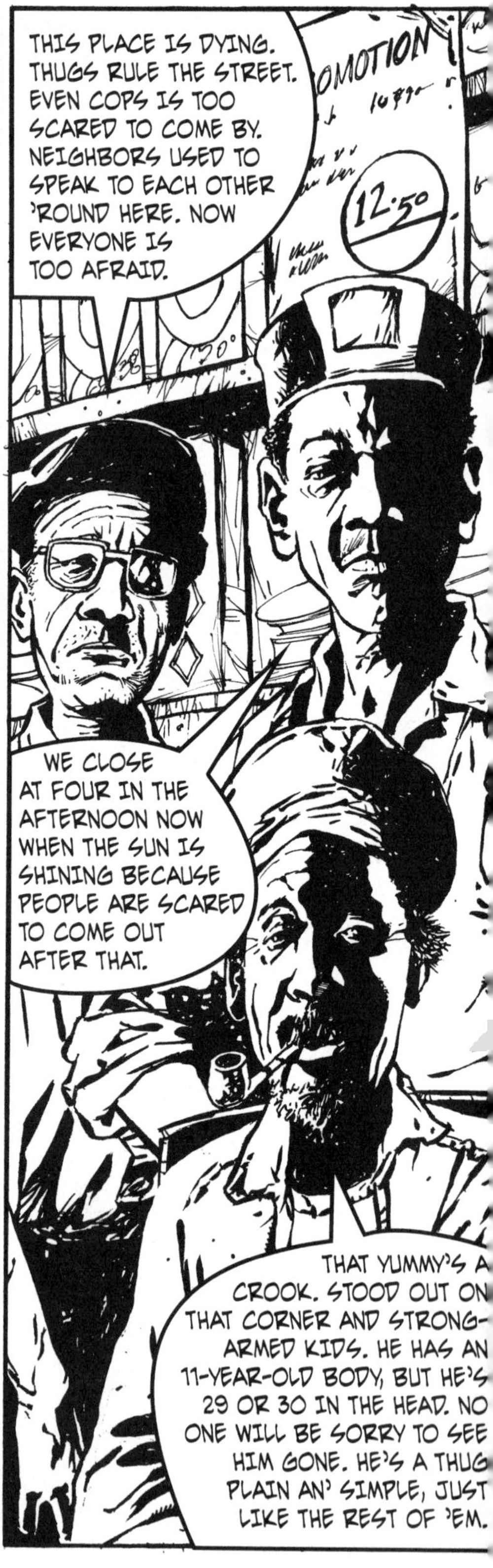
THIS PLACE IS DYING. THUGS RULE THE STREET. EVEN COPS IS TOO SCARED TO COME BY. NEIGHBORS USED TO SPEAK TO EACH OTHER 'ROUND HERE. NOW EVERYONE IS TOO AFRAID.
12.50
WE CLOSE AT FOUR IN THE AFTERNOON NOW WHEN THE SUN IS SHINING BECAUSE PEOPLE ARE SCARED TO COME OUT AFTER THAT.
THAT YUMMY'S A CROOK. STOOD OUT ON THAT CORNER AND STRONG-ARMED KIDS. HE HAS AN 11-YEAR-OLD BODY, BUT HE'S 29 OR 30 IN THE HEAD. NO ONE WILL BE SORRY TO SEE HIM GONE. HE'S A THUG PLAIN AN' SIMPLE, JUST LIKE THE REST OF 'EM.

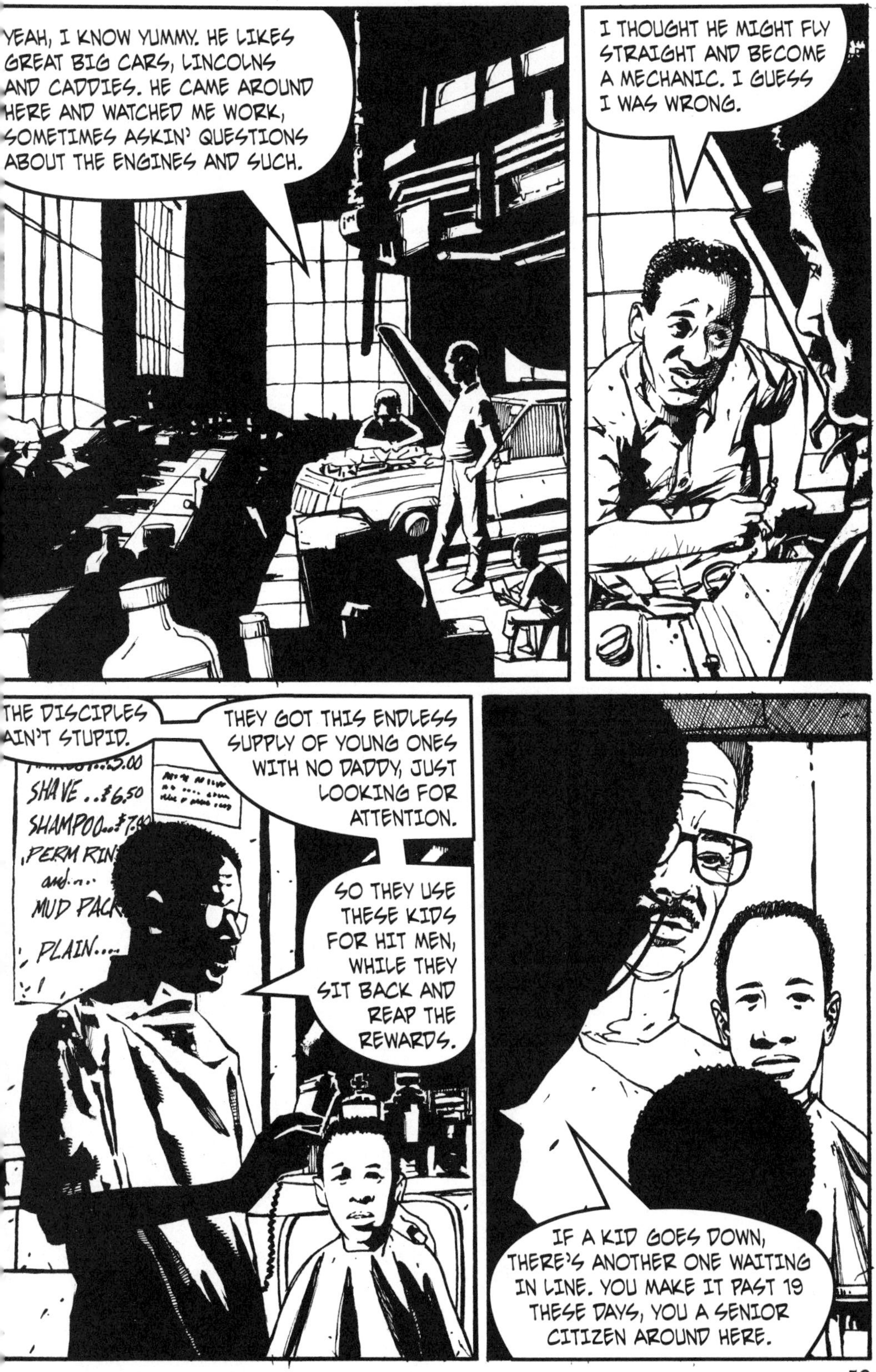
YEAH, I KNOW YUMMY. HE LIKES GREAT BIG CARS, LINCOLNS AND CADDIES. HE CAME AROUND HERE AND WATCHED ME WORK, SOMETIMES ASKIN' QUESTIONS ABOUT THE ENGINES AND SUCH.
I THOUGHT HE MIGHT FLY STRAIGHT AND BECOME A MECHANIC. I GUESS I WAS WRONG.
THE DISCIPLES AIN'T STUPID.
THEY GOT THIS ENDLESS SUPPLY OF YOUNG ONES WITH NO DADDY, JUST LOOKING FOR ATTENTION.
SHAVE ..$6.50
PLAIN....
SO THEY USE THESE KIDS FOR HIT MEN, WHILE THEY SIT BACK AND REAP THE REWARDS.
IF A KID GOES DOWN, THERE'S ANOTHER ONE WAITING IN LINE. YOU MAKE IT PAST 19 THESE DAYS, YOU A SENIOR CITIZEN AROUND HERE.

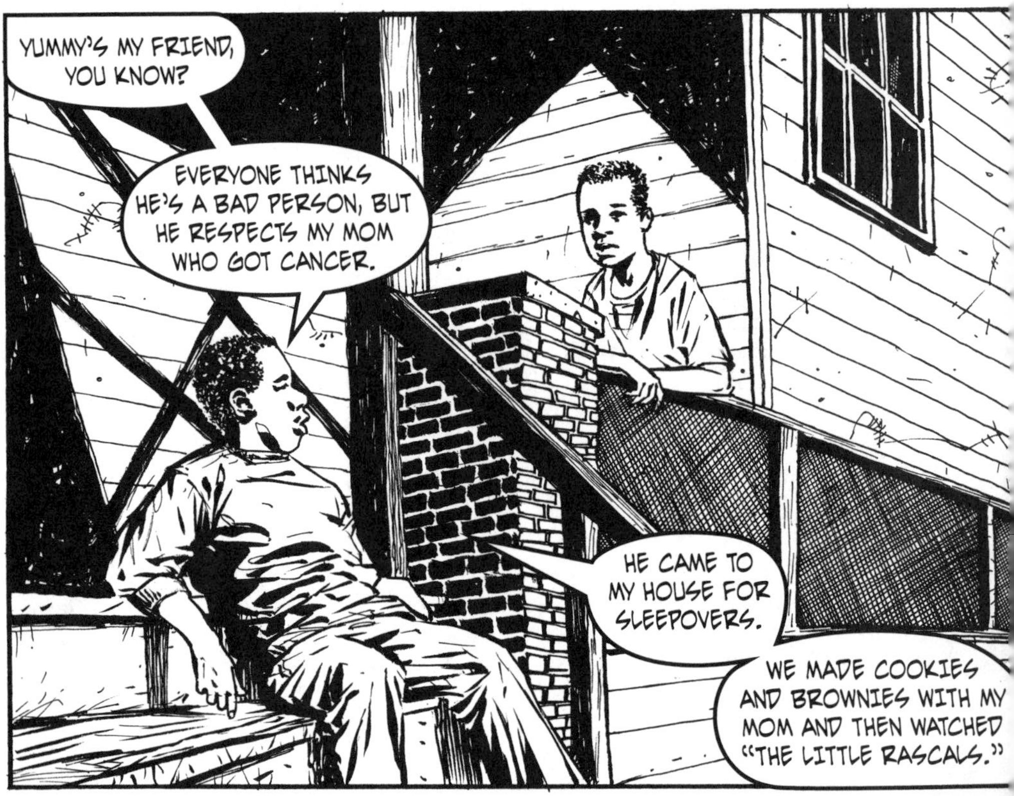
YUMMY'S MY FRIEND, YOU KNOW?
EVERYONE THINKS HE'S A BAD PERSON, BUT HE RESPECTS MY MOM WHO GOT CANCER.
HE CAME TO MY HOUSE FOR SLEEPOVERS.
WE MADE COOKIES AND BROWNIES WITH MY MOM AND THEN WATCHED "THE LITTLE RASCALS."

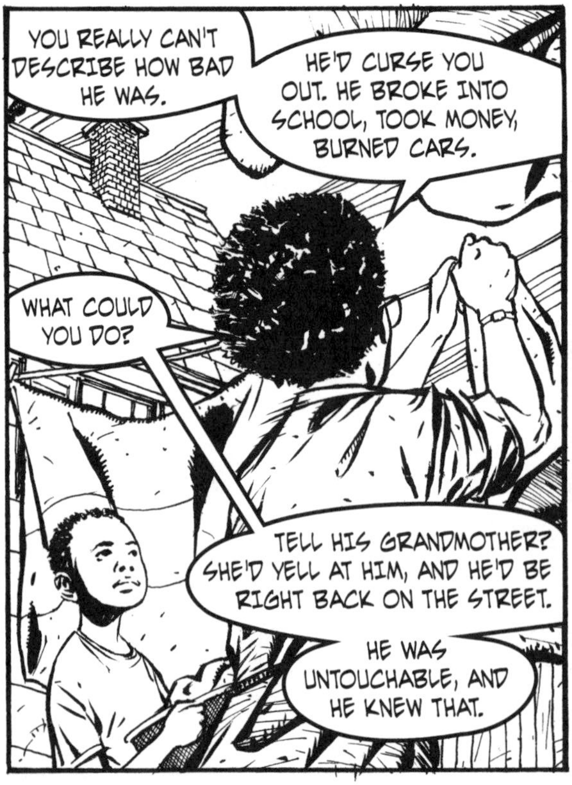
YOU REALLY CAN'T DESCRIBE HOW BAD HE WAS.
HE'D CURSE YOU OUT. HE BROKE INTO SCHOOL, TOOK MONEY, BURNED CARS.
WHAT COULD YOU DO?
TELL HIS GRANDMOTHER? SHE'D YELL AT HIM, AND HE'D BE RIGHT BACK ON THE STREET.
HE WAS UNTOUCHABLE, AND HE KNEW THAT.

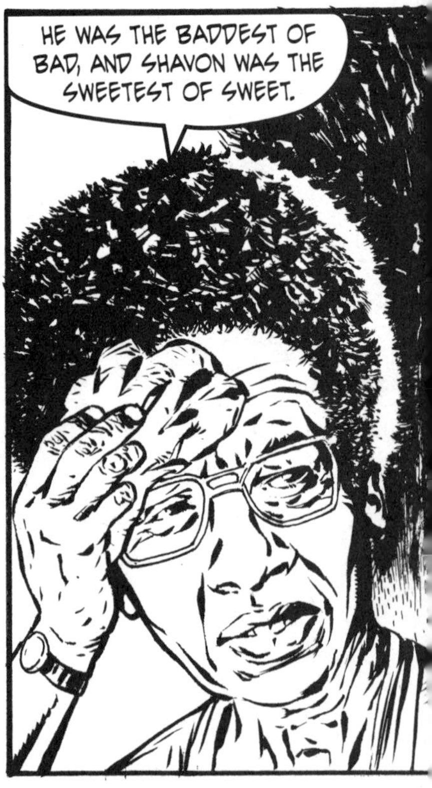
HE WAS THE BADDEST OF BAD, AND SHAVON WAS THE SWEETEST OF SWEET.

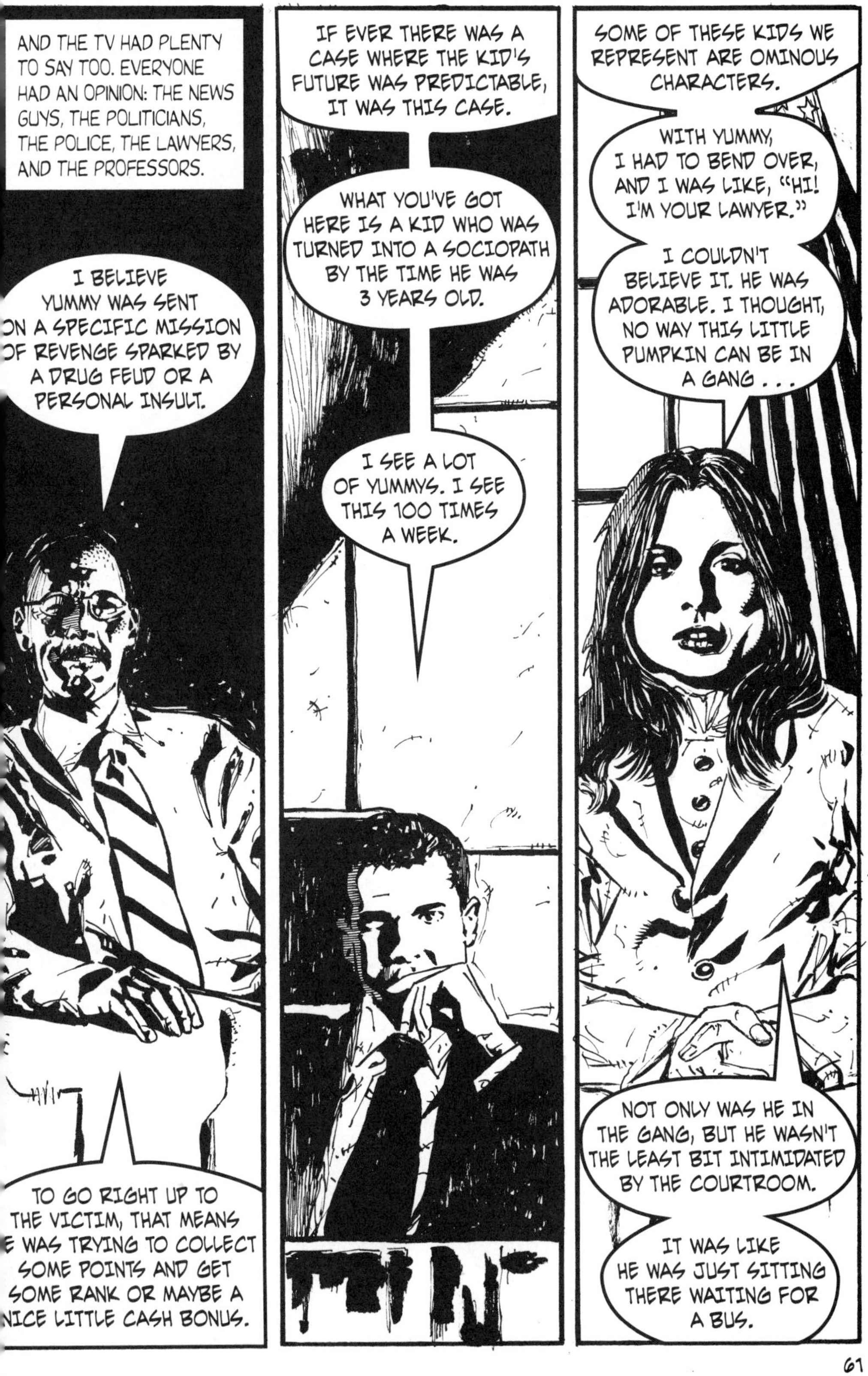
AND THE TV HAD PLENTY TO SAY TOO. EVERYONE HAD AN OPINION: THE NEWS GUYS, THE POLITICIANS, THE POLICE, THE LAWYERS, AND THE PROFESSORS.
I BELIEVE YUMMY WAS SENT ON A SPECIFIC MISSION OF REVENGE SPARKED BY A DRUG FEUD OR A PERSONAL INSULT.
TO GO RIGHT UP TO THE VICTIM, THAT MEANS E WAS TRYING TO COLLECT SOME POINTS AND GET SOME RANK OR MAYBE A NICE LITTLE CASH BONUS.
IF EVER THERE WAS A CASE WHERE THE KID'S FUTURE WAS PREDICTABLE, IT WAS THIS CASE.
WHAT YOU'VE GOT HERE IS A KID WHO WAS TURNED INTO A SOCIOPATH BY THE TIME HE WAS 3 YEARS OLD.
I SEE A LOT OF YUMMYS. I SEE THIS 100 TIMES A WEEK.
SOME OF THESE KIDS WE REPRESENT ARE OMINOUS CHARACTERS.
WITH YUMMY, I HAD TO BEND OVER, AND I WAS LIKE, "HI! I'M YOUR LAWYER."
I COULDN'T BELIEVE IT. HE WAS ADORABLE. I THOUGHT, NO WAY THIS LITTLE PUMPKIN CAN BE IN A GANG . . .
NOT ONLY WAS HE IN THE GANG, BUT HE WASN'T THE LEAST BIT INTIMIDATED BY THE COURTROOM.
IT WAS LIKE HE WAS JUST SITTING THERE WAITING FOR A BUS.

I HAD TO INTERVIEW HIM ONCE, AND WE PLAYED A GAME WHERE HE HAD TO COMPLETE A SERIES OF QUESTIONS.

I SAID, "COMPLETE THIS SENTENCE. I AM VERY _____," AND HE ANSWERED "SICK."

LATER, I ASKED HIM WHAT HE WANTED TO BE WHEN HE GREW UP AND HE SAID, "A POLICEMAN."

YUMMY AVERAGED A FELONY A MONTH FOR THE LAST YEAR AND A HALF. 23 FELONIES IN ALL BY THE TIME HE WAS 11. NOW YOU GOT OVER 1000 BLACK DISCIPLES LIKE HIM, ALL YOUNGER THAN 13. ALL WITH GUNS. IN THIS COUNTRY, 15 KIDS UNDER THE AGE OF 19 DIE BY GUNS EVERY DAY.

THAT'S 100 YOUNG MURDER VICTIMS THIS YEAR IN CHICAGO ALONE.

THIS YOUNG KID FELL THROUGH THE CRACKS. IF THIS CHILD WAS PROTECTED 5 YEARS AGO, YOU SAVE 2 PEOPLE.

YOU SAVE THE YOUNG WOMAN WHO WAS KILLED, AND YOU SAVE THE YOUNG OFFENDER.

EVEN PRESIDENT CLINTON HAD SOMETHING TO SAY ABOUT YUMMY. . . .

THE NUMBER OF GANG HOMICIDES HAS NEARLY TRIPLED SINCE 1980 IN ROBERT AND SHAVON'S HOMETOWN.

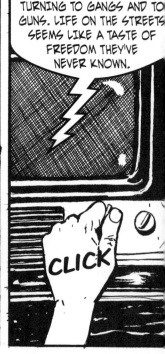

AT YOUNGER AND YOUNGER AGES, BOYS AND GIRLS ARE TURNING TO GANGS AND TO GUNS. LIFE ON THE STREETS SEEMS LIKE A TASTE OF FREEDOM THEY'VE NEVER KNOWN.

CLICK

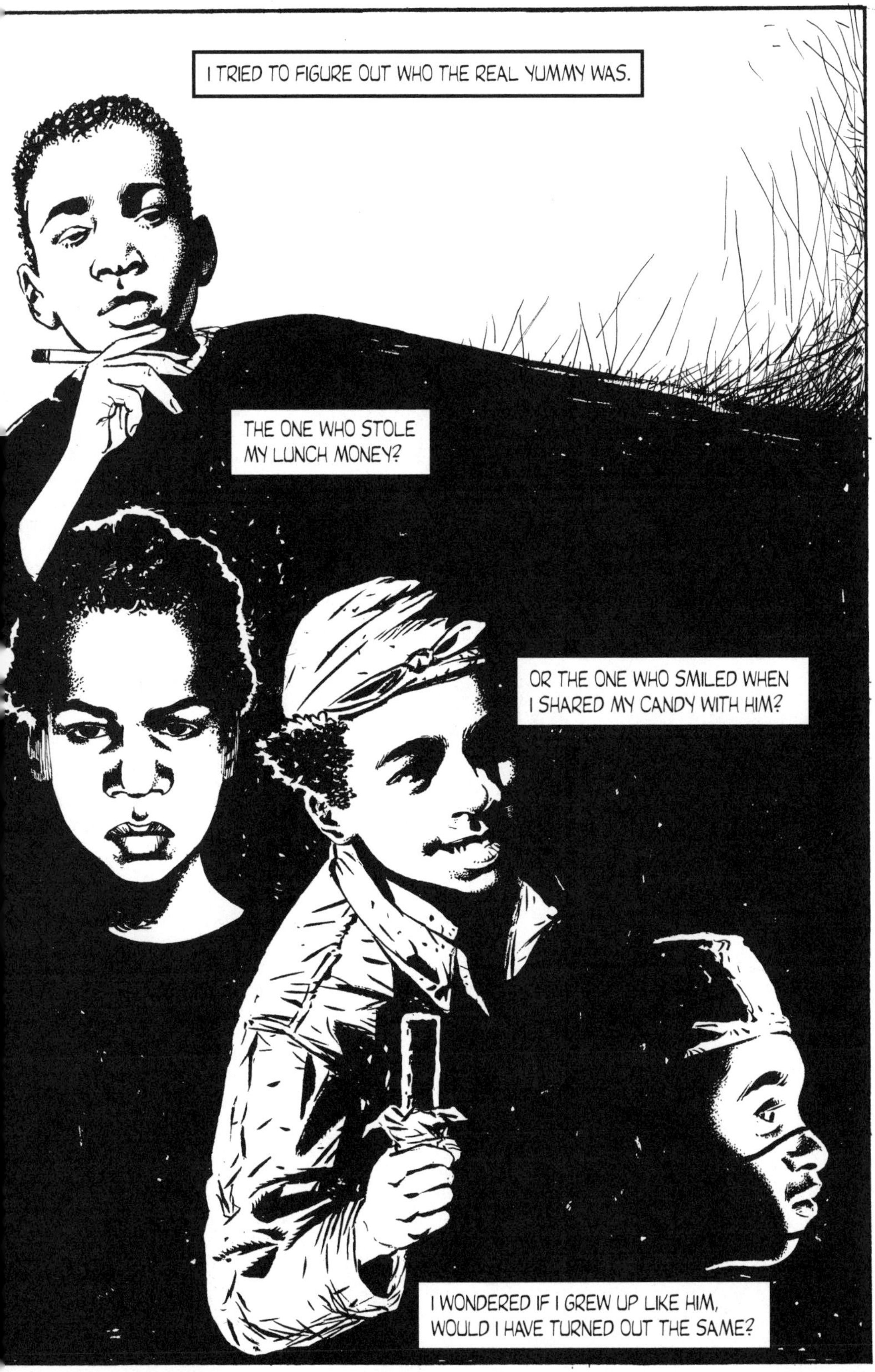
I TRIED TO FIGURE OUT WHO THE REAL YUMMY WAS.
THE ONE WHO STOLE MY LUNCH MONEY?
OR THE ONE WHO SMILED WHEN I SHARED MY CANDY WITH HIM?
I WONDERED IF I GREW UP LIKE HIM, WOULD I HAVE TURNED OUT THE SAME?

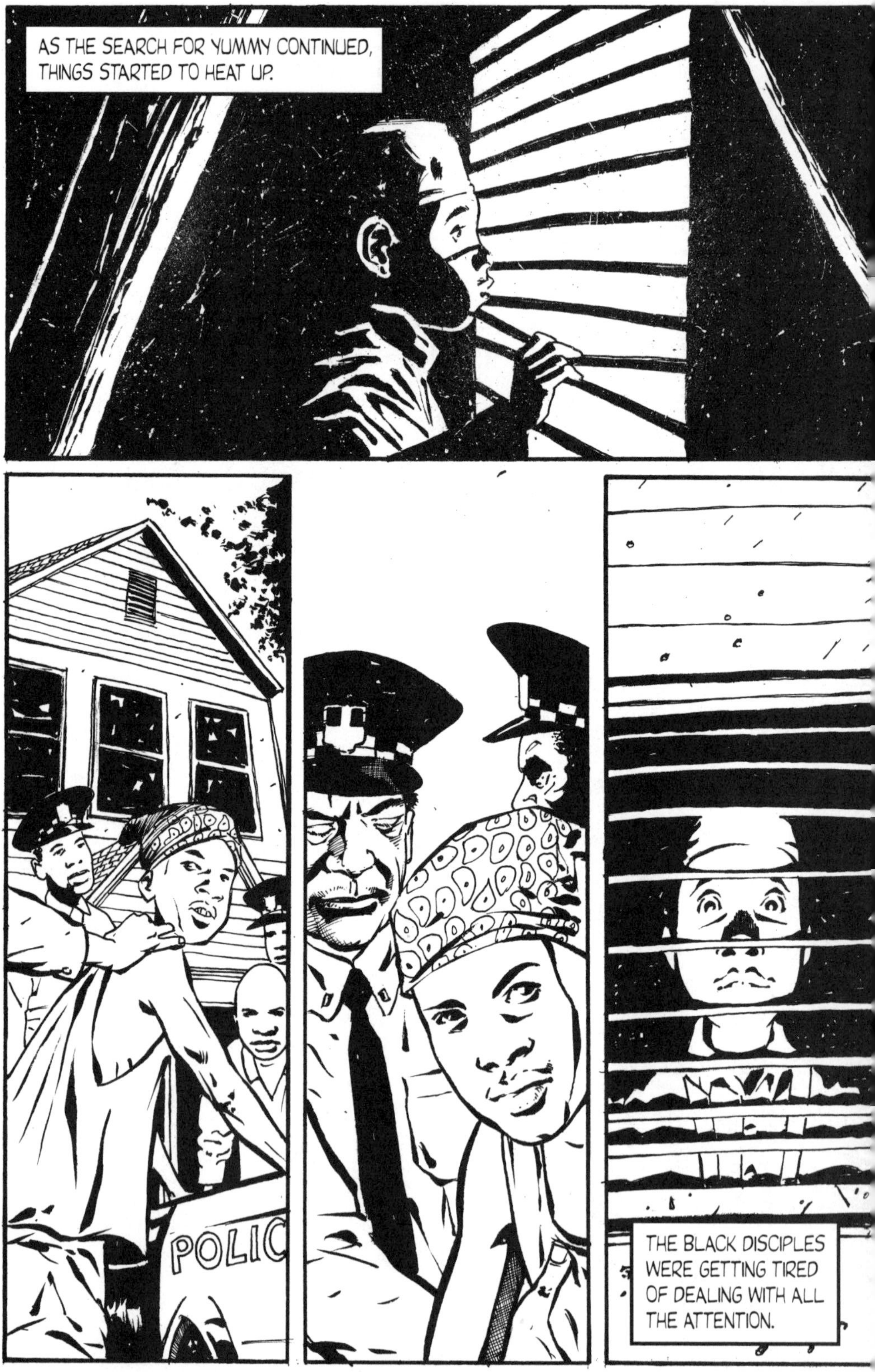
AS THE SEARCH FOR YUMMY CONTINUED, THINGS STARTED TO HEAT UP.
POLIC
THE BLACK DISCIPLES WERE GETTING TIRED OF DEALING WITH ALL THE ATTENTION.

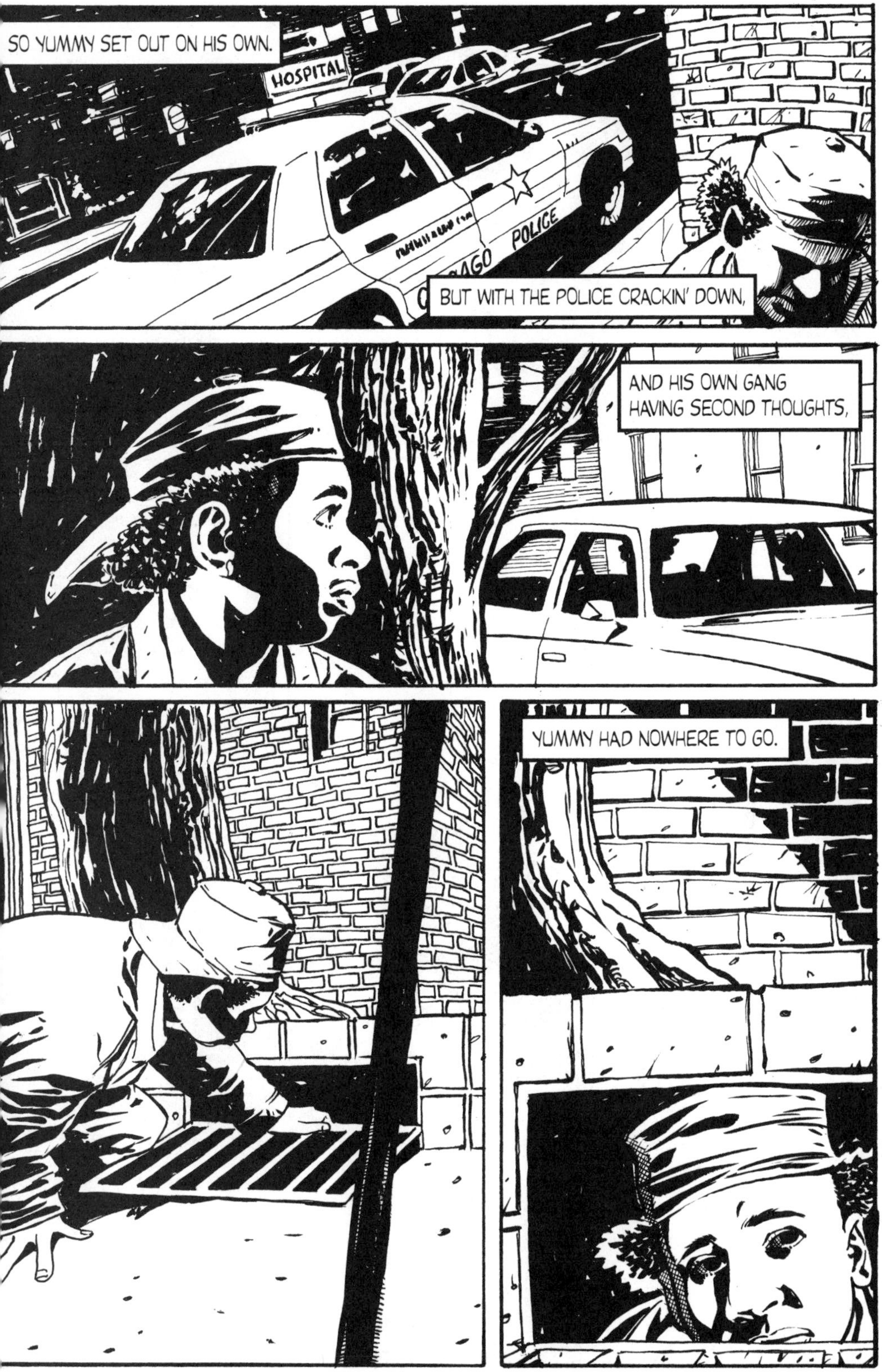
SO YUMMY SET OUT ON HIS OWN.
HOSPITAL
POLICE
BUT WITH THE POLICE CRACKIN' DOWN,
AND HIS OWN GANG HAVING SECOND THOUGHTS,
YUMMY HAD NOWHERE TO GO.

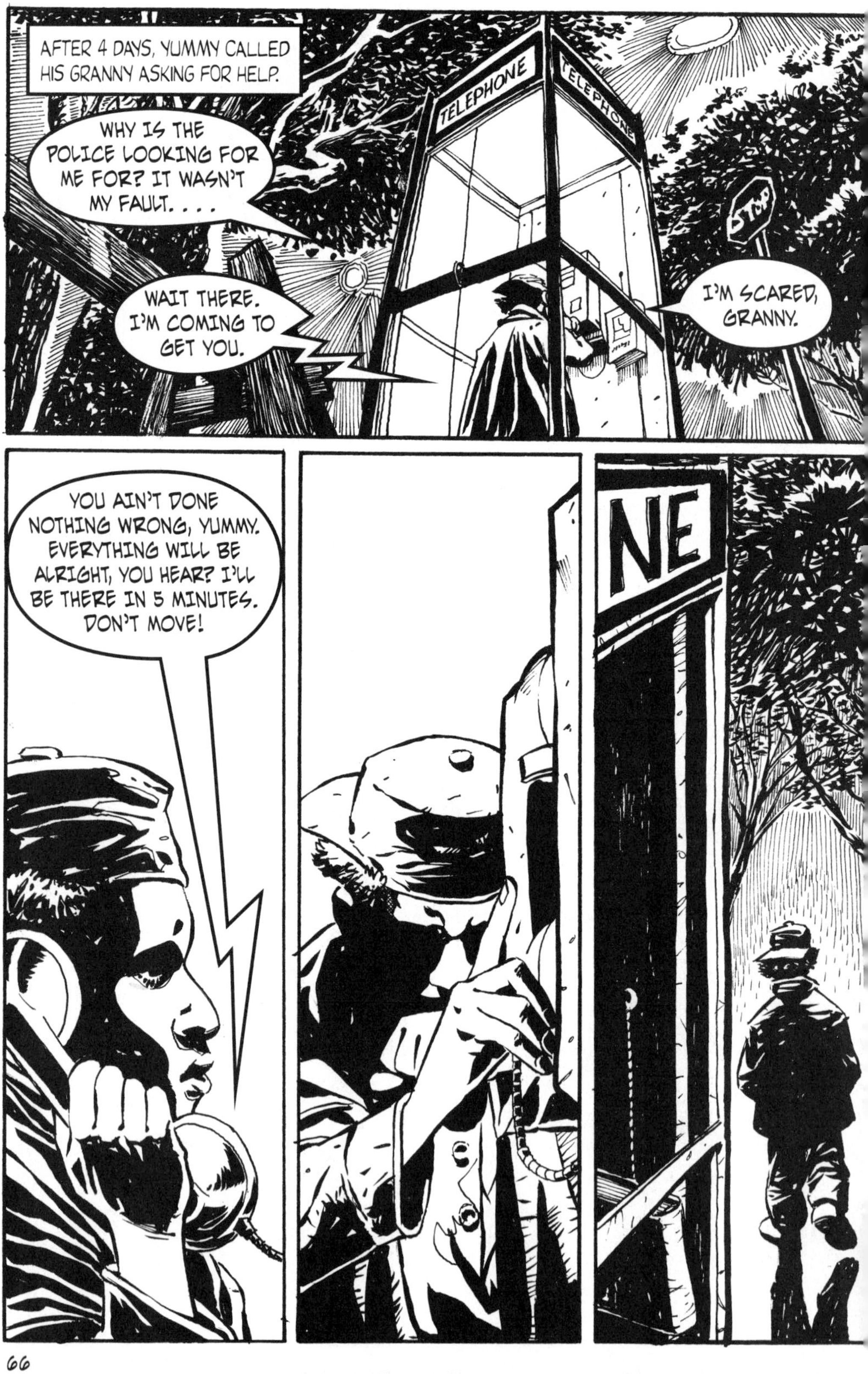
AFTER 4 DAYS, YUMMY CALLED HIS GRANNY ASKING FOR HELP.
TELEPHONE
TELEPHONE
STOP
WHY IS THE POLICE LOOKING FOR ME FOR? IT WASN'T MY FAULT. . . .
WAIT THERE. I'M COMING TO GET YOU.
I'M SCARED, GRANNY.
YOU AIN'T DONE NOTHING WRONG, YUMMY. EVERYTHING WILL BE ALRIGHT, YOU HEAR? I'LL BE THERE IN 5 MINUTES. DON'T MOVE!
NE

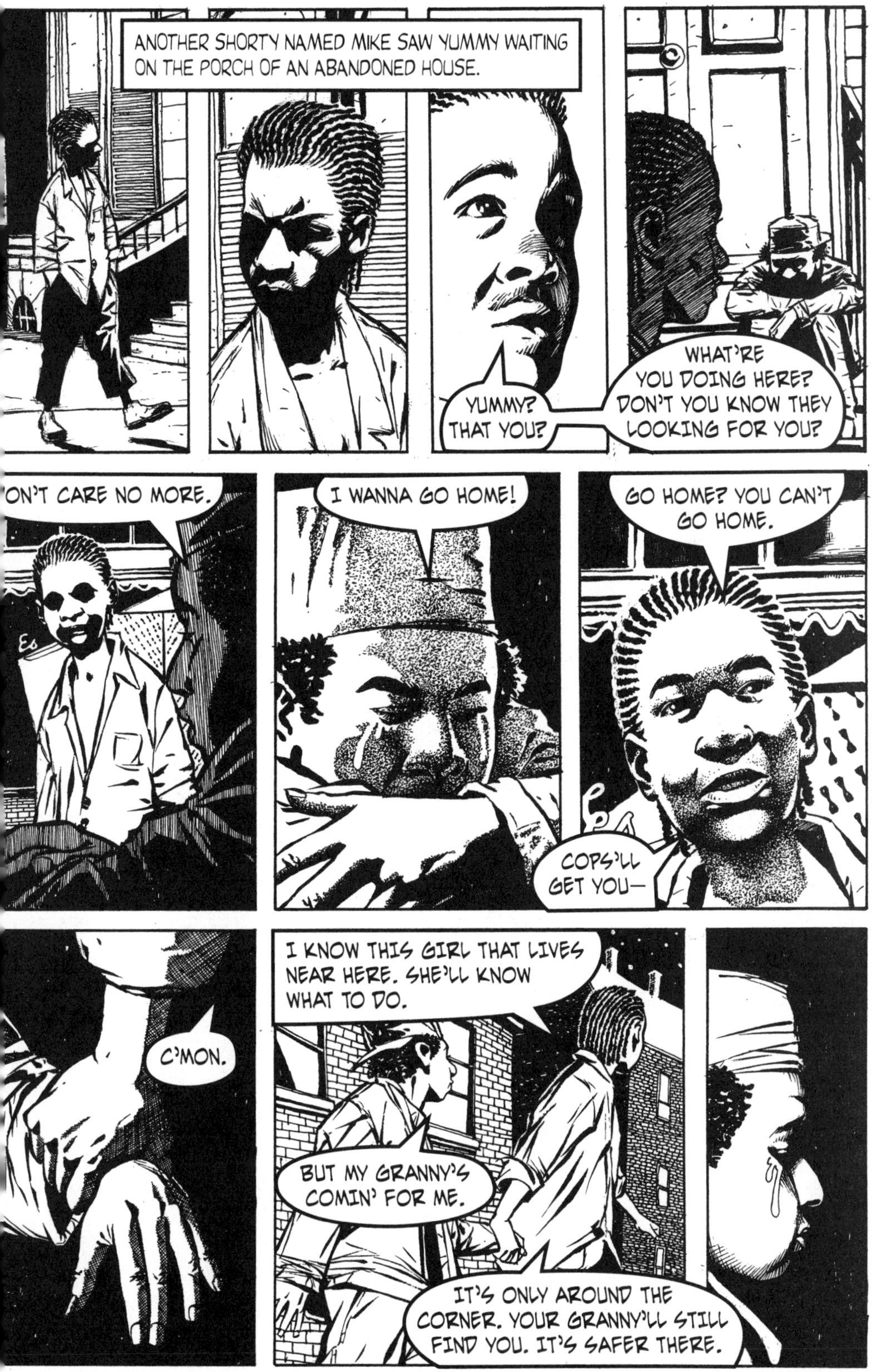
ANOTHER SHORTY NAMED MIKE SAW YUMMY WAITING ON THE PORCH OF AN ABANDONED HOUSE.
YUMMY? THAT YOU?
WHAT'RE YOU DOING HERE? DON'T YOU KNOW THEY LOOKING FOR YOU?
ON'T CARE NO MORE.
I WANNA GO HOME!
GO HOME? YOU CAN'T GO HOME.
COPS'LL GET YOU—
C'MON.
I KNOW THIS GIRL THAT LIVES NEAR HERE. SHE'LL KNOW WHAT TO DO.
BUT MY GRANNY'S COMIN' FOR ME.
IT'S ONLY AROUND THE CORNER. YOUR GRANNY'LL STILL FIND YOU. IT'S SAFER THERE.

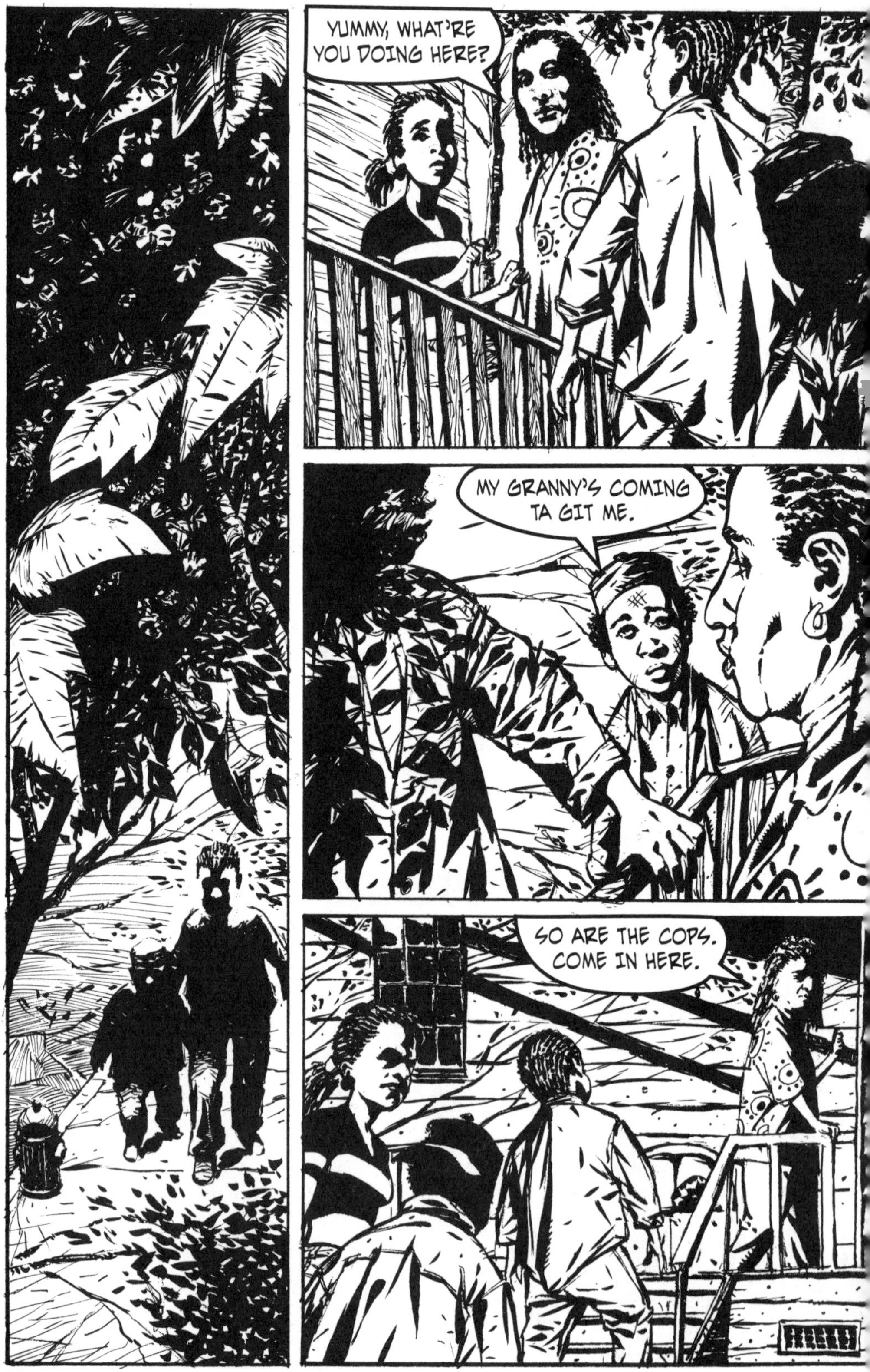
YUMMY, WHAT'RE YOU DOING HERE?
MY GRANNY'S COMING TA GIT ME.
SO ARE THE COPS. COME IN HERE.

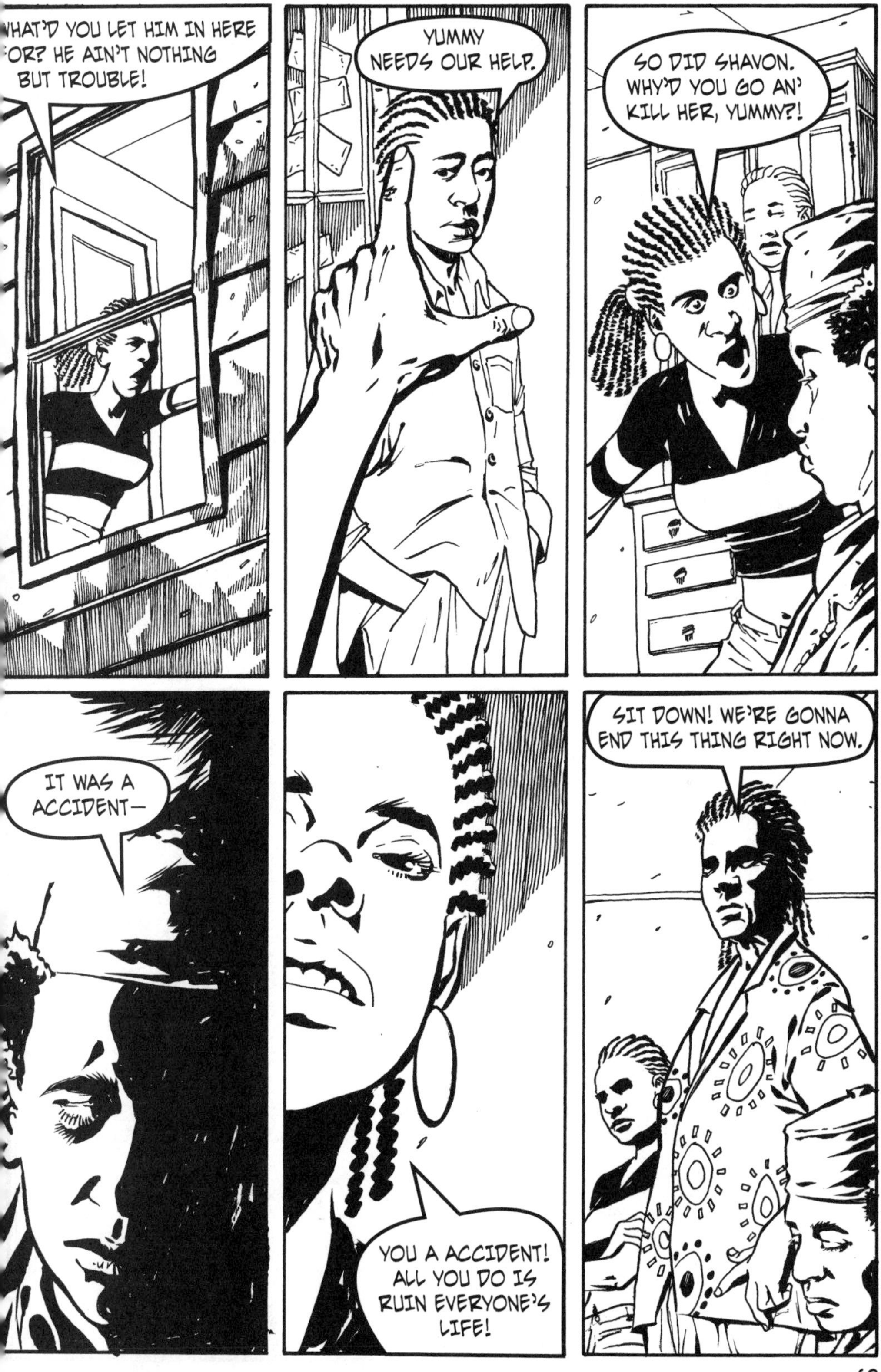
WHAT'D YOU LET HIM IN HERE FOR? HE AIN'T NOTHING BUT TROUBLE!
YUMMY NEEDS OUR HELP.
SO DID SHAVON. WHY'D YOU GO AN' KILL HER, YUMMY?!
IT WAS A ACCIDENT—
YOU A ACCIDENT! ALL YOU DO IS RUIN EVERYONE'S LIFE!
SIT DOWN! WE'RE GONNA END THIS THING RIGHT NOW.

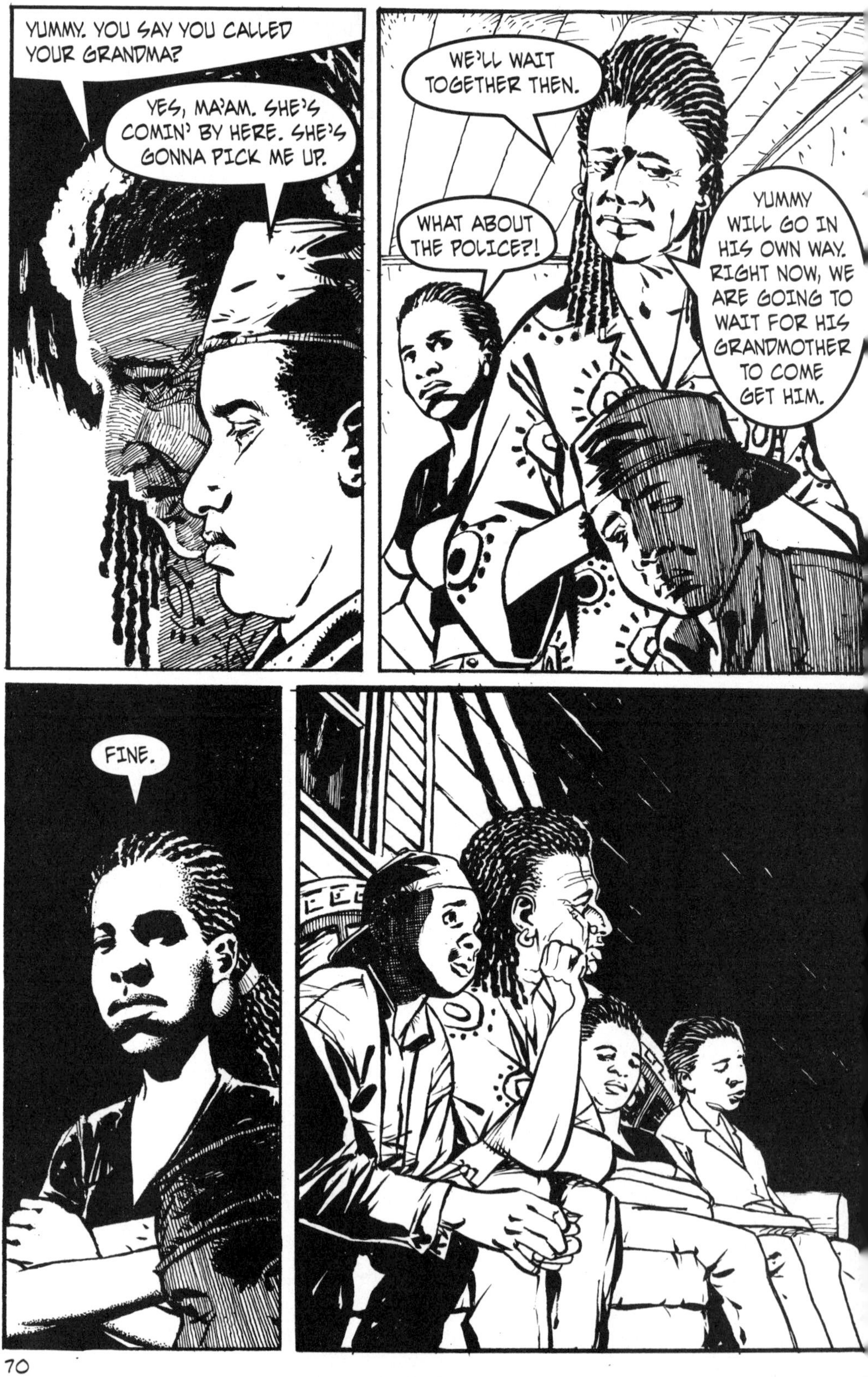
YUMMY. YOU SAY YOU CALLED YOUR GRANDMA?
YES, MA'AM. SHE'S COMIN' BY HERE. SHE'S GONNA PICK ME UP.
WE'LL WAIT TOGETHER THEN.
WHAT ABOUT THE POLICE?!
YUMMY WILL GO IN HIS OWN WAY. RIGHT NOW, WE ARE GOING TO WAIT FOR HIS GRANDMOTHER TO COME GET HIM.
FINE.

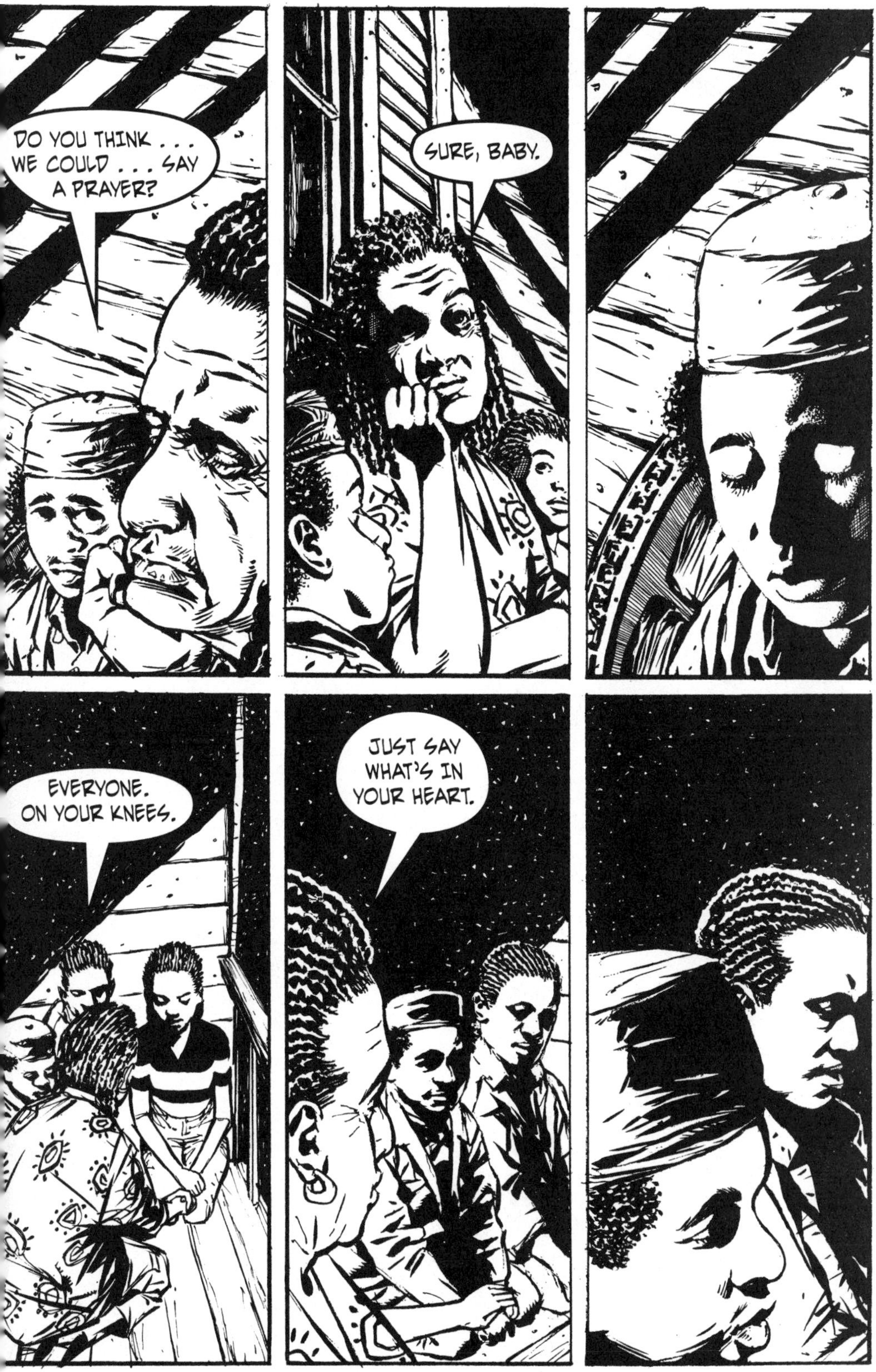
DO YOU THINK . . . WE COULD . . . SAY A PRAYER?
SURE, BABY.
EVERYONE. ON YOUR KNEES.
JUST SAY WHAT'S IN YOUR HEART.

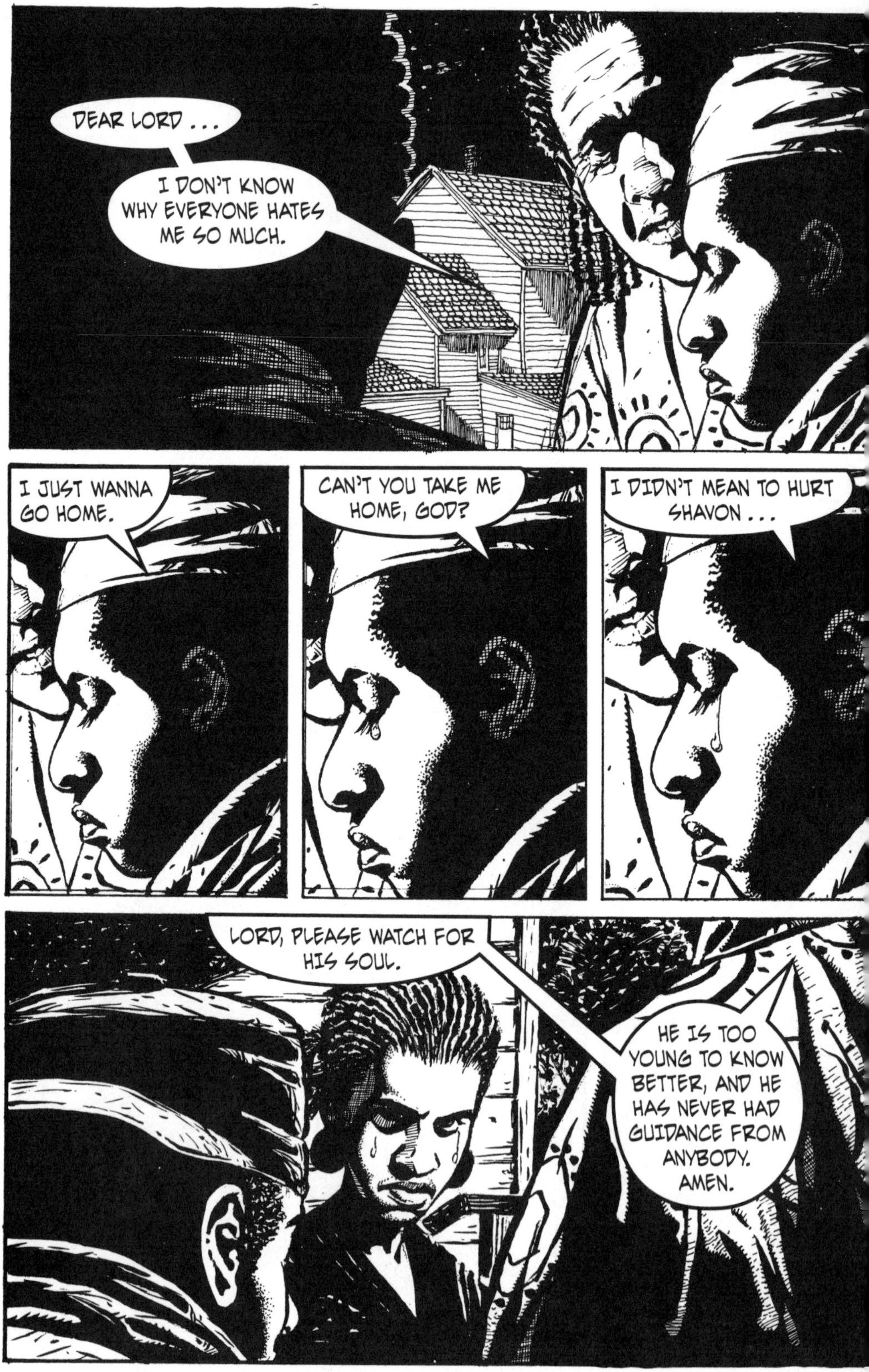
DEAR LORD . . .
I DON'T KNOW WHY EVERYONE HATES ME SO MUCH.
I JUST WANNA GO HOME.
CAN'T YOU TAKE ME HOME, GOD?
I DIDN'T MEAN TO HURT SHAVON . . .
LORD, PLEASE WATCH FOR HIS SOUL.
HE IS TOO YOUNG TO KNOW BETTER, AND HE HAS NEVER HAD GUIDANCE FROM ANYBODY. AMEN.

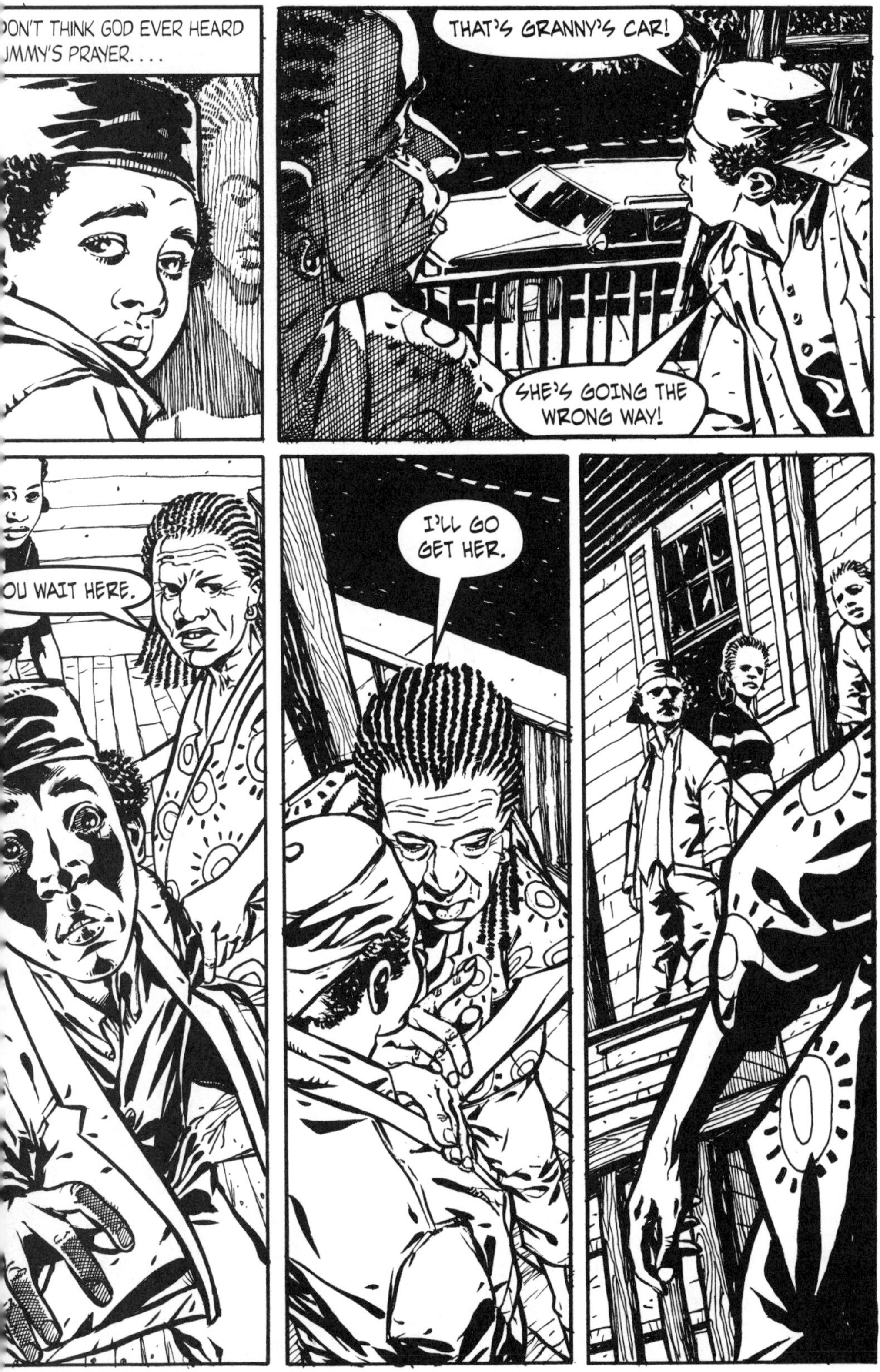
DON'T THINK GOD EVER HEARD
UMMY'S PRAYER....
THAT'S GRANNY'S CAR!
SHE'S GOING THE WRONG WAY!
OU WAIT HERE.
I'LL GO GET HER.

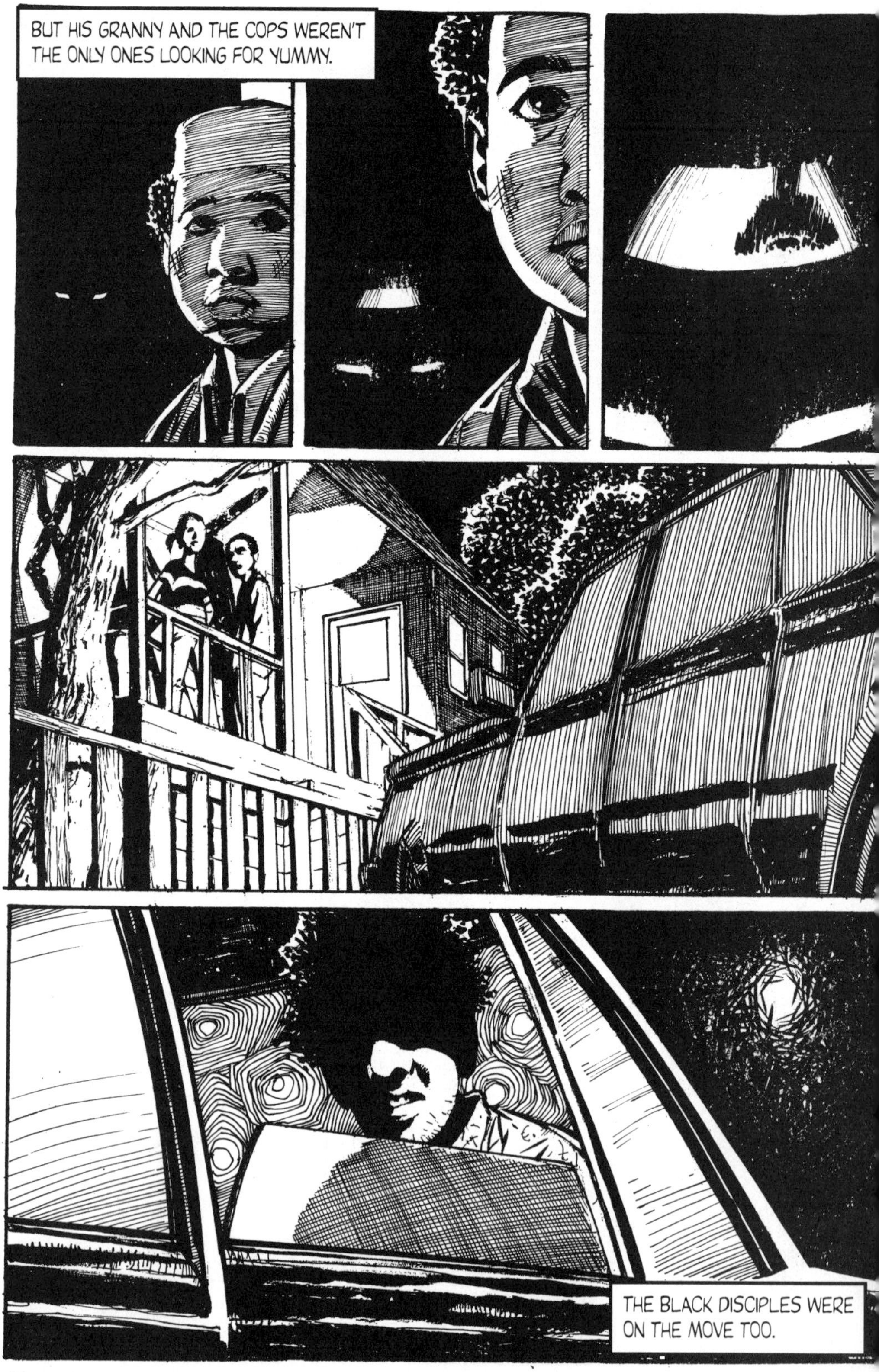
BUT HIS GRANNY AND THE COPS WEREN'T THE ONLY ONES LOOKING FOR YUMMY.
THE BLACK DISCIPLES WERE ON THE MOVE TOO.

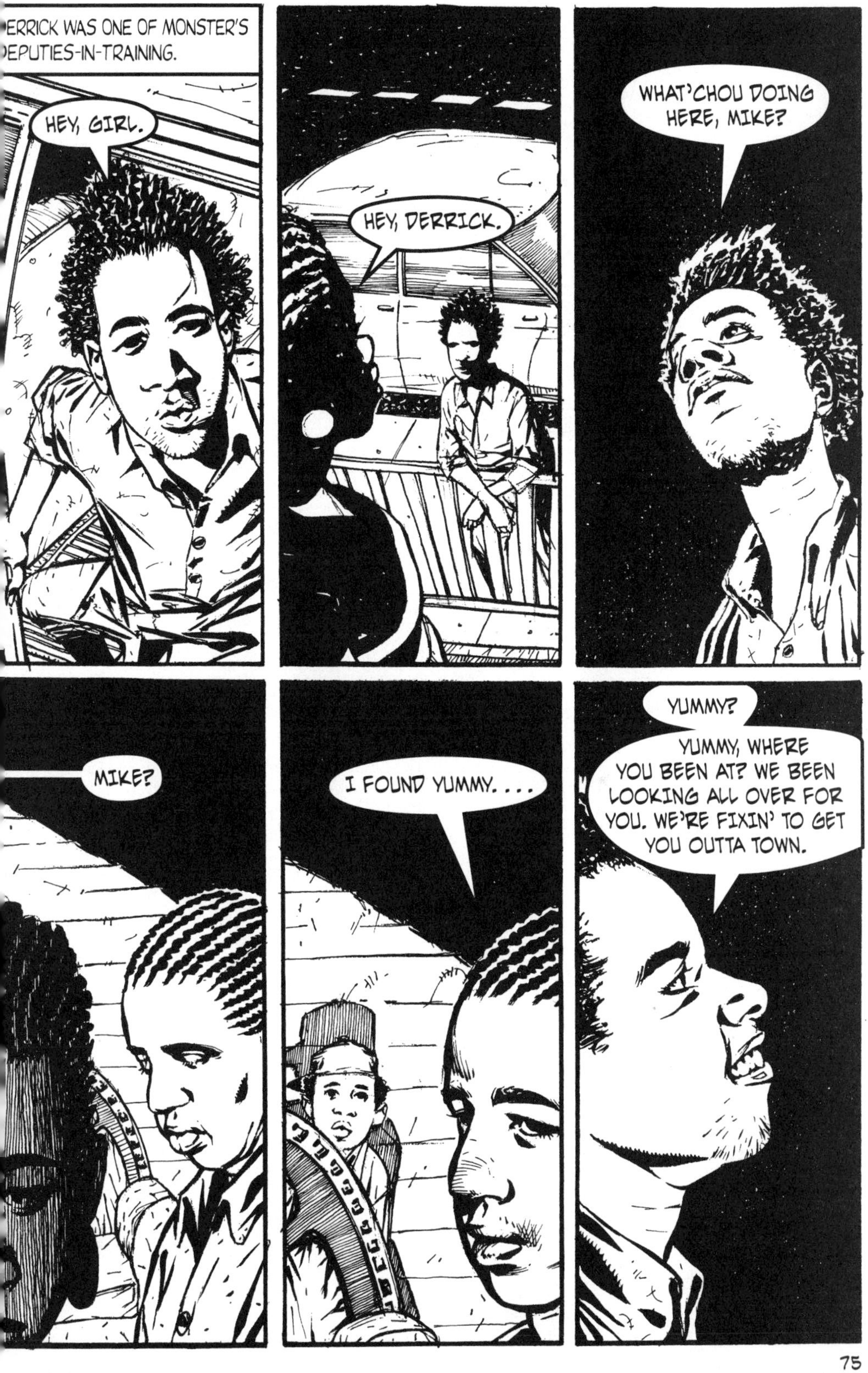

ERRICK WAS ONE OF MONSTER'S EPUTIES-IN-TRAINING.
HEY, GIRL.
HEY, DERRICK.
WHAT'CHOU DOING HERE, MIKE?
MIKE?
I FOUND YUMMY. . . .
YUMMY?
YUMMY, WHERE YOU BEEN AT? WE BEEN LOOKING ALL OVER FOR YOU. WE'RE FIXIN' TO GET YOU OUTTA TOWN.

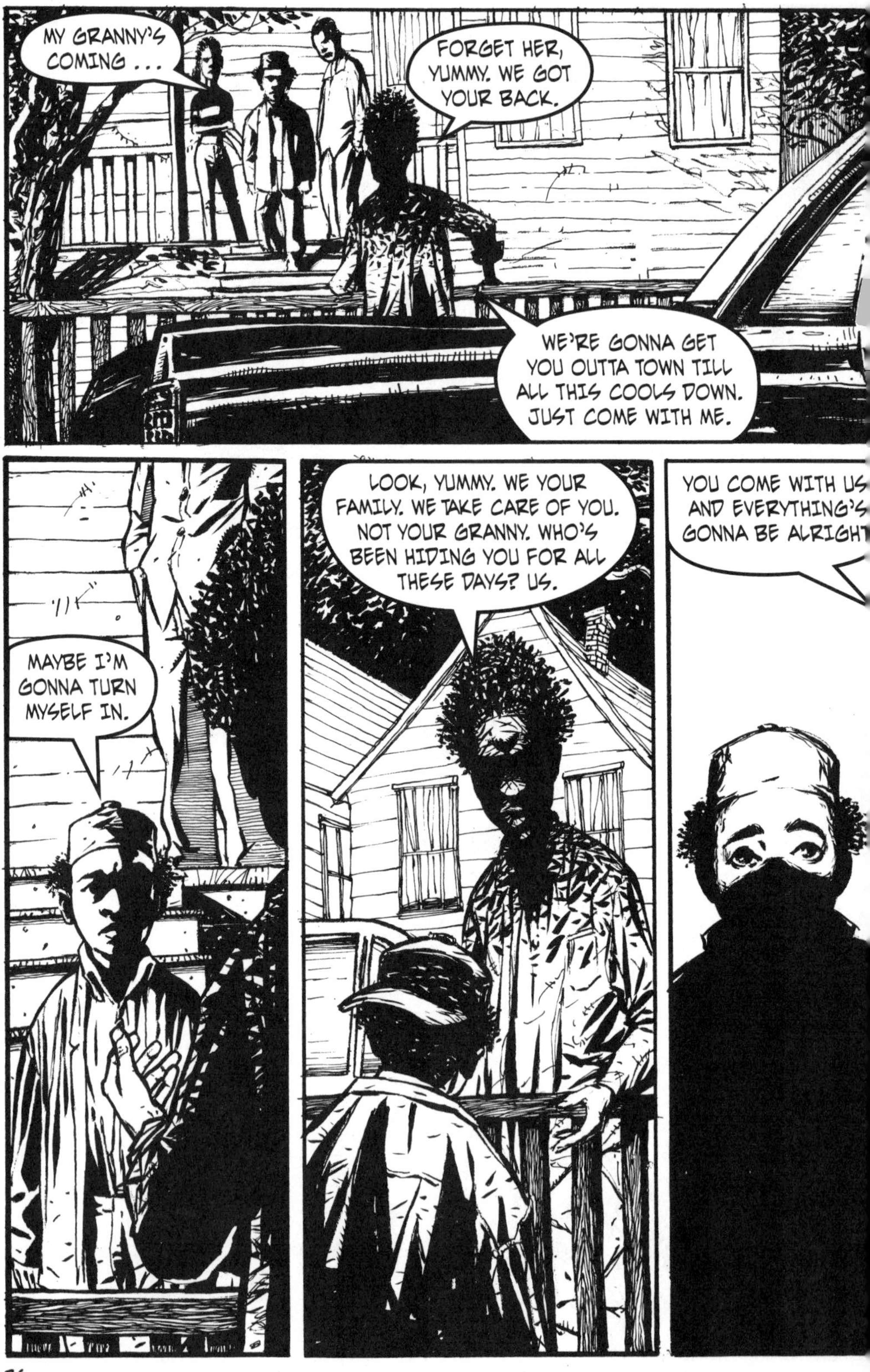
MY GRANNY'S COMING . . .
FORGET HER, YUMMY. WE GOT YOUR BACK.
WE'RE GONNA GET YOU OUTTA TOWN TILL ALL THIS COOLS DOWN. JUST COME WITH ME.
MAYBE I'M GONNA TURN MYSELF IN.
LOOK, YUMMY. WE YOUR FAMILY. WE TAKE CARE OF YOU. NOT YOUR GRANNY. WHO'S BEEN HIDING YOU FOR ALL THESE DAYS? US.
YOU COME WITH US AND EVERYTHING'S GONNA BE ALRIGHT

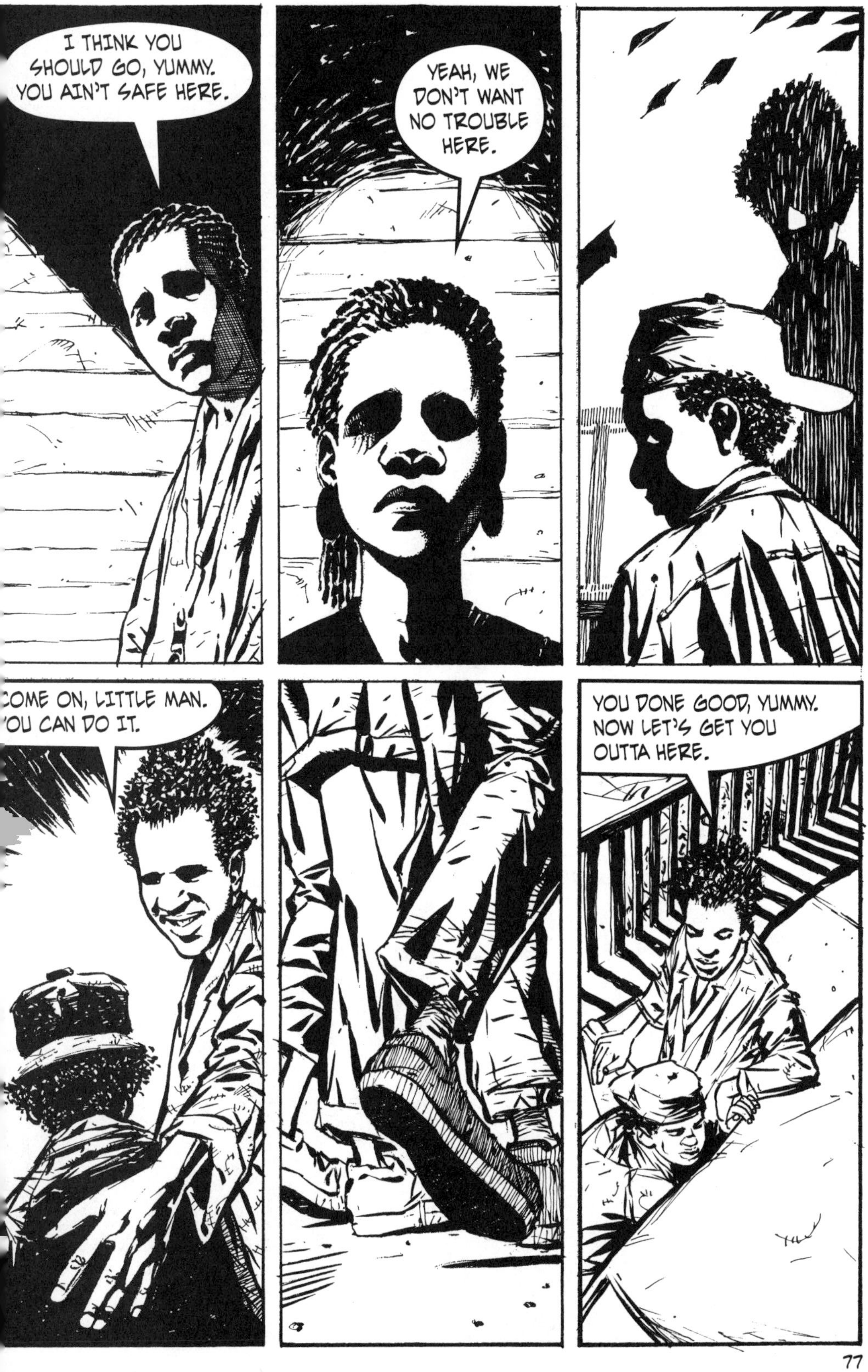
I THINK YOU SHOULD GO, YUMMY. YOU AIN'T SAFE HERE.
YEAH, WE DON'T WANT NO TROUBLE HERE.
COME ON, LITTLE MAN. YOU CAN DO IT.
YOU DONE GOOD, YUMMY. NOW LET'S GET YOU OUTTA HERE.

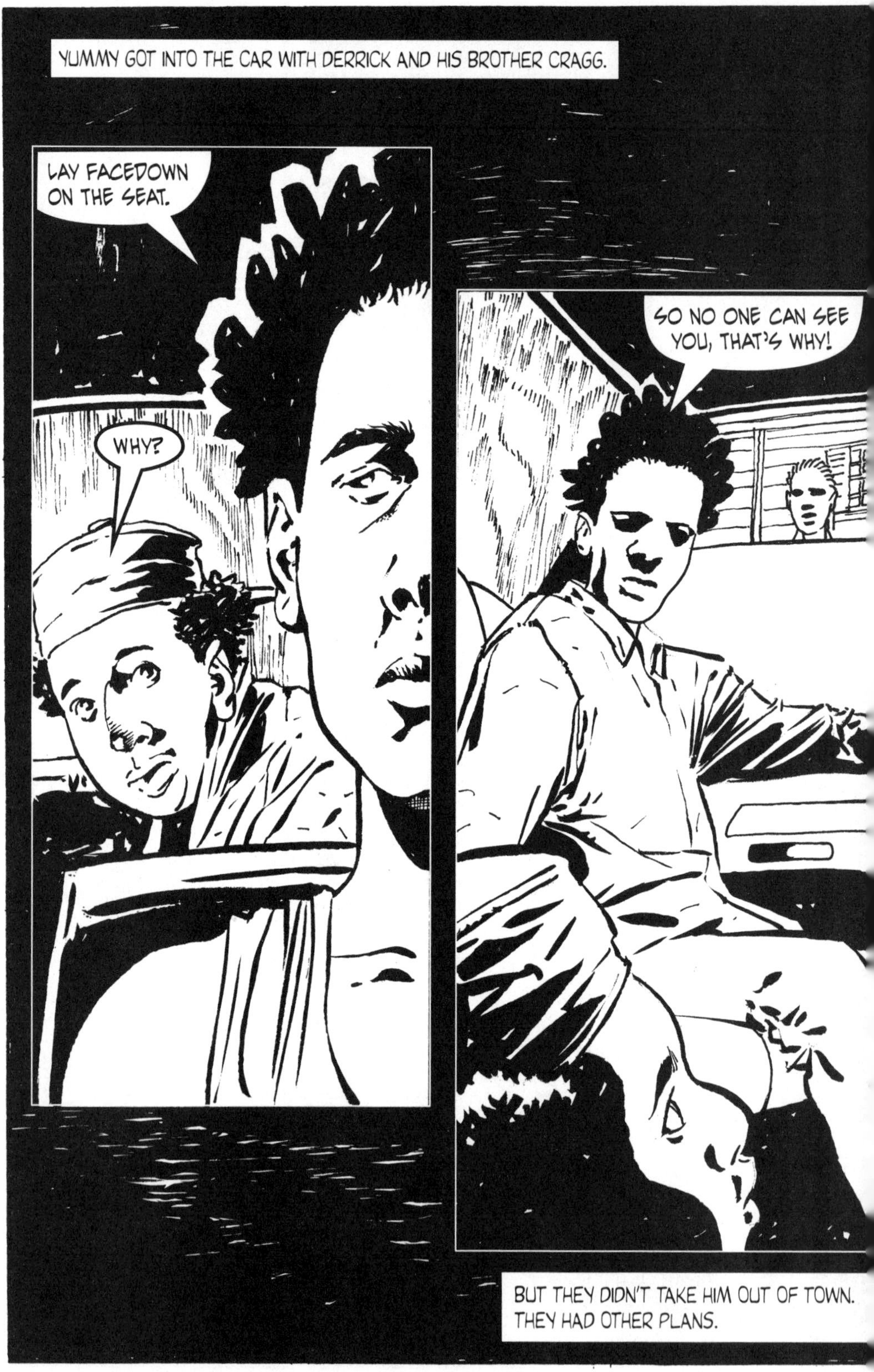
YUMMY GOT INTO THE CAR WITH DERRICK AND HIS BROTHER CRAGG.
LAY FACEDOWN ON THE SEAT.
WHY?
SO NO ONE CAN SEE YOU, THAT'S WHY!
BUT THEY DIDN'T TAKE HIM OUT OF TOWN. THEY HAD OTHER PLANS.

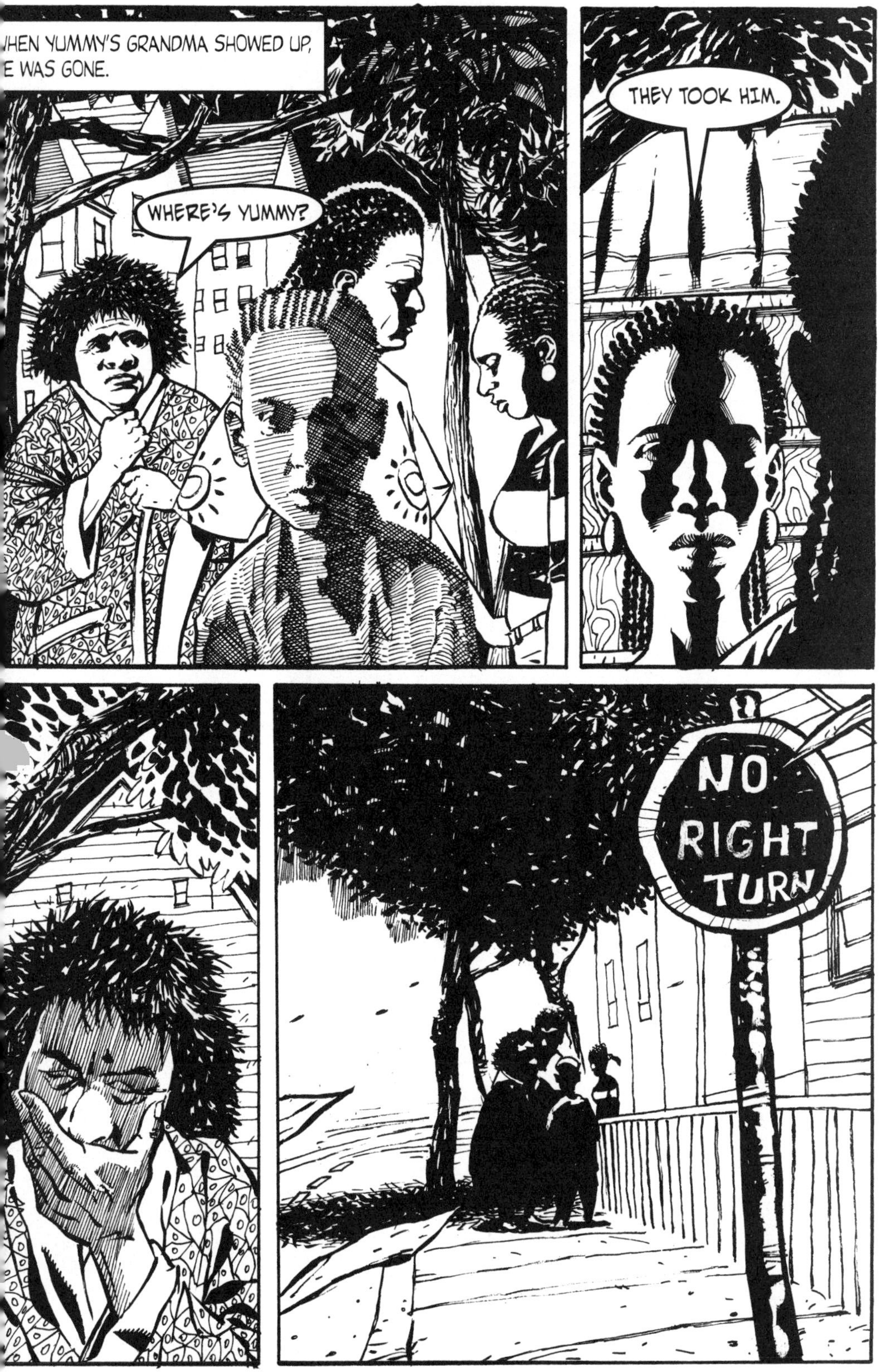
HEN YUMMY'S GRANDMA SHOWED UP, E WAS GONE.
WHERE'S YUMMY?
THEY TOOK HIM.
NO RIGHT TURN

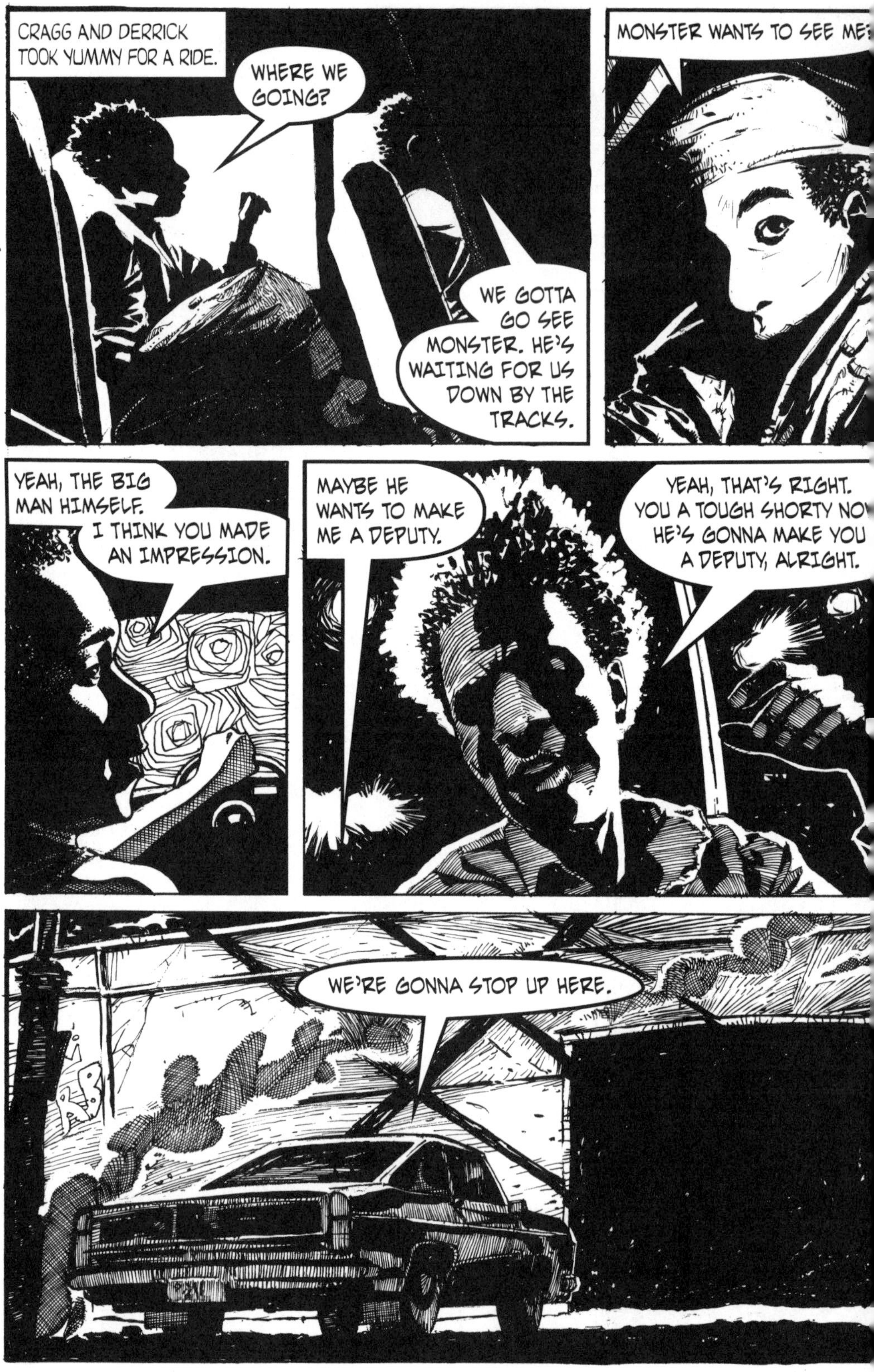
CRAGG AND DERRICK TOOK YUMMY FOR A RIDE.
WHERE WE GOING?
WE GOTTA GO SEE MONSTER. HE'S WAITING FOR US DOWN BY THE TRACKS.
MONSTER WANTS TO SEE ME?
YEAH, THE BIG MAN HIMSELF.
I THINK YOU MADE AN IMPRESSION.
MAYBE HE WANTS TO MAKE ME A DEPUTY.
YEAH, THAT'S RIGHT. YOU A TOUGH SHORTY NOW. HE'S GONNA MAKE YOU A DEPUTY, ALRIGHT.
WE'RE GONNA STOP UP HERE.

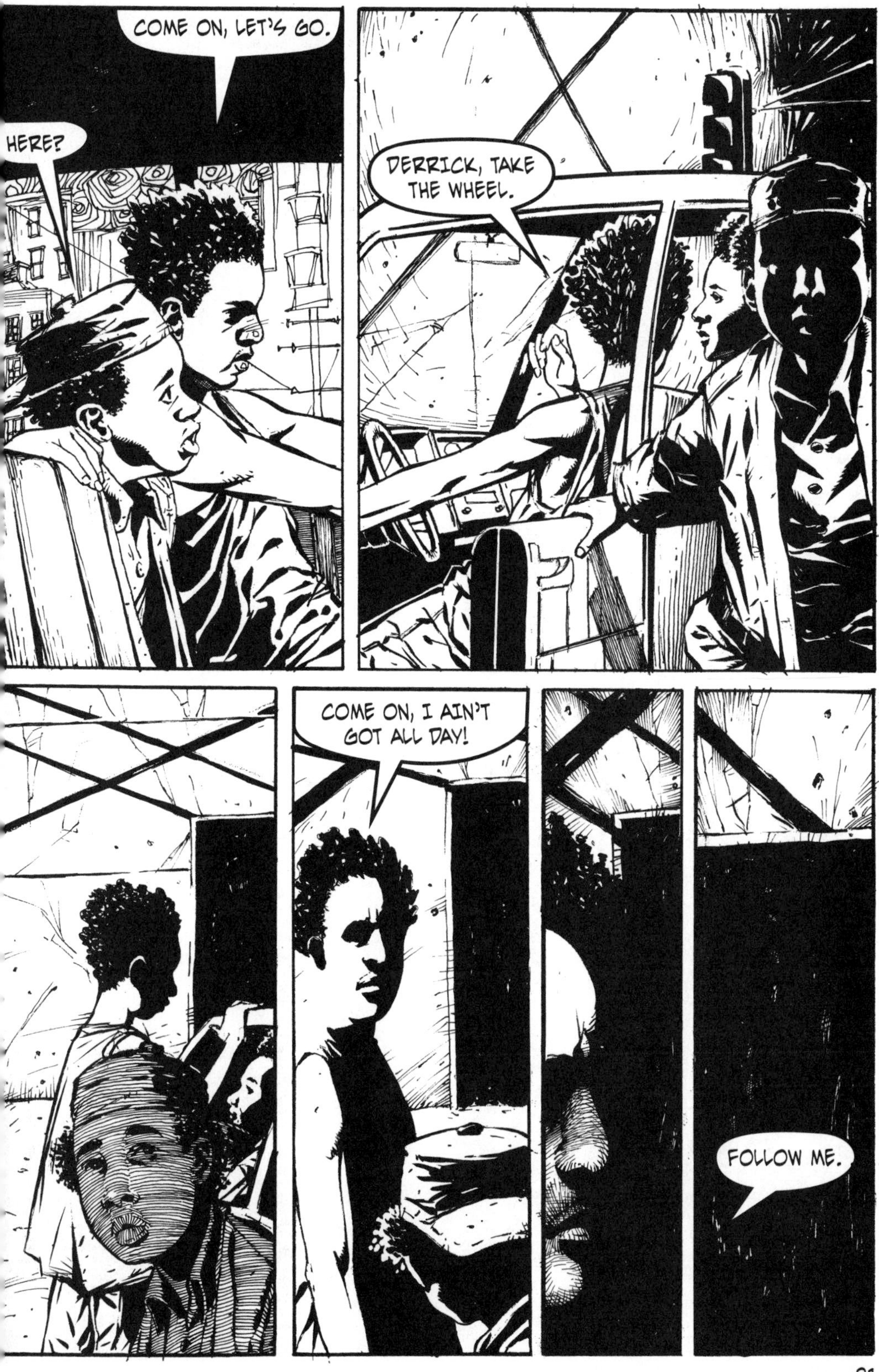
COME ON, LET'S GO.
HERE?
DERRICK, TAKE THE WHEEL.
COME ON, I AIN'T GOT ALL DAY!
FOLLOW ME.

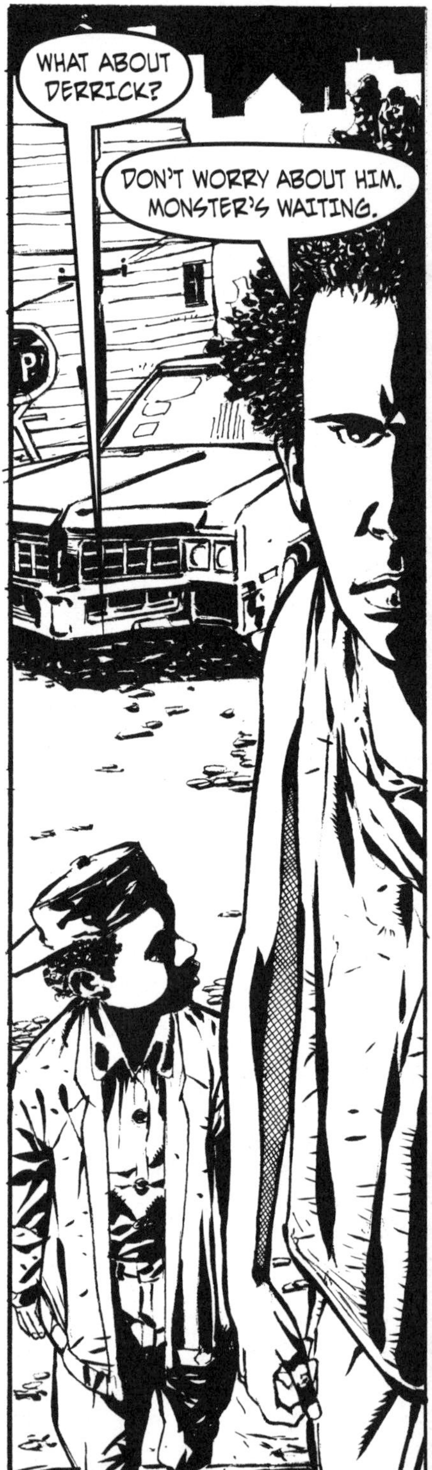
WHAT ABOUT DERRICK?
DON'T WORRY ABOUT HIM. MONSTER'S WAITING.

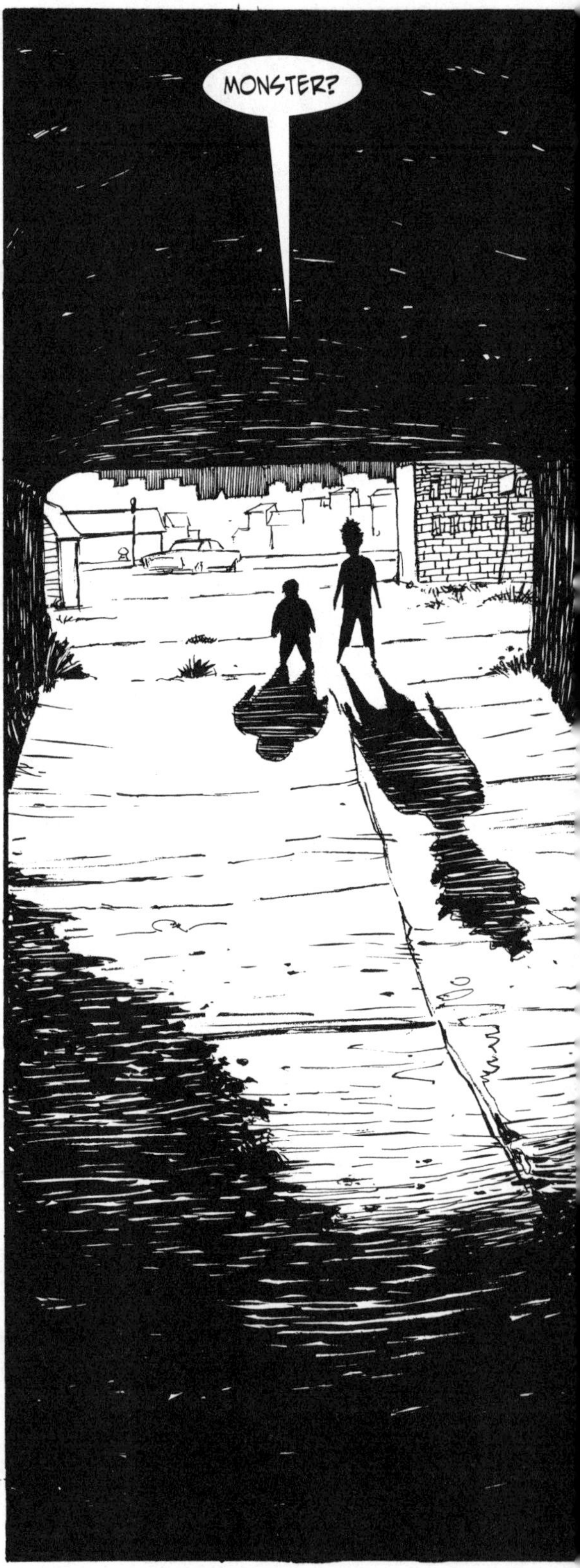
MONSTER?

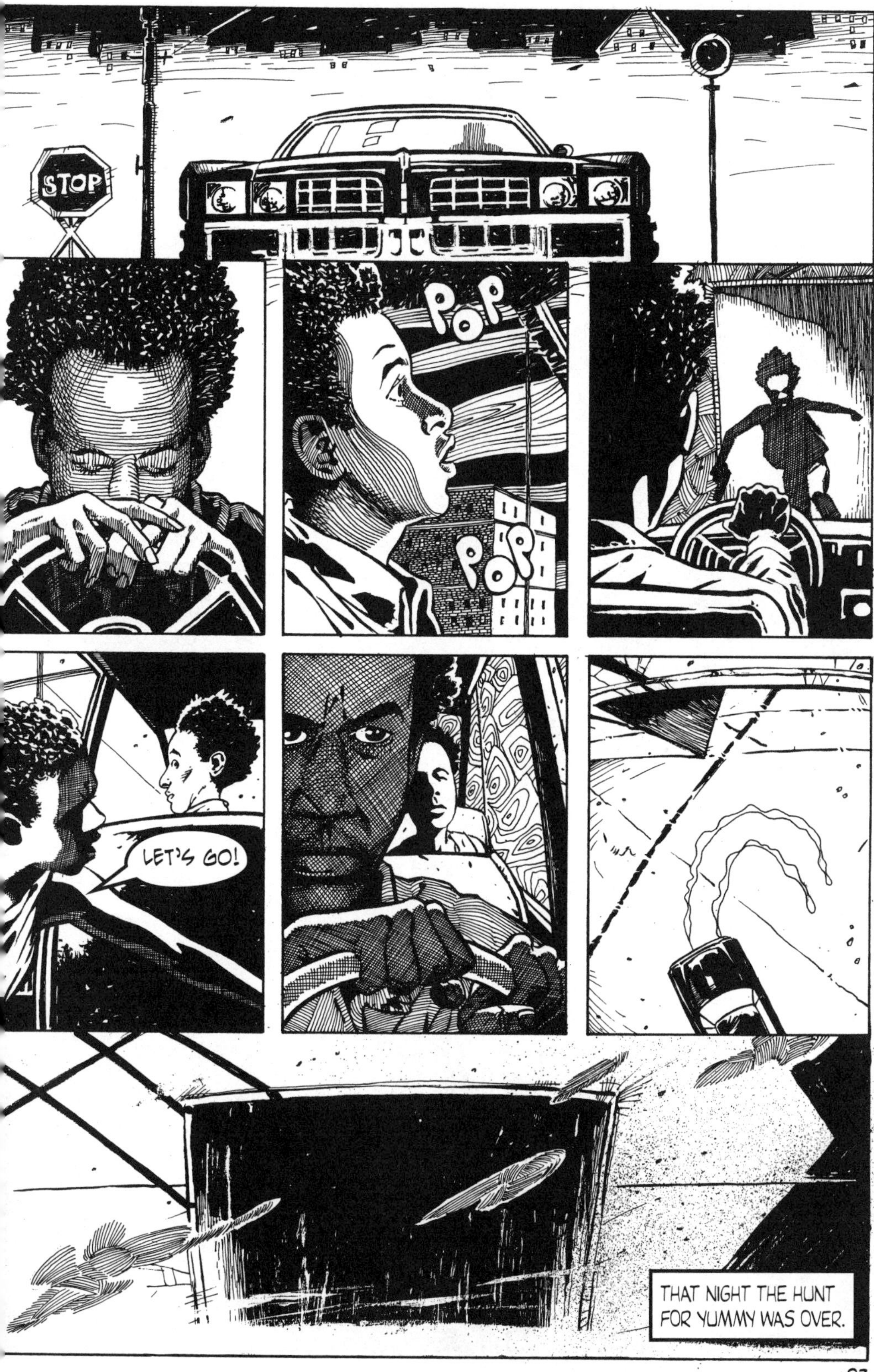
STOP
POP POP
POP POP
LET'S GO!
THAT NIGHT THE HUNT FOR YUMMY WAS OVER.

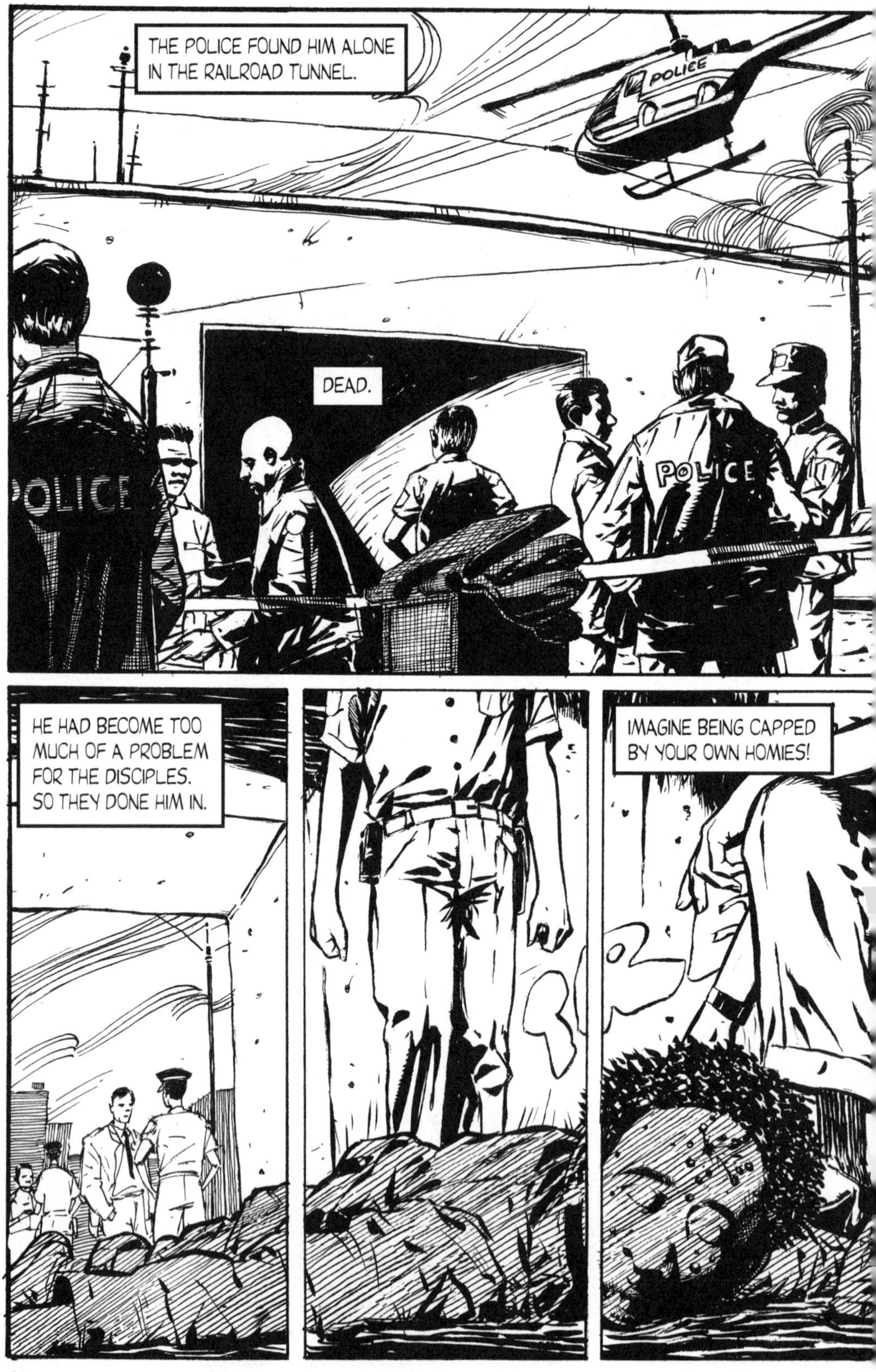
THE POLICE FOUND HIM ALONE IN THE RAILROAD TUNNEL.
POLICE
DEAD.
POLICE
POLICE
HE HAD BECOME TOO MUCH OF A PROBLEM FOR THE DISCIPLES. SO THEY DONE HIM IN.
IMAGINE BEING CAPPED BY YOUR OWN HOMIES!

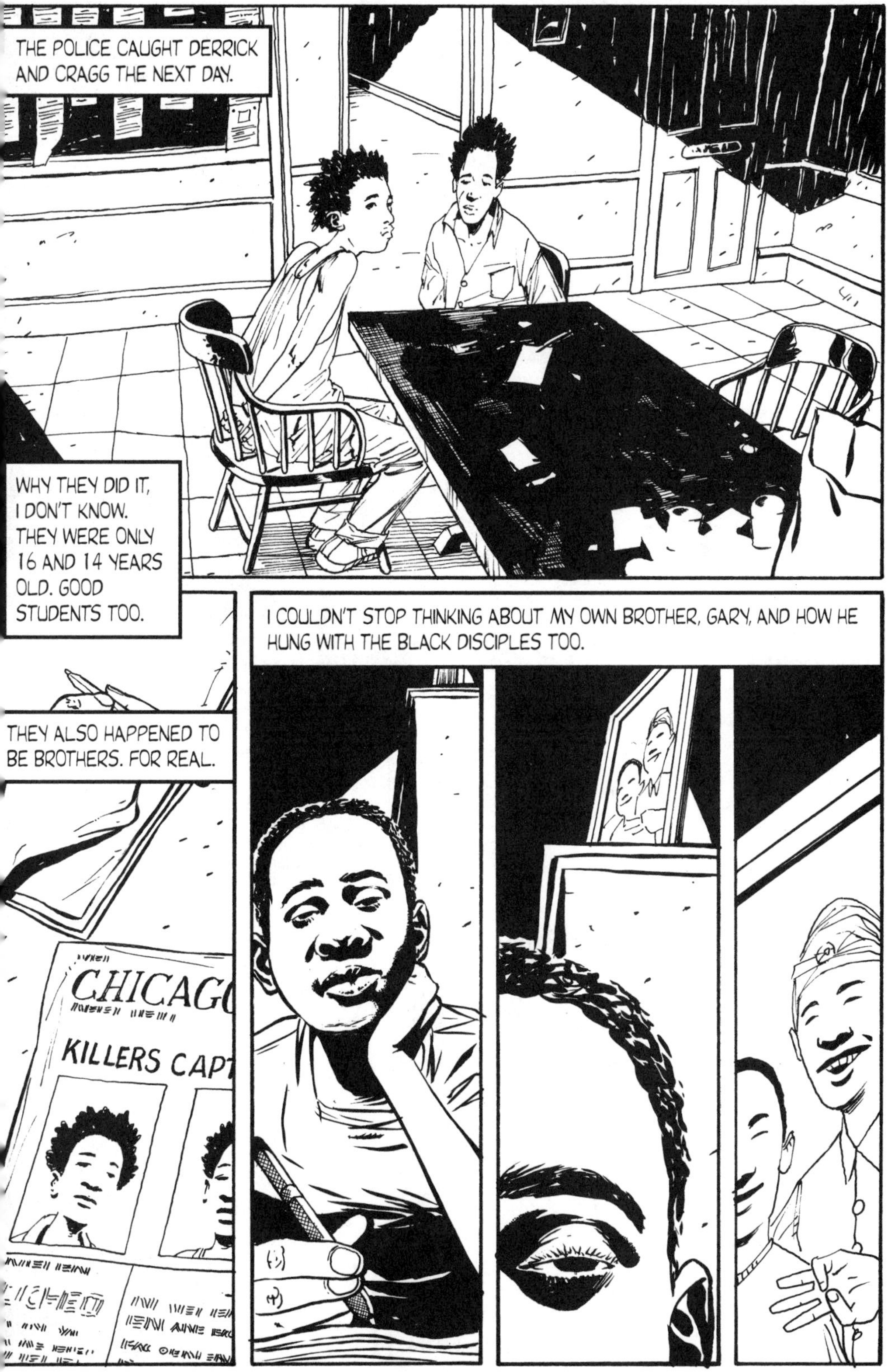
THE POLICE CAUGHT DERRICK AND CRAGG THE NEXT DAY.
WHY THEY DID IT, I DON'T KNOW. THEY WERE ONLY 16 AND 14 YEARS OLD. GOOD STUDENTS TOO.
THEY ALSO HAPPENED TO BE BROTHERS. FOR REAL.
CHICAGO
KILLERS CAPT
I COULDN'T STOP THINKING ABOUT MY OWN BROTHER, GARY, AND HOW HE HUNG WITH THE BLACK DISCIPLES TOO.

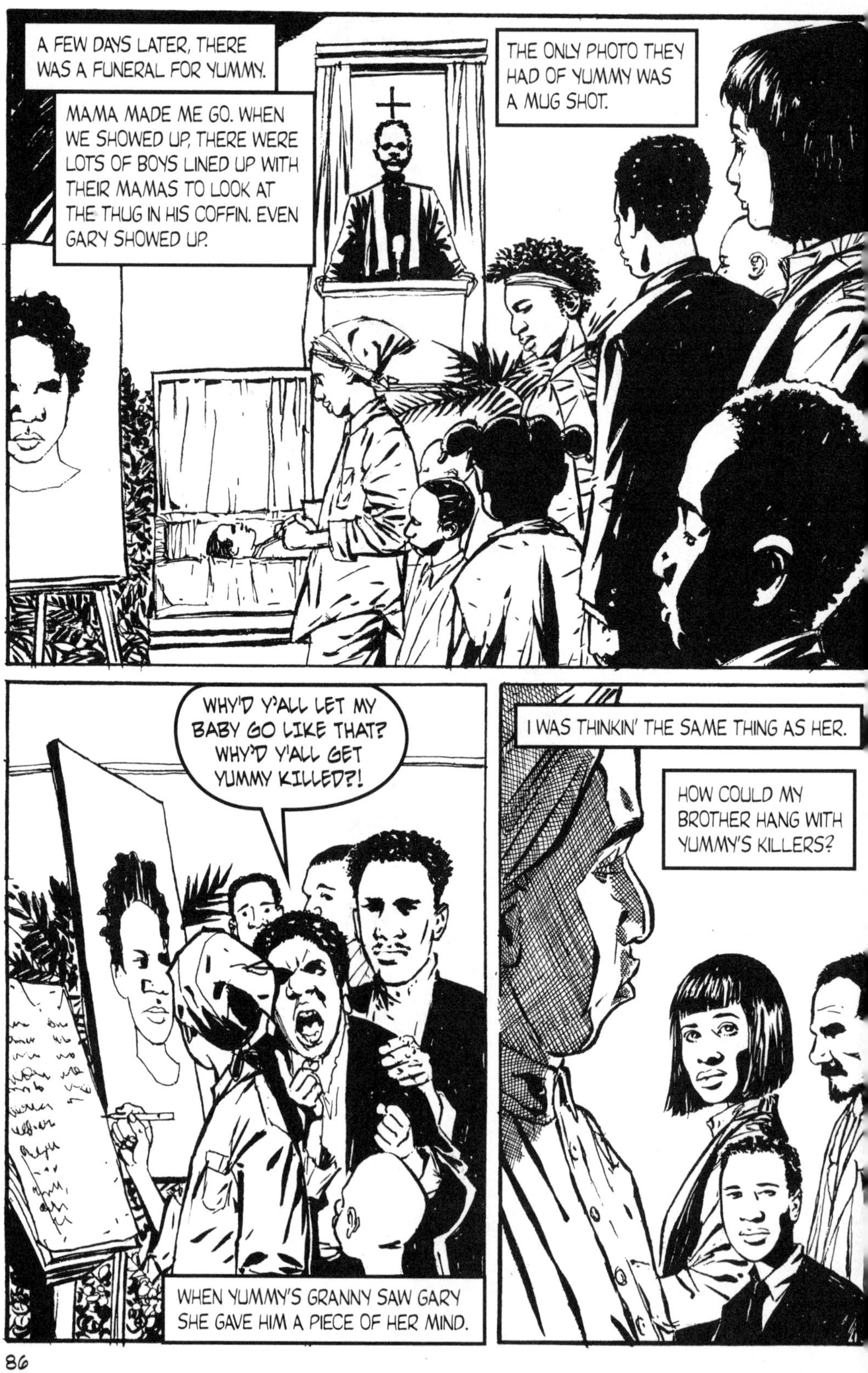
A FEW DAYS LATER, THERE WAS A FUNERAL FOR YUMMY.
MAMA MADE ME GO. WHEN WE SHOWED UP, THERE WERE LOTS OF BOYS LINED UP WITH THEIR MAMAS TO LOOK AT THE THUG IN HIS COFFIN. EVEN GARY SHOWED UP.
THE ONLY PHOTO THEY HAD OF YUMMY WAS A MUG SHOT.
WHY'D Y'ALL LET MY BABY GO LIKE THAT? WHY'D Y'ALL GET YUMMY KILLED?!
WHEN YUMMY'S GRANNY SAW GARY SHE GAVE HIM A PIECE OF HER MIND.
I WAS THINKIN' THE SAME THING AS HER.
HOW COULD MY BROTHER HANG WITH YUMMY'S KILLERS?

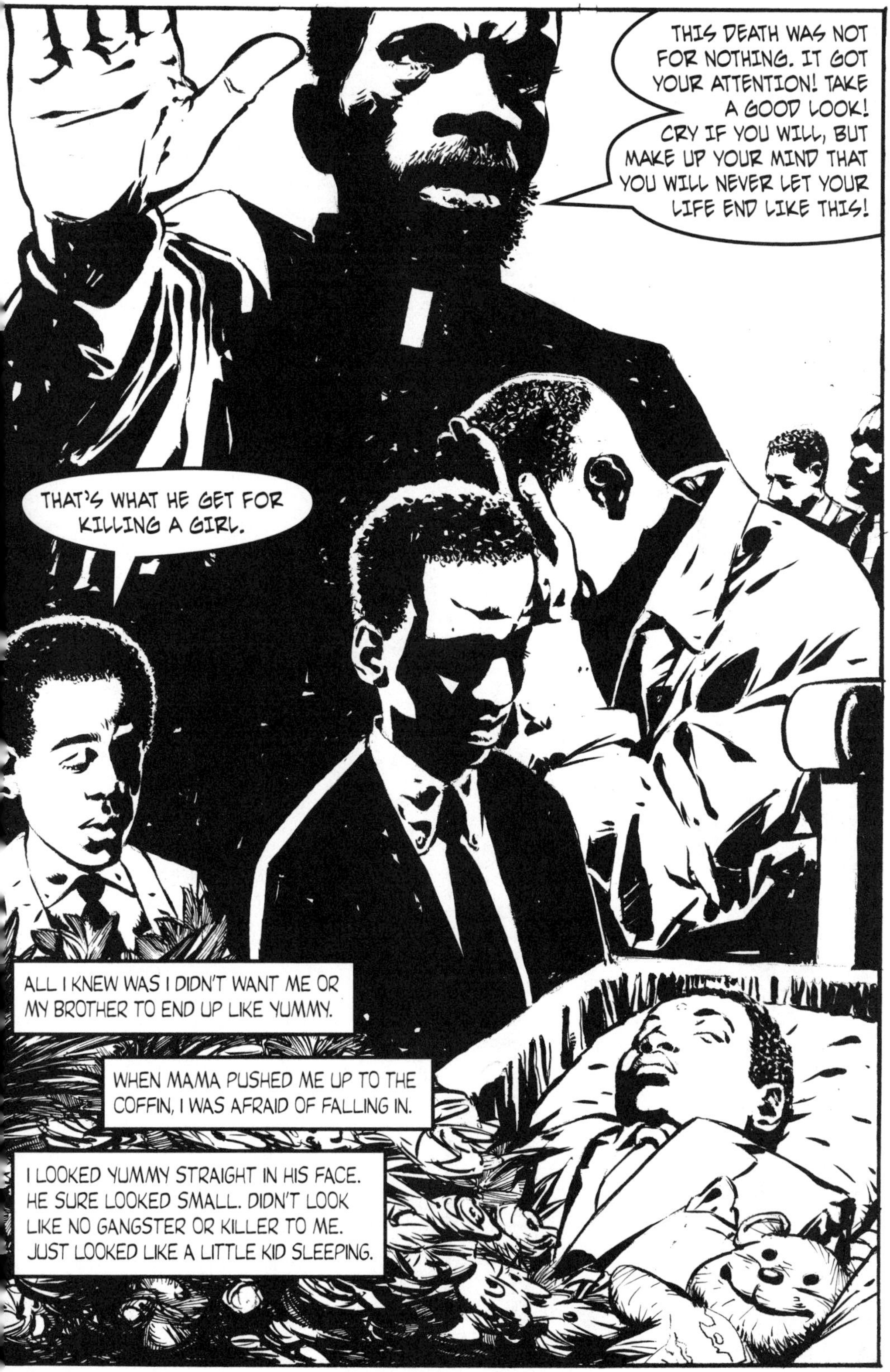
THIS DEATH WAS NOT FOR NOTHING. IT GOT YOUR ATTENTION! TAKE A GOOD LOOK! CRY IF YOU WILL, BUT MAKE UP YOUR MIND THAT YOU WILL NEVER LET YOUR LIFE END LIKE THIS!
THAT'S WHAT HE GET FOR KILLING A GIRL.
ALL I KNEW WAS I DIDN'T WANT ME OR MY BROTHER TO END UP LIKE YUMMY.
WHEN MAMA PUSHED ME UP TO THE COFFIN, I WAS AFRAID OF FALLING IN.
I LOOKED YUMMY STRAIGHT IN HIS FACE. HE SURE LOOKED SMALL. DIDN'T LOOK LIKE NO GANGSTER OR KILLER TO ME. JUST LOOKED LIKE A LITTLE KID SLEEPING.

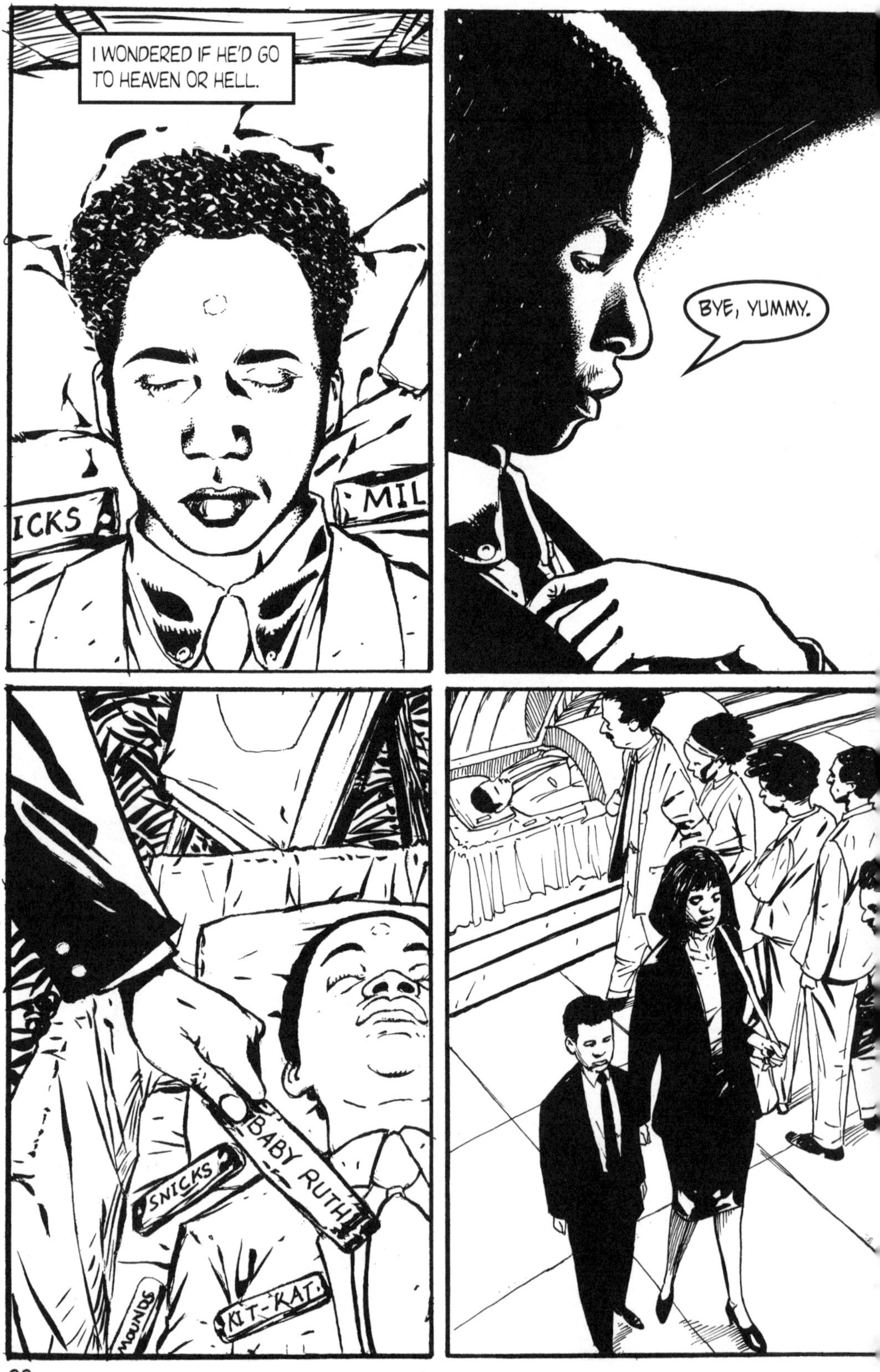
I WONDERED IF HE'D GO TO HEAVEN OR HELL.
ICKS
MIL
BYE, YUMMY.
BABY RUTH
SNICKS
KIT-KAT
MOUNDS

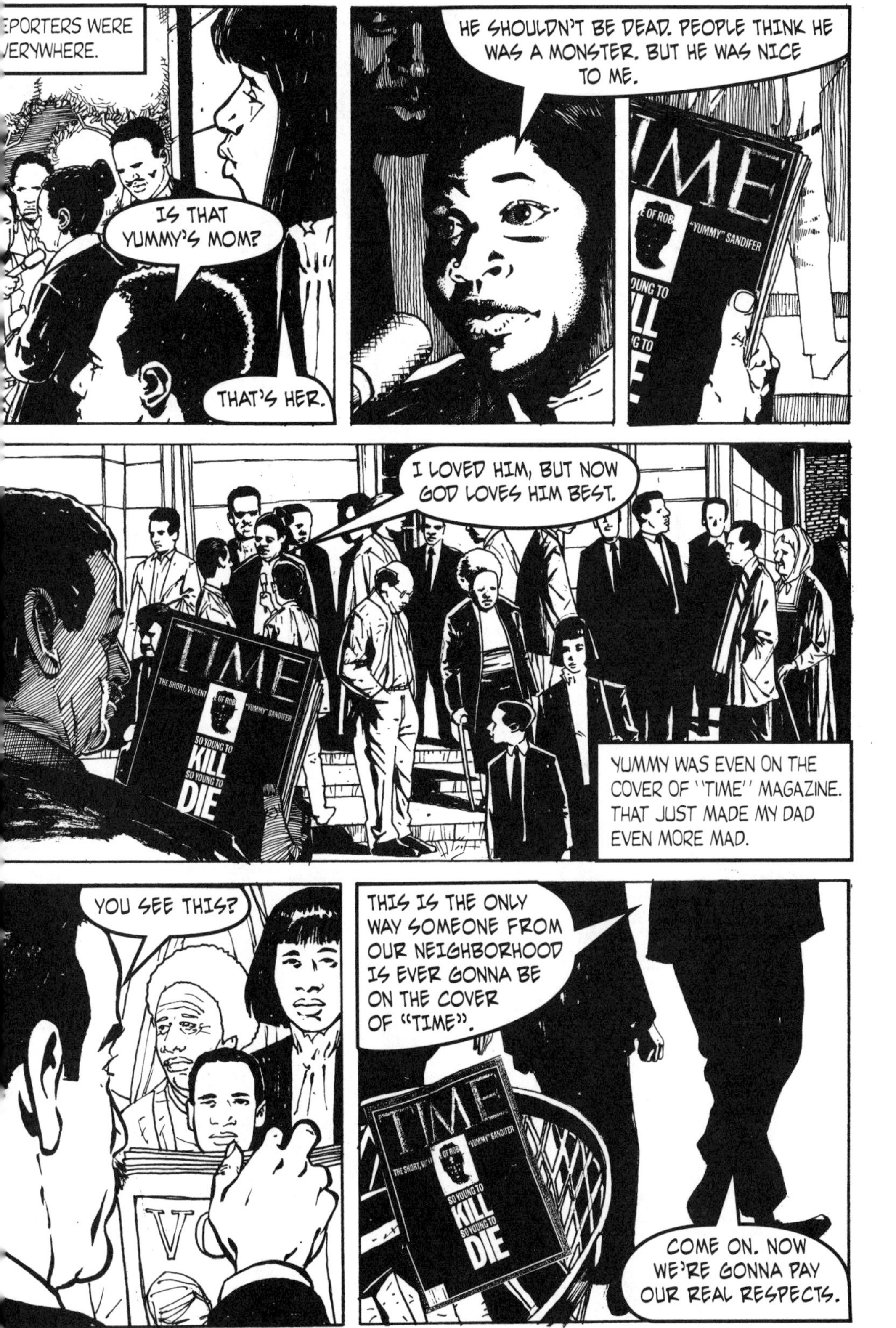
EPORTERS WERE VERYWHERE.
IS THAT YUMMY'S MOM?
THAT'S HER.
HE SHOULDN'T BE DEAD. PEOPLE THINK HE WAS A MONSTER. BUT HE WAS NICE TO ME.
I LOVED HIM, BUT NOW GOD LOVES HIM BEST.
TIME
THE SHORT, VIOLENT
OF ROB
"YUMMY" SANDIFER
SO YOUNG TO KILL SO YOUNG TO DIE
YUMMY WAS EVEN ON THE COVER OF "TIME" MAGAZINE. THAT JUST MADE MY DAD EVEN MORE MAD.
YOU SEE THIS?
THIS IS THE ONLY WAY SOMEONE FROM OUR NEIGHBORHOOD IS EVER GONNA BE ON THE COVER OF "TIME".
COME ON. NOW WE'RE GONNA PAY OUR REAL RESPECTS.

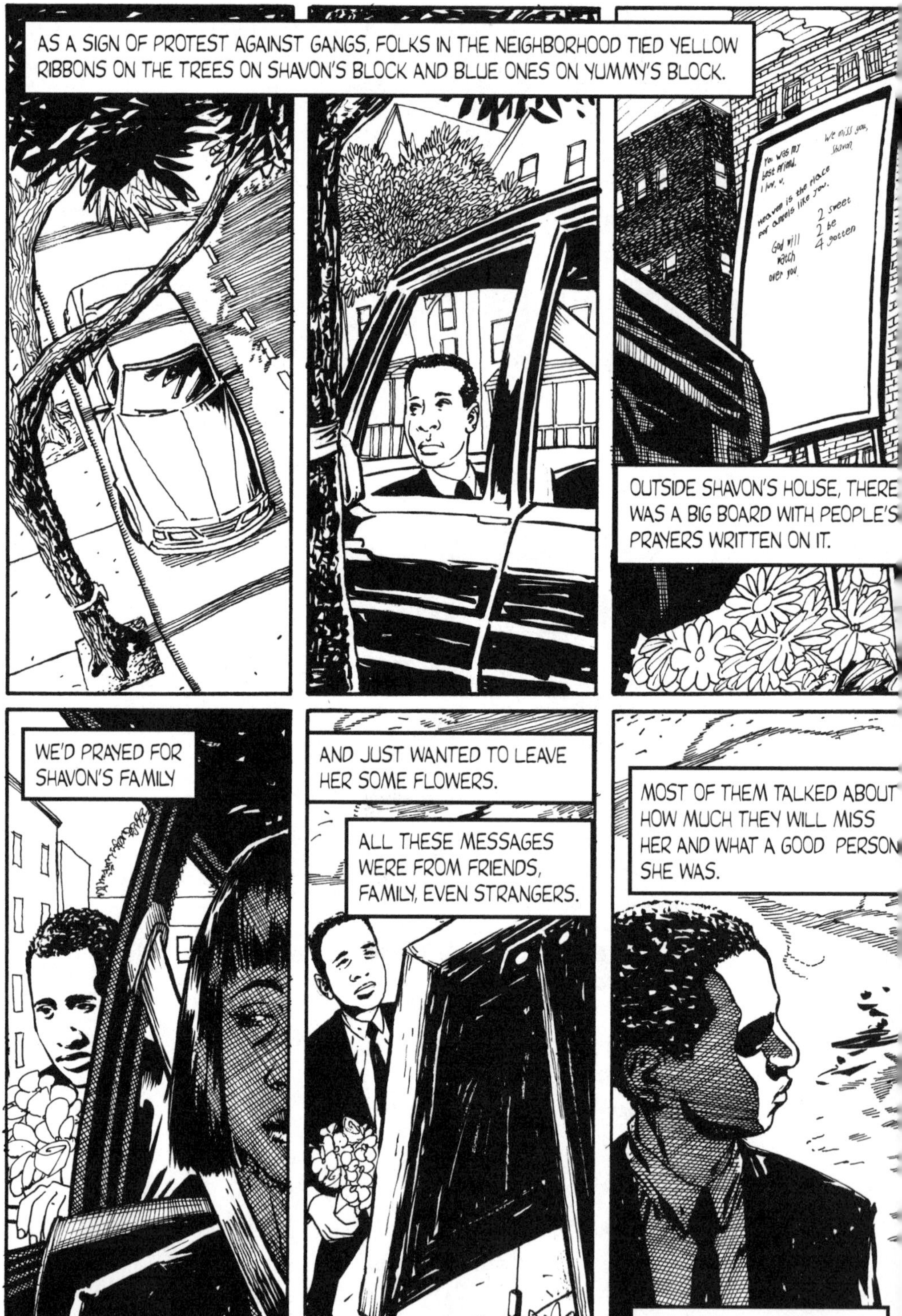
AS A SIGN OF PROTEST AGAINST GANGS, FOLKS IN THE NEIGHBORHOOD TIED YELLOW RIBBONS ON THE TREES ON SHAVON'S BLOCK AND BLUE ONES ON YUMMY'S BLOCK.
We miss you, Shavon.
You was my best friend. I luv. u.
Heaven is the place for angels like you.
God will watch over you.
2 sweet 2 be 4 gotten
OUTSIDE SHAVON'S HOUSE, THERE WAS A BIG BOARD WITH PEOPLE'S PRAYERS WRITTEN ON IT.
WE'D PRAYED FOR SHAVON'S FAMILY
AND JUST WANTED TO LEAVE HER SOME FLOWERS.
ALL THESE MESSAGES WERE FROM FRIENDS, FAMILY, EVEN STRANGERS.
MOST OF THEM TALKED ABOUT HOW MUCH THEY WILL MISS HER AND WHAT A GOOD PERSON SHE WAS.
BUT WHAT CAN YOU SAY TO SOMEONE WHO'S DEAD?

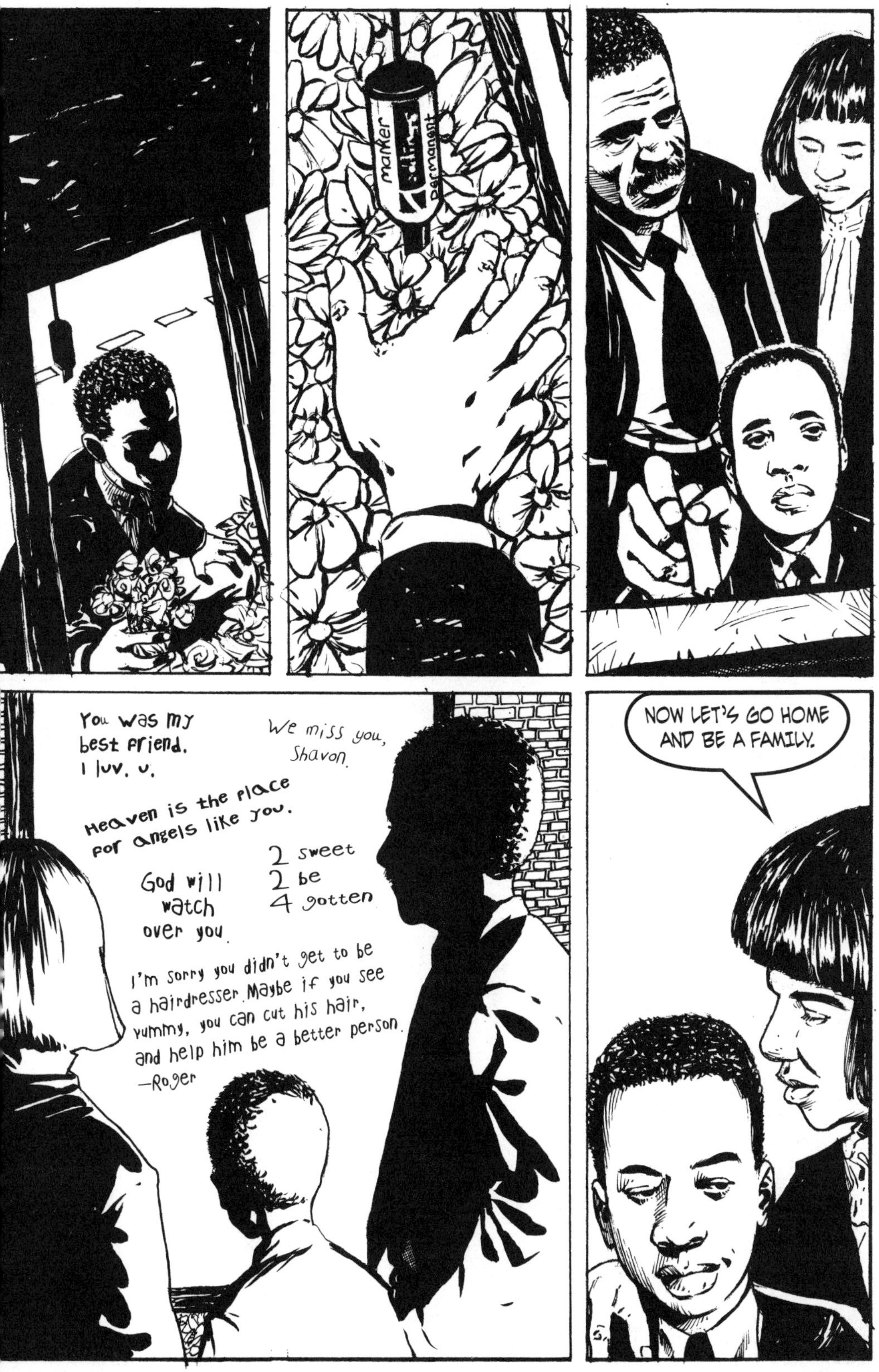
marker
permanent
You was my best friend. I luv. u.
We miss you, Shavon.
Heaven is the place for angels like you.
God will watch over you.
2 sweet 2 be 4 gotten
I'm sorry you didn't get to be a hairdresser. Maybe if you see yummy, you can cut his hair, and help him be a better person. —Roger
NOW LET'S GO HOME AND BE A FAMILY.

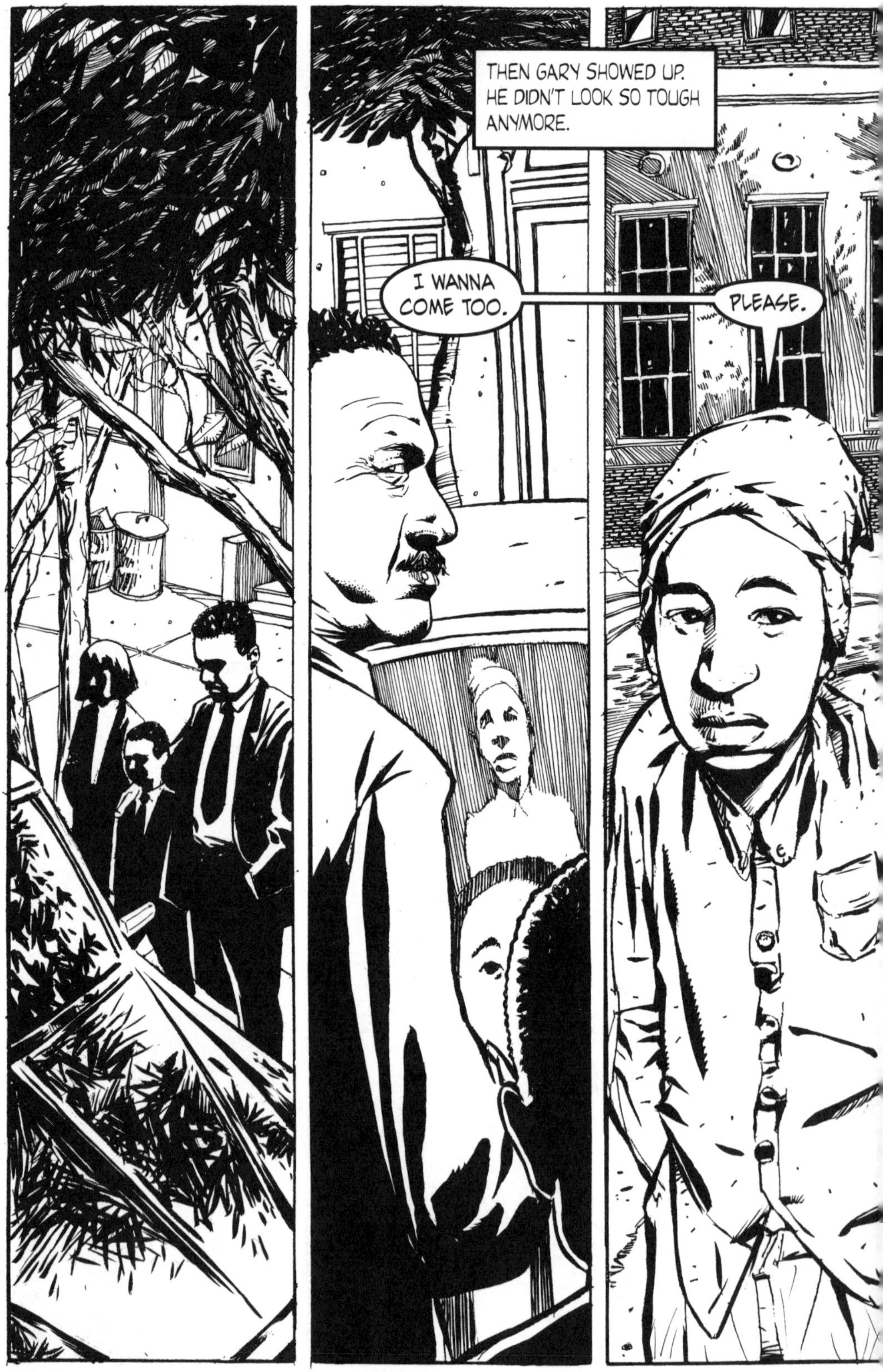
THEN GARY SHOWED UP. HE DIDN'T LOOK SO TOUGH ANYMORE.
I WANNA COME TOO.
PLEASE.

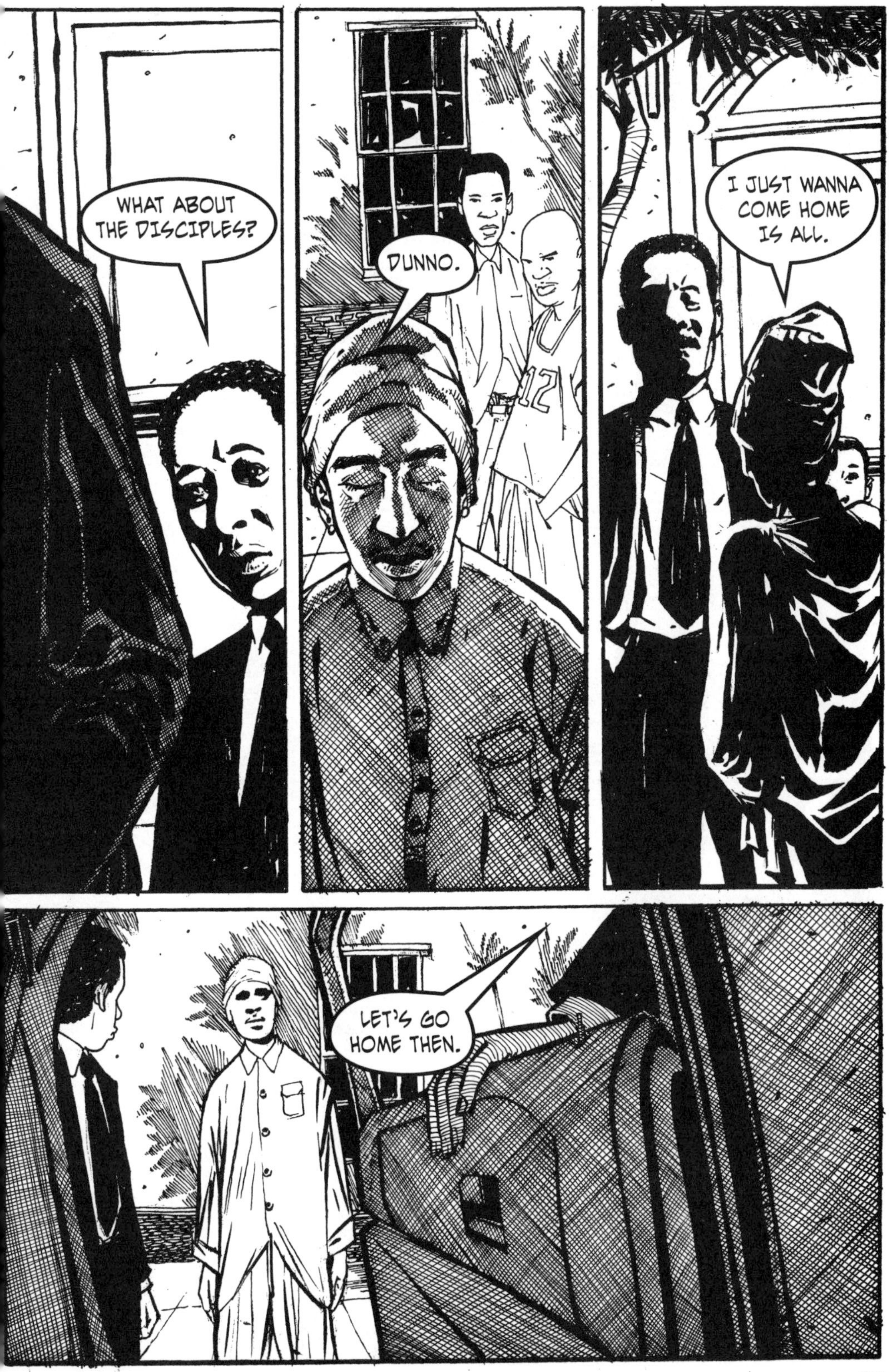
WHAT ABOUT THE DISCIPLES?
DUNNO.
12
I JUST WANNA COME HOME IS ALL.
LET'S GO HOME THEN.

I DON'T KNOW WHICH WAS WORSE, THE WAY YUMMY LIVED OR THE WAY HE DIED.

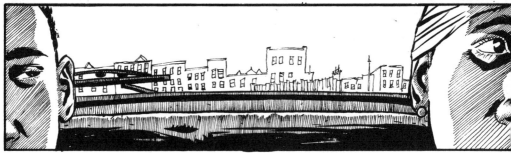

BUT IF WE CAN LIVE THROUGH ALL THIS CRAZINESS AND STAY A FAMILY . . .

MAYBE THAT'S WORTH FIGHTIN' FOR.

AUTHOR'S NOTE

"Sometimes stories get to you; this one left my stomach in knots. After three days of reporting, I still couldn't decide which was more appalling: the child's life or the child's death."

—Jon D. Hull, *TIME* magazine, September 1994

When Yummy's story first broke, I was teaching in South Central Los Angeles. Some of my students came from dysfunctional homes; some had siblings or parents in jail; some had family members who had been killed in the gang wars. More than a few times, I'd heard announcements come over the PA system for memorial services for students who had been killed. I even worked with a teen who, when he wasn't around gangs, acted like any sweet, innocent kid. But on the streets, he had already become a hard-core gangbanger.

I remember following Yummy's story day by day. A couple of students had heard about it and we argued whether he was a victim or a bully. When Yummy was found dead and all the facts came out, I wasn't sure who the bad guy was. There were no winners in this story, only losers. Even the president at the time, Bill Clinton, talked about how the violence had to stop.

Some things changed after Yummy's murder, and some things stayed the same. The infamous projects in Chicago's Southside were torn down. Many of the people who had lived there had to move, but the gangs just moved with them. Yummy's murderers were tried as adults and remain in prison. The Black Disciples are still a powerful force.

So, was Yummy a cold-blooded killer or a victim? The answer is not black-and-white. Yummy was both a bully *and* a victim—he deserves both our anger and our understanding. Other answers, however, may be clearer. Like the preacher at Yummy's funeral said: make up your mind that you will not let your life end like Yummy's. Easier said than done, no doubt. But if you can find a way to make the choice of life, then other decisions may be easier.

Choose wisely.

—G. Neri

AUTHOR'S SOURCES

I followed Yummy's story daily as it unfolded in the coverage of many Chicago news organizations. To that end, the *Chicago Tribune* and the *Chicago Sun Times* were the main resources in real-time news. Later, the following sources were extremely useful in their critical analysis of different aspects of the story. —G.N.

Circuit Court of Cook County. *People v. Hardaway*. Transcript no. 1-97-1204. 1st District, September 10, 1999.

Gibbs, Nancy R., Julie Grace and Jon D. Hull. "Crime: Murder in Miniature." *TIME*, September 19, 1994.

Jones, Andrew. *Robert Sandifer Murder*. FITV, Chicago, 1994.

Jones, LeAlan, and Lloyd Newman. "Ghetto Life 101." New York: Sound Portraits, 1997.

———. *Our America: Life and Death on the Southside of Chicago*. New York: Washington Square Press, 1997.

Knox, George Ph.D. *Gang Threat Analysis: The Black Disciples*. Chicago: National Gang Crime Research Center, 2004.

Wedemeyer, Alex. *Chicagoland: Inside the Map Project*. WildOnions.org, 2002–2005.